Praise for ~~The Boy Under the Table~~

'Gritty [and] shocking, but not without hope.'
The Australian

'Trope paints a compassionate picture of how grief and despair can dramatically alter and shape our lives.'

Joanne Sim, *Melbourne Weekly*

'A gutwrenching story of fear and loss.'
Daily Telegraph

'A hard book to put down.'

Pittwater Life

'The pace is unrelenting and the story is utterly engrossing.'

Book'd Out.com

Nicole
TROPE

The Boy Under the Table

ALLEN&UNWIN
SYDNEY•MELBOURNE•AUCKLAND•LONDON

Allen & Unwin
83 Alexander Street
Crows Nest NSW 2065
Australia
Phone: (61 2) 8425 0100
Email: info@allenandunwin.com
Web: www.allenandunwin.com

Cataloguing-in-Publication details are available
from the National Library of Australia
www.trove.nla.gov.au

ISBN 978 1 74331 474 6

Internal design by Lisa White
Set in Minion by Midland Typesetters, Australia

10 9 8 7 6 5 4 3 2 1

To Mom, Dad and David who know how much this means
and
Mikhayla, Isabella and Jacob who mean everything

Tina

The boy was tied up under the table, scrabbling his way through an empty packet of biscuits, licking his fingers to gather the crumbs.

The kitchen was freezing; Tina could see the warmth of her breath in the air. It got like that sometimes in winter. The cold got trapped inside.

Her first glance had made the boy a dog, just a mongrel tied up to the table leg, but a second glance told the truth. People saw what they wanted to see. Tina hadn't wanted to see the boy. She thought she had perfected the art of tunnel vision. There were a lot of things she didn't want to see.

But she saw everything in the kitchen, everything.

She felt it too. The despair in the air had a familiar feel. Hopeless defeat. It came off the boy in waves and she had to hold on tight to prevent it knocking her over.

1

There was a thick piece of rope tied around the boy's ankle and another thick piece of rope tied around his neck. Both pieces of rope were connected to the central table leg.

It was one of those old fold-down laminate tabletops that had been around in the 1970s. Tina came from a house with the exact same tabletop, although in her house it had been replaced with a stone benchtop that swept away the past and looked to a future of steel appliances and automatic vacuum cleaners.

The rope was short. The boy couldn't have made it onto either of the bench seats alongside the table. Not without strangling himself.

The knots on the rope looked like they meant business. What did they call them—sailors' knots?

They would not be loosened. They would not give way. The boy wasn't going anywhere.

Tina began to breathe in a little of the boy's despair. It crept up her spine and tingled at her neck. Right now she wasn't going anywhere either. Her first instinct had been to run. When she had recognised what was tied up under the table she wanted to run screaming from the house, but she knew enough to wait and keep her mouth shut. She was in real trouble. Panic was stupid.

A rancid sweet smell filled the space. Tina wrinkled her nose.

The boy was skinny to the point of nothingness and dirty enough to be an animal. His lips and fingers were tinged with blue. His breath formed puffs of cloud in front of his face. His huge watery blue eyes met hers for a moment and then darted away.

The man smiled down at the boy and gave him a pat as though he were, in fact, greeting the family dog. The man's nondescript face was enveloped in a smug grin.

'See what I have here?'

Tina heard the unspoken words as though the man had shouted them aloud. There was no reply worth making. Instead she swallowed a piece of the boy's despair and stared at the wall.

His body had become a statue as soon as the man's hand made contact. He was perfectly still on his bed of newspapers. When faced with attack most animals instinctively know to become motionless. If you didn't move and you didn't breathe it was possible that you would not be seen. The boy's skinny ribcage filled with stale air while he waited for the hand to leave his head.

Tina held her breath as well. If the man did more than pat the boy she would have to do something. She would have to do anything. There are some things that cannot be tolerated. If he did more than pat the boy Tina would not survive. She was completely sure of that.

She looked away from the man and the boy and tried to convey the idea that the only thing she was interested in was her twenty dollars.

Twenty dollars, twenty whole dollars, twenty precious dollars.

Those were the words she kept repeating in her head, hoping they would blot out all the other words making a grab for her attention.

The man looked back at her, almost daring her to ask about the frozen starving child under the table. Wanting her to ask?

Tina met his stare. She was here for her twenty dollars. That was it.

The man nodded at her. He had chosen well. Tina could see him putting her into the harmless category. She was someone who wouldn't make trouble. If you want someone to keep your secret, pick the person who has more secrets than you.

He was right. Tina knew now that she had made a mistake with the man. If she got out of the house it would be a bonus. If she got out unscathed it would be a miracle. Her best hope was silence. Silence and acquiescence. If she did make it out the only story she would have to tell would be the one about her own survival. She would be quiet and she would acquiesce, agree, comply, assent, concede and concur with whatever the man wanted.

'Fuck you know a lot of big words for a kid,' Ruby had said. 'How come you didn't just stay in school? What are you doing here anyway?'

Tina had shrugged her shoulders like she hadn't been asking herself those questions ever since she packed her bags and headed to a place she could lose herself in.

On the day she left she went to the station because trains took you away and she needed to be away. She got on a train waiting for a plan to form, waiting for an idea to take hold, but her thoughts were trapped in anger and grief and she could not get past these emotions. So she sat on the train and stared out of the window and let the click clack of the rails decide for her. The train passed through station after station and each time the doors opened Tina leaned forward and looked for a reason to get off the train. Each time she let the doors close again without leaving her seat. Then the train stopped at Kings Cross and when the doors slid open the platform was teeming with people. In the warm gust of air that blew into the train Tina heard a woman laugh. The woman laughed loud and long and Tina got off the train, wanting to find the woman. Wanting to find the laughter. She found herself in the Cross instead and she roamed the streets that never emptied, feeling lost. Safely lost.

So she stayed.

Her lack of money kept her there and her desire to disappear from a life she could no longer live meant that she stayed longer than she should have. Not that anyone, anyone at all, *should* ever stay in the Cross.

Nothing shocked Tina anymore. Ruby's words and her red leather mini had shocked her at first. Ruby's sallow skin and the sores on her arms that she scratched at constantly but always covered with makeup had drawn her eyes. She had felt a jolt of stunned recognition at seeing the real deal. She had forced herself to look at her shoes so she could pretend she hadn't seen.

The people putting needles in their arms as casually as though they were drinking coffee had shocked her too, and the filth and the all-pervasive anger had been terrifying. But it had been two years now and she barely registered the horror of her surroundings anymore.

She didn't see what she didn't want to see. The women on the street were pretty girls waiting for a date and she was a princess waiting for her prince. The world could be a lot easier to deal with if you lived mostly inside your own head. Probably all the same ugly, sick, twisted stuff went on behind the pretty fences of her childhood anyway.

She had built herself a fairly impressive wall in the last two years, but then she had been building that long before she got to the Cross. She could watch the world shit itself up right in front of her and not feel a thing. Sometimes she thought that any feeling at all would have been a luxury, but nothing got through. It meant that nothing could hurt her but it also meant that nothing could move her either. It was a price she was willing to pay. It was one interesting fucking trade-off.

The boy under the table was quietly battering against her walls, but she held firm.

'Take care of yourself first, before you think about anything else,' Ruby had said.

Ruby handed down the same advice that had been given to her. She had been in the Cross for five years and it was a tradition to help the newbie.

Some didn't help. Some led the younger kids in the wrong direction and then didn't stick around to pick up the pieces. But Ruby liked to educate. Knowledge is power and all that shit.

Usually Tina knew better. Ruby had taught her better. Usually she knew better than to get into a car with one of them. Usually she would never have dreamed of allowing one of them to take her to his house. Usually she would never have put herself in this situation.

Usually it wasn't fucking freezing and she wasn't fucking starving.

Twenty bucks could stretch to cover a week if she was careful.

She could almost taste the burger and fries, but before she was allowed to put any food in her mouth she had to put something else down her throat.

'You know it's just a blow right?' she said.

''Course I do, luv, that's what we agreed. I just thought it would be more pleasant if we got out of the rain.'

She had been standing on the street for almost an hour when he came along. An hour of cars that sped past and an hour of the wind biting at her body. An hour of the trickling rain down her back that the umbrella did little to stop. An hour of thinking time.

There had been no one to talk to. Everyone else had given up and gone home but Tina had stayed.

Tina is a determined student with a great deal of potential.

When she saw the gold sedan finally slow down she had breathed a sigh of relief. She had watched him go past three times already.

She opened her coat so he could get a proper look. The window slid down and she leaned in just a little, squeezing her breasts together. She was wearing a tight red singlet with a back mini and sky-high silver heels.

All ready for the club dontcha know.

'Cold, isn't it?' he said.

'You've got that right,' she said, and smiled. *Like me, want me, like me, want me.*

'How much?'

'Twenty for a blow, fifty for the whole thing.'

'Twenty is good.'

'I can meet you in the alley at the back.'

'It's really cold. Why don't you get in here?'

'Okay,' she said. Her mouth responded before her body processed the idea. The car was filled with heat. She could feel it coming out of the window. It was irresistible.

'Stupid, stupid girl,' Ruby would have said.

'My house is just a few blocks away. It will be better there— for both of us.'

Tina knew she should get out of the car. But she just sat there and nodded. She was so grateful to be out of the rain. She willed her legs to move but they knew what was good for them. Her legs stayed put.

She sat there and let him drive off. It was so cold. Tina never knew that cold could become your whole body, not until she spent a night on the streets. It burrowed in through your clothes and went straight for your lungs and your bones. It became all you could think about. You could not imagine ever being warm again.

So she sat in the car and she let him drive and she tried not to see the boy under the table. The little boy under the table licking the empty biscuit packet. The little boy who should not have been there.

Tried/failed.

'I want my money now,' said Tina. She glanced around the kitchen again, sniffed at the air. The smell must have been coming off the boy because the kitchen was spotless. It was clean enough to be in one of those adverts that tried to convince the public that their crappy lives would be perfect if they could just kill enough germs.

Her mother was like that. Her kitchen cabinet was stacked with the best germ killers. A whole arsenal dedicated to wiping out anything that dared to live on her surfaces.

In the clean kitchen in the man's house not a single thing was out of place. Even the tea towels were folded into perfect squares and sitting together on the draining board.

Not a single thing out of place except for one thing so very out of place.

The man's car had been clean as well. Free of the usual debris of a life lived moving from one place to another.

No coffee cups or water bottles or burger wrappers. Nothing.

Nothing but the pine smell and the heat.

In the kitchen Tina stamped on her fear and forced herself to look around. She was in enemy territory. Time to work out the lay of the land.

'If you're dumb enough to let one of them drag you home always plan an escape route,' Ruby had said. 'But mostly don't be dumb enough to let one of them take you home.'

Ruby carried a knife, hidden from prying eyes. Tina had never needed a knife. Correction: Tina had never needed a knife before.

She could see a small window and a back door that the man had locked three different ways after they used it to enter the house.

Shit, she thought. You could turn one lock and get out before you got caught. If you were quick you could maybe turn two locks. Three would be impossible.

She looked at the window again.

There was something a little off about the window. Tina stared at it without staring at it and then she realised what she was seeing.

The latch was broken. It was hanging off the window at an odd angle. With a little bit of work she could get through it in no time. It was a small imperfection in the perfectly maintained space.

She kept the triumphant detail to herself. She stared at her feet and went over the movements that would get her through the window and out of the house.

The man held out a crisp twenty-dollar note.

There it was.

Who said money can't buy happiness? No one who had ever been hungry, that's for sure.

Tina grabbed the note and stuffed it right down the bottom of her cloth backpack, underneath her wallet and the few bits and pieces of her life she carried around.

It stopped her thinking. That was the one benefit of hunger. Nothing else mattered. Nothing else occupied your thoughts.

'Come into the lounge room,' he said. 'I've got the heat on in there.'

It was a lot warmer in the lounge, and Tina felt her hands begin to thaw again. The boy under the table was wearing a pair of shorts and a torn T-shirt.

I'm just here for my money, Tina thought.

The man sat himself down on a leather recliner. He unzipped his pants and opened them a little.

Tina felt the bile rise in her throat as it did every time.

'Just think of the money,' Ruby had advised.

'Sometimes it's good to feel a woman's lips,' said the man, giving her a creepy smile.

Tina said nothing. She got down on her knees.

'Don't talk to the fuckers. Just do your thing and leave. They love to think that we actually enjoy it because they are so special and so different from every other fuck who ever handed us twenty bucks. Well fuck 'em, I say. They're all the same,' Ruby had said.

Tina had listened and learned, grateful for eighteen year old Ruby and her brash kindness.

'They'll love you.' Ruby was looking at Tina's clear skin and green eyes. 'You still look like a little kid. How old are you, anyway? Don't shit me.'

'Fifteen.'

'Shit, you look twelve. All the daddies in their four-wheel drives will be after you. Poor bitch.'

The man groaned and it was over.

'Can I use your loo?'

'Yeah, sure, it's over to the right. You could stay awhile, you know. I'd be willing to pay extra. I could make dinner.'

And we could play house, thought Tina. *Do I give the kid under the table a pat as well?*

Tina looked at the man. He was so clean. No extra hair on his face and he smelled of soap. He was even cleaner than his house, but the kid under the table told her that there was plenty of dirt where she couldn't see it. Black stinking dirt.

'I'm good,' she said. 'I have to get back. Billy will look for me.'

'Billy your pimp?' asked the man.

People were stupid. The whole fucking world was raised by the television. Tina nodded. 'Big bloke from Tonga. You must have seen him when I got in your car. I told him I was coming here. He usually likes to follow me to make sure he gets his money.'

'Now let me tell you about Billy,' Ruby had said. 'He's the best fucking thing I ever thought up.'

The man knew there was no Billy but he wasn't one hundred percent sure. None of them ever were. Mostly they didn't take the chance.

In the bathroom Tina used some of the man's mouthwash. She used it twice. She wiped her hands on the white towel and then she wiped her nose as well. She made sure the towel was lying perfectly straight again.

There was a uniform hanging just outside the shower. Tina felt her heart in her throat until she looked closer. It was the wrong colour for a cop's uniform. The blue was different and the pants could have belonged to anyone but the badge made it official. But it was just a security guard's uniform. Just a security guard.

'Jumped-up fucks. Think they're more dangerous than they are,' Ruby had said about the ones who told them to move away from the front of the ritzy stores.

'Jumped-up fuck,' said Tina softly, enjoying the sound of the words and the memory of Ruby.

The man was dozing in his recliner.

'I'm going now,' said Tina, focusing on the large fireplace and the iron poker standing next to it.

'I'll give you a lift,' said the man, opening his eyes. He stood and zipped up his pants. He had been more awake than asleep; waiting for her. Listening for her.

'Nah thanks. Billy just rang me. He's waiting around the corner.'

'Oh,' said the man, and he gave Tina a small smile. 'I didn't hear a phone ring.'

Tina sniffed and said nothing. You can't argue with silence.

'Why don't I just walk you to his car? I'm sure Billy would appreciate me taking care of you. You can't be too careful these days.'

Tina's heart began to hammer in her neck. She knew exactly who she had to be careful of. She had to play this right or she was fucked.

'I'm going now,' she said in what Ruby called her teacher voice. 'I'm going alone and if you want to see me again you know where to find me.'

'Always let them know they can see you again,' Ruby had told her. 'The stupid fucks like to think it's been a fucking date!'

The man gazed at Tina for a moment and then he seemed to come to the conclusion that staying inside was easier. The possibility of 'Billy' was a risk he was not prepared to take.

He sat down again.

Tina nodded again and turned to make her way through the kitchen and out the back door.

The boy was curled up as small as he could make himself and he was whimpering and shivering in his sleep.

She moved her arm without thinking but quickly clenched her fist and shoved it in her pocket. He was not hers to touch. But whose was he? Could the man who had made him a dog be his father? Did he belong to the clean man?

Tina felt her stomach contract. *Don't look, don't look, don't look.*

Acid burned her throat but she kept going until she was out of the house and down the path. When she got to the road she started to run and she didn't stop until she hit the main road. She ran with the exhilaration of having done it again and survived. She ran with the joy of having made the mistake of going with the man but living to tell the tale. She ran to keep warm and to get out of the rain. She ran but she would never be able to run far enough. She couldn't quite believe her luck. The man had taken her home when he could have just had his blow in the car. There was a chance that he had wanted the warmth of home but there was also a chance that he wanted her in his house for something else entirely.

He had wanted her to see the boy. He had smiled and waited for her to show some reaction. He wanted her to see his prize. 'Sick fuck,' said Tina to the night air. She pushed the man and the boy from her mind and concentrated on moving her body. She was feeling lucky tonight. The universe only offered you so many chances.

The first time she did it she thought the disgust and self-loathing would kill her but they didn't. Hunger could kill you, cold could kill you. All your thoughts could do was torture you so you wished you were dead. Big difference.

She felt her feet pound along the pavement and listened to the click of her heels.

She could run fast in heels now. Being able to run was important. Ruby had made her practice.

In a few minutes she was back where she started.

It wasn't far to her usual spot. She could make it back to the house from her squat in ten minutes if she wanted to. But why would she want to?

Doug

There were times when Doug would forget. It would only be for a moment but he would forget.

He'd be driving the ute, rounding up the sheep. Jarred and Sean would be calling to each other, trying to keep the horses moving in the right direction, the dogs would be barking and he'd be so focused on making sure he didn't let any of the sheep stray he would forget about his boy.

He would watch the young boys—boys whose lives centred around the pub and the girls who they could meet there—and he would smile as they whistled and made jokes. He would feel the sun on his body and breathe in the smell of the sheep.

And he would forget.

It would only be for a moment and then it would all come surging back like a wave hitting the beach. Like a tsunami destroying everything in its path. And he would have to stop the ute because he couldn't breathe properly. His eyes would prick with salt and his throat would scratch and his lungs would collapse under the memory.

The boys would carry on without him for a few minutes as he tried to get his body under control. They knew now just to carry on. At first they had looked lost. They had stopped too and ignored the sheep and looked at him, wondering what to do.

He was the boss. He was supposed to carry on regardless. If he stopped what were they supposed to do?

Now they just went on with the work and waited for him to get himself together. It had happened enough times that they knew to pretend the ute hadn't stalled right in the middle of the sheep. They kept on talking and laughing and moving the stock, and even though the jokes had a hollow sound they kept making them.

They didn't know what to say to him. When he first came back they had mumbled words of sympathy to their shoes. They were young, so very young. Doug had never felt the gap between his age and theirs so acutely. He felt ancient now. He had been regarded as a man who'd kept everything going through the worst years on the farm. The old men in town had nodded at him with respect when he ventured in for a cold one.

Now he was an object of pity.

The old men in the pub didn't meet his eye. They offered to pay for his drink but they didn't make the offer to him. They spoke to Will, the bartender and owner. Will would shuffle up to him slowly and whisper the gift of a beer. Doug never took it. A beer bought because you were a mate or because you'd survived the drought along with the others or because you could be counted on to lend a hand or give a bit of advice was different from a beer bought because you had been stupid enough to fuck up your whole life.

People respected strength. They took advantage if they felt pity.

He had caught the boys slacking off in the weeks after he came back and he had to pull out his own old-man voice and give them a reason to get back to doing things his way.

They were just boys really. Jarred was only seventeen; he only shaved every second day. Sean was nineteen but so innocent Doug knew he was still waiting to find the right girl.

Doug had yelled and thrown things and used some pretty foul language and the boys had jumped back into line.

If only everything could be solved that simply.

He was always struck by the irony of his ability to keep his sheep safe. To keep them from straying and getting lost.

He had lost his child.

It sounded ridiculous. You lost your keys and your sunglasses. You lost your job and, if the bad luck had you in its sights, you lost your house and your farm.

What kind of person lost a child? And to lose him in a place where there were so many other kids? Thousands of families went to the Easter Show every year. Thousands of families and thousands of kids and all of them went home stuffed with food and loaded up with toys and whatever other crap they could find. But not Lockie.

Not the Williams family.

At first they hadn't been worried when they found Sammy in the stroller alone, her cheeks flushed with sleep and her hair damp with sweat. Lockie had been too excited to stand still. He had been darting ahead of them all day.

'Did you see that, Dad, did you see that? Look at the people—have you ever seen so many people? Wow, what's that, Dad? Can I have an ice cream? Can I have a toffee apple? Can I, Mum? Can I, Dad?'

So they weren't worried when he wasn't standing where they had told him to stand. They had lost him for a few minutes more than once, but even though they had scolded a little they had both been made indulgent by his excitement, his enchantment with everything. And they hadn't even told him that he would be able to choose the bounty of two show bags yet.

Two show bags, one filled with toy cars and another with chocolate sat unopened in his bedroom. Doug had bought them hurriedly on the last day and he had to take what he could get. He was worried that when they found Lockie he would be disappointed to have missed out. So he bought the bags and showed them to Sarah, who thought it was a good idea.

They had both refused to lose hope.

Refused. To. Lose. Hope.

Lockie would be found.

The judging and prize presentation in the cake-decorating section had been boring for the kids. The speeches went on and on. Lockie had worked himself up into a whine until Sarah reminded him of the promised lamington.

The one distinct feeling Doug remembered from the time he now thought of as *before* was a feeling of pride. The whole day he had felt puffed up with pride.

He had been so proud of Sarah, beating all those Sydney people for the prize. She was a true artist. The kids' birthday cakes were always the talk of the town. He had also been proud of his kids, of the way they launched themselves into the excitement of the Show. He had stopped once and watched as they walked along in front of him—Lockie occasionally grabbing Sammy's hand to point out something he wanted her to see as Sarah pushed the empty stroller, waiting for Sammy to grow tired of walking. He had felt the kind of happiness he knew most people never got to feel.

Sarah's mother had hated him from day one. Her daughter was meant to marry a lawyer or a doctor. She was supposed to drive a fancy car and live in a house in a leafy suburb like the one she'd grown up in. The idea that Sarah might marry a farmer had never even entered Sarah's mother's mind.

They had met at a mate's wedding. He'd taken time away from the farm to come up to Sydney, which had been pretty stressful. In those days he was still running things mostly by himself.

He hadn't expected to fall in love with anyone, let alone a north shore girl from a private school.

Sarah always said she came up to him because he was the only one who hadn't drunk himself into a stupor. It wasn't that he didn't like to drink, but he was planning to drive back down to the farm that night.

They had sat out under the stars together and listened to the dancing going on inside and Sarah had handed him her life to be discussed and examined. She hadn't asked for much from him and Doug preferred it that way. If he had something to say he liked to get it said, but otherwise he liked to listen. You learned to live in the silence when you ran a farm alone. Either you loved it or you went mad.

Sarah was bored with all the university boys. 'Their conversations just circle around the same topics,' she said. 'I don't want to discuss the meaning of life anymore. I want to start living a real life, a life that has meaning because you work hard and get something done.'

If he was honest with himself, Doug knew that he had caught her at the right time. She was looking for an adventure and it was either him or a year in London. From the day he married her he was always aware that she might just wake up one day and be done with him.

Sometimes at night, when the heat stopped him sleeping, he wondered what he would do if she ever left him for a life in the city. He couldn't imagine it.

She seemed happy most of the time, especially after the kids came, but he knew the isolation got to her every now and again.

Doug understood how there could be days when you questioned your own sanity, days that could not be separated from one another. The routine never changed and sometimes those repetitive days could chafe at a person; especially if they were used to a different kind of life.

There had been days in the beginning, when he was just getting started, that he found himself singing every song he could remember, beating the silence with words. Beating the silence and stopping the endless thoughts from going round and round in his head. It didn't happen so much since he'd hired the boys and found Sarah but now, in the time he knew was *after*, in the time he was terrified would be the rest of his life, the thoughts were so terrible he sometimes hummed under his breath so that the monotone of his voice gave him something else to focus on. Sarah stopped the thoughts in her own way. She had grown used to being on the farm but things were different now. No one could get used to this.

He had known when he married Sarah that she would need more than just the farm. Four years ago, when Sarah started making cakes, it was like she had found a part of herself she had been looking for. Doug hadn't understood at first, but then she had shown him the cake she had made for Lockie's fourth birthday—a train made out of icing running across chocolate tracks that went over cake mountains. He had been in awe.

Winning the prize at the Show was the culmination of years of work. Sarah had glowed on the podium. She had lit the place up. She always lit the place up. They were so alike, she and Lockie. They both shined regardless of where they were.

She had won the prize and then, as the applause died down, they had returned to their kids. Sammy was too big for a stroller but she hated all the walking. She was fast asleep in the sea of people, not bothered by the noise or the movement of her stroller as people bumped into it.

But Lockie was gone.

'Oh that boy,' said Sarah, her face still flushed with her success. 'He drives me mad sometimes.'

At that moment, the only thing Doug was feeling was irritation. 'He's probably in here somewhere. But he has to learn that he can't just wander off. He needs to accept that sometimes he has to be responsible for Sammy.' It was important that Lockie grew up knowing how to take care of someone other than himself. There were times when the farm needed both him and Sarah. Times when the floods came and the stock had to be moved, times when the fires came and the stock had to be saved. Lockie would need to be responsible during those times.

Doug circled the room a few times and then moved outside. It was only after about twenty minutes of looking that he considered the possibility that Lockie might actually be lost. Again he felt irritation flare. The boy was going to lose his ride on the rollercoaster for this infraction. Doug never once considered the possibility that they would not find him, though. Kids didn't just disappear. They were always somewhere. They were down by the river when they knew they weren't allowed unless accompanied by an adult. They were climbing trees when they should have been doing their homework. They were hiding under the bed waiting to be found. Kids didn't just disappear. It was only after they had enlisted the help of the security guards and announcements were being made that he began to think they might be in real trouble.

Kids didn't just disappear unless someone made them disappear.

'Relax, mate,' the head of security said. 'We've never lost one yet.' Lots of kids wandered off at the Easter Show, he told them. They were always found, usually somewhere near the food.

Doug had tried to relax, to stay calm, but he could feel the panic building inside him.

The place was too big.

There were too many people.

Lockie could be anywhere.

The police were called. It took hours for everyone to leave the showgrounds because every family was stopped. Every parent was questioned and every child identified. It was way past midnight when everyone had finally gone home, and still they had not found Lockie.

The head of security changed his tone. The police held whispered conversations in groups. They began to look at him with sympathy in their eyes.

Doug felt his heart slow down. There was a ringing in his ears. He was underwater and he couldn't swim.

Lockie was gone.

They had lost one.

Sammy had gone from impatience to hunger to exhaustion. She didn't understand what was happening.

Sarah sat next to the pram twisting her hands. She did not cry. She didn't cry for days, but every time Doug went near her he could hear her muttering the word 'please'. 'Please, please, please, please.' It drove Doug mad and he had to move away because he wanted to hit her, to snap her out of her trance. He had never lifted a hand to his wife or his children, but now he had to close his fist and dig his nails into his palm to keep himself from lashing out.

Sarah didn't believe in hitting children; she believed in time out and consequences. It was different to the way Doug had been raised but he had come around to the idea. The thought of anyone—especially himself—hurting Sarah and the kids was almost too much to bear.

Doug sometimes wondered, after, if whoever had taken his son had hit him. When he did think about someone hurting his boy he could feel his hands curl into fists. He would embrace the rush of heat that came with the anger because at least it was a different feeling to the sorrow and despair. Anger felt constructive. He wanted to kill everyone, even himself. But as fast as the anger came it would recede and he would be back at the place he hated to be. Mired in his own helplessness. There was fuck-all he could do.

They had stayed on even after the Show closed. They stayed at the motel in Sydney for a month, living on microwave food and waiting. At least, Doug and Sammy had eaten. Sarah had begun her existence on dry bread and coffee. She told him she couldn't swallow anything else. Doug went back to the Show every day and walked up and down the aisles of the different pavilions, paced around the rides and food stands, even though he knew that wherever Lockie was, he was not there. The anger and the fear rose and crashed and twisted inside him. Every time there was a sighting their hopes would rise, only to be dashed. People only wanted to help, but after he and Sarah had gone on television all the freaks came out of the woodwork.

Lockie was in Canada.

Lockie was in the city, living as a girl.

Lockie had been drowned in the harbour.

Lockie had run away because he'd been abused. (Sarah had woken up for that one. Her denial was so vehement that the police didn't push it any further.)

None of it came to anything. The police divers found nothing. There were only dead ends.

He had called Pete and Pete had come. Pete had wrapped his arms around Doug the same way as he had at the funeral for Doug's father. Back then, he had let Doug know that he would step in for his old friend and be around when Doug needed a guiding hand. Now he came because having a cop— even a small town cop—on your side was a good thing. But eventually the city police just found Pete annoying. His belief in the basic goodness of human beings was misplaced in the city.

'Where's Lockie?' Sammy asked every day.

'We're looking for him,' Doug told her.

She had stopped asking the question lately and Doug had taken it as a sign. It was time to give up. Lockie was never coming home.

He had started saying it to himself as he worked, repeating the words again and again—'He is never coming home'— in the hope that eventually they would sink in and he could accept the truth.

He wanted to die sometimes. He wanted to get into bed and not have to wake up.

He wanted to die but he had to take care of Sarah and Sammy.

When they had to return home because they were running out of money and the farm was suffering, Doug felt like he was leaving his boy to die alone. He had felt his heart tear as they pulled out of the city in the ute. The drive down had been filled with Lockie's voice and demands for ice cream and bathroom breaks. The drive home was silent. Sammy and Sarah slept most of the way back.

When they stopped for food only Sammy could eat.

There was an unreality about the days and months that followed. Doug was alone, trapped in his bubble of pain. He wanted to help Sarah but he couldn't help himself. What words could soothe her? What words could soothe any of them?

He and Sarah didn't talk anymore.

They exchanged words about dinner and the farm and what avenue they should pursue next but they had nothing to say to each other.

Sarah blamed him.

Doug could see it in her face. She blamed him but that was okay. He blamed himself. He should never have left the kids.

He should have let someone else carry the cake when they asked for it to be put on the podium, but he was so damn proud of Sarah. It felt like his whole world was being applauded. It felt like the end of the bad times. The rain had begun to fall and the sheep were getting fat. After so many years of questions from the bank and late-night discussions about selling the farm they were finally back on track, and now Sarah had won first prize.

Sixty seconds. It couldn't have been more than that. He had kept saying it to the police and even though they eventually began to give him strange looks he couldn't stop saying it.

At home Sarah had shut down. The doctor had given her sleeping pills and she took them every night. She turned her back to him and slept until she was forced out of bed.

Doug lay awake. He could not take the pills. He had tried them once after Dr Samuels had given them to Sarah. That night his dreams were filled with rage and fear and he could see Lockie running in front of him but he couldn't catch him. When he eventually did grab hold of him, the boy was not Lockie. Lockie was gone. The next morning he reversed the ute into the side of one of the sheds. After that, he hadn't taken any more of the pills.

Instead he lay awake and stared at the ceiling and replayed the day in his head over and over again wondering what he had missed.

Someone had taken his child.

It was an inconceivable thought.

Every morning since it had happened he woke up convinced that it was just a dream, that he would find Lockie in his pyjamas eating his breakfast on the couch when he was supposed to be in the kitchen.

All those rules meant fuck-all now. Sarah just let Sammy do as she pleased. Doug would have given his right arm to be able to yell at Lockie for spilling milk on the couch. Literally—his right arm. He had already made that bargain with God and the universe, but if that wasn't enough his life was also available. If Lockie could come home safe he was willing to give up his own life. He was completely certain about that.

The moment right between waking and tuning into the day was the one moment he looked forward to most of all. In that moment everything was still the same. His family was whole and the nightmare they had been living was just that—a nightmare.

Then reality would hit and he would feel his whole body sink into the mattress with the devastation that accompanied him throughout the rest of the day.

He missed Lockie so much it was an ache just above his heart. He had thought that he might be having a heart attack but the ache never changed. It just stayed that way day after day. When the lambs began to appear he thought of Lockie feeding the babies whose mothers rejected them. When the canola was ready he thought of Lockie running hell for leather through the plants with the pure joy of energy and space.

When Sammy said something funny he thought of Lockie laughing.

He thought of Lockie.

He thought of Lockie.

He thought of Lockie.

When his son's birthday had come along he had tried to be strong. He had helped Sarah wrap the presents and put them in Lockie's room but then he ran out of strength.

He had taken a six-pack and gone to the shed. In the morning he had stayed away from the house. When he finally did go home he found his wife curled up in his son's bed. Sammy was eating peanut butter out of the jar with a spoon. The house that Sarah was so proud of was littered with dirty clothes and empty packets of biscuits. Sammy was wearing the same clothes she had worn the night before. Bits of chocolate biscuit clung to her cheeks.

'Mum is sleeping and sleeping and sleeping,' said Sammy.

They were falling apart.

Doug heard his father's voice then, reminding him of his role. 'The man of the house keeps it all together, boy. Do you understand me? When the stock are dying and the heat bakes your bones you have to keep it all together so that when the rain falls again your family is still there with you.'

Doug had kept it together. He stopped drinking and he took over for Sarah. If she got up and looked after Sammy he went to work, but on the days she stayed in bed he looked after Sammy and got her to school. Or he called Pete's wife, Margie.

He got through the day by sticking to the routines Sarah had established and he didn't hope life would go back to normal one day. He knew better than that. Regardless of what he told Sarah and Sammy, he knew that this terrible sense of desolation would be his for life.

He tried to imagine being an old man and telling someone about the boy he had lost but he could never picture it. He could never picture Sarah sitting next to him on the veranda, watching over their grandchildren, though he had been able to picture it once. The image had been so clear to him, and on nights when he felt he might be losing her it had been a comfort.

Now he could no longer see them together in some bright future. He could not see them together at all. All he saw was himself—alone with only the faintest memory of his golden family.

He saw a man who had lost everything, and it had only taken sixty seconds.

Tina

Two burgers and two cartons of fries later, Tina was basically asleep on her feet. She knew she should have tried to fit in a few more jobs before she headed home but it was freezing and the streets were nearly empty.

Winter in the Cross was a lousy time to be alive.

Tina pulled out a packet of cigarettes and gave herself a treat. Each pack had to last a week. They were so fucking expensive. She gazed up at the ceiling of McDonald's and waited for the manager to kick her out for smoking. She and Arik were almost friends. He would slip her some extra food if he could, but he always kicked her out for smoking. Rules were rules. Tina didn't mind. She still remembered a life where everyone imagined that the world could be controlled by rules. She thought back on that life and now she knew what she had given up, how much she had given up, and there were times when she questioned her choices. Not all the time, just every day and every night. Tina allowed herself a grim smile.

She watched the empty streets and enjoyed the smoke filling her lungs.

The rain had stopped but the wind was making up for it.

She didn't think about the boy. Every time his short, dirty blond hair and runny nose crossed her mind she didn't think about him. The man could not be the boy's father. Any evil fuck could have a child but Tina could not bear the thought of that man being the boy's father. If the boy belonged to someone else, if the man had taken what was not his to take, then where had he found the boy? And what did he want him for? He told her it was good to 'feel a woman's lips' so whose lips had he been feeling?

'Jesus Fuck,' said Tina out aloud. The food rose in her stomach and she sucked heavily on the cigarette to keep the burgers where they belonged. She finished her cigarette without having to go outside. Arik was a good bloke. He knew how cold it was. She could imagine him looking up from his desk at the back and sighing in frustration at the thin curl of cigarette smoke filling his store. She was sure he would have kicked anyone else out.

He had a wife and two little girls at home and he told Tina to go home every time he saw her.

'You don't belong here, Tina. You know things can only get worse. Go back home, go back to school. Do something else with your life.'

Arik was studying to be a lawyer. He had plans. One day he would have a house in the suburbs and drive one of those cars that made you smile every time you got into it. One day his wife wouldn't be cleaning other people's houses while she took care of her kids and tried to study to be a teacher.

Arik had a lot of *one days* in his future.

He was a lot older than Tina, but when she listened to him talk Tina felt like a grandparent listening to an eager child. She didn't have the heart to tell him what could happen to his dream life in the suburbs. All those painted fences and electric garage doors hid a lot of the same things you saw on the streets in the Cross. Just because the package was beautifully wrapped didn't mean it wasn't still full of shit.

Tina never planned beyond that day, that hour, that minute. What for?

The boy's face drifted across her mind again. He couldn't have been more than nine.

Timmy had been eight, but he was a big eight. At least, he had been a big eight. He was really small towards the end. Just skin stretched over bones really.

'This is my daughter Christina and my son Timothy,' her mother had said.

'Tim and Tina,' laughed the man who they would come to know as Jack. Jack the do-gooder. Jack the Christian. Jack the substitute daddy.

He thought a few months at church would turn them right back into a real family.

A few sermons would make them forget everything that had happened before he arrived. It was almost funny. Some adults never grew up. They stopped believing in the Tooth Fairy and Santa Claus but they held on to the idea of a kindly old man looking down from the clouds.

Tina found it easier to believe in the Tooth Fairy. At least she performed a simple economic transaction. Your teeth for money. Easy.

She wasn't sure exactly what a belief in the kindly man in the sky got you. Her mother and Jack had prayed every night, begging for Tim to be saved. Jack believed, really believed right up to the end, that Tim would pull through.

Tina watched her brother shrink and knew better. All she could hold on to was the anger that warmed her. It was still there right in the churning pit of her stomach. Nothing would ever make it go away.

Tina hated Jack from day one even though he was good to Tim when he got sick.

Jack hated her back. He wanted her to be something she couldn't be.

God wants us to keep our language pure, Christina. You do not need to use such profanity.

It's Tina, said Tina. *Just Tina.*

You carry the name of our Lord, Christina. He was sent to save us. You should thank God every day for sending Him. God wants your gratitude. God wants us to humble ourselves before Him, Christina. You must pray on your knees. God wants you to attend church so that you may hear His glory, Christina. God wants, Christina, God wants.

Fuck what God wants, Tina thought but she had chosen to keep silent in front of Jack. Her mother smiled at Jack and her mother laughed at Jack and her mother prayed with Jack. Her mother was happy with Jack. He had succeeded where Tim and Tina had failed. Tim was too sick to do anything and Tina had been raising herself ever since the divorce. Mothers can't just check in when they feel like it.

Give her time, Jack, she would hear her mother say when all the bedroom doors were closed.

Why does she have to be so belligerent, Claire? Why can't she just get along with us? Why does every discussion have to be an argument?

I know, she's very difficult. She and Tim are so close, I don't know what will happen to her when it's all over.

I can see how upset she is, Claire. I know that she feels powerless but if she could just look to God she would know that He is watching over her and she can turn to Him for help.

I know that, Jack. I can see you're working hard to help her but when I look at Tim it all seems hopeless.

We have to believe he'll be fine, Claire. God needs our faith and our belief or He cannot perform miracles.

I believe, Jack, I do . . . I'm just a little tired tonight.

Christina needs to pray with us. She needs to believe as well.

Oh, Jack, I don't think that's going to happen. I'm not sure what Christina believes anymore.

There were moments that it all came back and, try as she might, Tina could never control the flow of memories. What surprised her most at the time and what still continued to surprise her was how quickly things could transform. Your world could implode in an instant. When she was ten she had the perfect family. Mum, Dad, Tim and a dog named Buster. It was so boring and predictable it was pathetic. It was a life that belonged in a commercial for the latest family car. But then her father decided he'd had enough of family life. None of the commercials ever used that sort of family. The sort of family where one parent just decides he doesn't want to deal with it all anymore. Can't sell a car to that type of family.

Those were the actual words he used. *I've had enough of this whole family thing, Claire. Sorry.*

And then he was gone. He never called, he never sent money. He just wiped them out of his life. It seemed impossible to Tina that someone could do that. After that they were no longer boring and predictable. She was taking care of Timmy and her mother was either working or crying. Tina felt like one of those soldiers returned from the war. Shell-shocked.

Jack had been the one who was going to make it all right again.

Please, Christina, give him a chance. I need someone in my life, Christina. You don't know how hard it's been.

Tina had laughed at that. *You're right, Mum; I have fuck-all idea how hard it's been.*

They wanted her to go for counselling, especially after Tim, but it just wasn't going to happen. No way was she going to change for some arsehole do-gooder. Tim had been eight and he would never be nine. No amount of talking would change that.

You can't keep blaming me, Christina; it wasn't my fault he got sick.

I'm not blaming you. I know it wasn't your fault.

You're lying, Christina. I see the way you look at me. You think I'm a bad mother. You think I should have noticed sooner. You don't understand how hard it is to be a mother, a single mother. I've held it all together, Christina, and I can't look at you when you judge me like that. I can't even look at you.

So don't look, Mum. Look somewhere else. Look where you have been looking all the time that he was sick. Look there.

Well, her mother didn't have to look at her now.

There was nothing left for her afterwards. Her mother still worked, only now she came home to cook dinner for him, to talk to him, to fuck him. There was even talk of another child. Her mother was doing exactly what her father had done, wiping the slate clean and starting again. Just because she whined about wanting to be a family again didn't make it any different.

There was nothing left for Tina. Her mother didn't act like someone who had lost a kid. She just got on with it.

Everyone grieves in their own way, said Jack. *Try to be patient and understanding, Christina. You have to pray, Christina. Only through prayer will you find the answer. Only through God will you see a purpose. Your mother is at peace with God's purpose.*

Is she high on prayer then? Tina had asked as her mother raced up and down the house cleaning and singing.

You have the devil in you, Christina, said Jack.

I think the devil is too busy to bother with me, said Tina.

And do you want to know something else, Christina? God knows of your disdain for Him. God knows that you have no faith in your heart. If you had faith you could have saved Tim. You could have saved him if you had prayed from your heart and if you had given your soul to God.

Tina had felt tears choke her.

I'm sorry, Christina. I did not mean ... you can be a very difficult child, Christina.

You don't have to worry about that, Jack, since I'm not your child. She knew Jack's words came from anger and frustration but they burned themselves into her very being.

Jack didn't back off. He wouldn't leave her alone. His desire to convert her took over their lives. He seemed incapable of having any conversation with her that did not involve God. Tina stayed out at friends' houses or at school activities or she just wandered the local shopping centre. But she had to come home. And each time she came home Jack had more control over her mother.

Meal times became sermons after Tim died. She wasn't allowed to eat in her room. She wasn't allowed to watch television.

In this house we pray before we eat, Christina, Jack said.

In this house we dress in appropriate clothes, Jack said.

In this house we honour your mother and we accept the guidance of adults, Jack told her.

It was my house before it was your house, Tina said.

Jack had remained silent on that point but her mother darted around the table and slapped her hard. Her hand cut across Tina's face so quickly that after the sting was gone Tina could not be sure it had even happened. It had never happened before, not even when her mother could not hide her despair at having to raise two children on her own. It had never happened until Jack came.

This is Jack's house now, Christina, her mother had yelled. *Jack's house and my house. Do you understand me?*

Tina had been stunned. Her mouth had opened and closed but there were no words available to her. Jack had bowed his head and refused to look at her but she could see the twitch of his mouth, hiding his smile.

She had known that she would not be able to stay, known it then and there but she had waited, holding on to Tim's memory. Holding on to who he had been because her mother seemed so desperate to forget.

Of course Tim had been more Tina's kid than anything else. Tina lost a kid. She had actually felt her heart break in two inside her chest. It was a slicing pain that left you stunned. Half the time she couldn't breathe properly. The constant lump in her throat made eating hard.

Too bad mothering couldn't be a part-time job.

No one in the Cross knew about Tim. Why would they?

And if she saw his face every time she passed a boy about the same age what difference did it make?

Jack kept using the word 'heal'.

Tina and her mother were in the process of healing; they had to heal and soon they would be healed. But Tina knew that was a load of shit. Tim's death wasn't some broken bone that could be fixed. Nothing could fix that. It pissed her right off the way everyone expected her to regenerate her heart the way she could regenerate skin on a cut.

She cleared the table and stubbed out her cigarette in the garbage bin. She raised her hand to Arik before she left but didn't wait to see if he waved back.

Out in the street she pulled her coat tightly around her and played with the money in the pockets. It felt good to have a little in her pocket again. She had been stupid with the money she made last week. Books were too expensive, even when they were second-hand. Books were a place to go even on the harshest of days, but even though she restricted herself the same way she did with her cigarettes, they were still finished too soon. She read when she woke up in the afternoon. She read in the dying light of the day and escaped into other worlds where at least the author was in control. People did all sorts of things to escape the Cross. Tina hid in the pages of a book. It was the warmest place she could find. She had tried the library once, using an old student ID card to join. The librarian had shrugged her shoulders and accepted the address that was so far away from the Cross. When Tina brought the book home to her house, her residence, her dwelling, her current domicile, someone had trashed it while she was out. She hadn't gone back after that. Afraid to be asked for the book or the money for the book. Tina felt an unpleasant twist in her stomach whenever she walked past the building now, upset at having betrayed the librarian's trust.

The library used to be a sanctuary. Now it was just one more place she couldn't go. Tina's mother had taken her to the library every week, filled with pride at how quickly her daughter got through a book. She had taken her to the library *before*. Before everything.

Tim had loved the library as well. He liked books about monsters and when he got bigger he liked books about mysteries. He added 'detective' to the list of things he wanted to be when he grew up. What books did the boy under the table like to read? Did his mother take him to the library? Did he have a mother?

If the clean man was not the boy's father and if he had taken him, Tina knew that someone must be looking for him. She wanted someone to be looking for him.

Tina made her way slowly through the freezing streets until she came to the building where she would spend the night. It was four weeks away from demolition. The notice got pinned up and torn down every week. The bloke from the council was one determined little fuck. Tina sighed at the thought of having to find somewhere else to live. When she first found her way to the Cross she had slept on a park bench for a few days. It was the height of summer and the park was always filled with people. She slept in fits and starts, terrified of anyone who came near her. Everyone was a threat then, and if she hadn't met Ruby she would probably have tried to make her way back home. But she had met Ruby in McDonald's over a dawn breakfast. Then she had stayed with Ruby for a while, until Ruby got jittery. If there was one thing Tina could pick up on, it was when she had worn out her welcome.

She climbed the stairs, not even noticing the smell anymore. She had never imagined that she would get used to the putrid smells in the Cross, but here she was, living among them and surviving. 'Adapt or die, baby,' Ruby had said.

In the unit on the second floor, four young boys were asleep on the floor. Young only described their chronological age. The boys had been in the Cross for longer than Tina had. They'd already lived a couple of lifetimes each.

'You're a bright girl, Tina,' Arik always said. 'You could be anything you wanted to be.'

'We're all pretty clever here in the Cross, Arik. Just surviving keeps you on your toes.'

Inside a few candles were almost at the end of their lives, sending flickering shadows onto the walls. There was an old crappy couch in the living room but not much else. Tina knew better than to start collecting stuff. She tried only to keep things she could carry when she moved. She would be leaving this building soon and who knew how long she would be in the next place, wherever that would be.

Mark lifted his head when he heard her come in.

'Hey, Teen, good night?'

'Nah, completely fucked. No one's even on the street. You?'

'Shit, but I did get a couple. Have you eaten?'

'Yeah, thanks, but I have to make the money stretch. I don't know if I'll get anywhere tomorrow either.'

Mark wouldn't let her starve but every dollar she took from him was a dollar he didn't have. Mark had a habit. He needed the money or he went completely crazy. Wild, mad, lunatic, insane.

Ruby had introduced Tina to Mark.

'This is my baby brother Mark,' Ruby had said, and then she'd laughed because Mark's dark skin couldn't have come from the same family as Ruby's tilted eyes.

'Ruby likes to look out for the young ones,' Mark said. 'I was only eleven when I got here.'

'That's really young. Were you scared?'

Mark laughed. 'Not as scared as I was at home.'

When she was moving around every night Mark always found her and told her where he would be. It was strictly a friendship. Neither could stand to be touched once they had finished working. Tina was never really sure which gender Mark would choose to be with if he could choose. As it was he had a habit to feed and a wall to stand against, waiting for men with money to feed it.

Then Mark and his posse, as he called them, found this place. Tina was amazed. She had no idea how these boys who did such terrible things to themselves could still believe in anything, let alone the concept of a group who could protect and care for each other. But they did and they liked having Tina around. Sometimes she forgot herself and told one of the boys to take a shower or another to eat something. They always looked at her like she was crazy but Tina could sense the momentary warmth it gave them—the idea of someone looking after them.

Mark had insisted that Tina be allowed to stay in the unit and then he insisted that she be given the bedroom. The boys hadn't protested much. Patrick and Alex were too far gone most of the time to care anyway and Adam liked her. The unit had the advantage of being on the second floor. No leaking from above and no water from the streets. The kitchen had already been wrecked by some former tenant and the walls were covered in graffiti tags but it was a home of sorts.

Tina didn't know who used the other units in the building. The residents didn't exactly exchange information. Once she and the boys had moved in no one tried to get them out. Even among the people with nothing to their names and nowhere to go there was a kind of code. Once a squat had been claimed that was it.

Tina gave Mark a small, weary smile. One battle-scarred soldier to another. 'Met a fucking psycho tonight,' she said quietly. The words didn't really express what she wanted to say but there was no point in pushing Mark into any sort of long discussion. His concentration was shot.

'They're all psychos,' whispered Mark.

'Yeah.' And that was all Tina could say. Part of her wanted to tell Mark about the boy, about his blue eyes and his skinny blue fingers. The words hovered on the tip of her tongue and then she swallowed them along with her guilt over the boy and her fear for him and the loss and despair she had seen in his body. 'Yeah,' she repeated. 'They're all fucking psychos.'

When he was level Mark would offer Tina money, but when he needed a hit he would turn into a bit of a psycho himself and demand it back. Tina knew better than to trust him when he said it wouldn't happen again. Boys or men, they were all the same.

'Don't believe one fucking thing they say,' Ruby had warned her, but Tina had already learned that lesson for herself.

Mark's last low had been a bit brutal. Her arm had only been bruised but it felt broken and there was all the crap of having to deal with the hospital. It was easier to let Mark keep his money. Mark was Mark and they all had their issues.

Mark pulled his sleeping bag up to his ears and closed his eyes. He was finished talking. The sleeping bag was warm. It was made for the coldest of winters. Tina blew him a kiss and went through to her bedroom. There was an old foam mattress on the floor with her sleeping bag.

The sleeping bags were the best job Mark and his friends had ever pulled. The bag had a hood and she could zip herself in completely. Some camping store in the city had thrown a massive sale and piled the footpaths with stuff to attract those with money to spend. Mark and the boys were just hanging around, waiting for the sun to set on a hot summer day. His friends told him he was full of shit to want the sleeping bags but Mark had been in the Cross long enough to know that summer would end.

Summer had ended but Tina knew that she would at least be warm in the cold squat when she slept. It wasn't a real home, but it was a place to come back to. The one thing she really missed was a bathroom. The one thing among the many, many other things.

The building had no water although it did, for some reason, still have electricity. She would have loved a heater but there was no way anyone wanted to draw attention to the building. They used the lights occasionally but a heater would probably give someone down at the electricity company the heads-up that they were using the space. They knew, everyone knew, but there was no need to throw a party and invite the council.

Tina took off her shoes and zipped herself into the sleeping bag. In the morning she would go to the gym for a shower. The gym membership was the most important thing she owned. It still had three months to go and Tina would savour every one of them. It was a parting gift from Ruby. At least that's how Tina liked to think of it.

Tina looked around the room in the dark while her eyes adjusted. She had been too tired to check her stuff tonight but she usually checked it every time she came in from being out on the streets. Three broken plastic boxes weighted down with bricks contained her clothes and her books. She made sure she never got attached to anything. If something meant enough to her, it went in the backpack that never left her side. Even now it was shoved in the sleeping bag with her.

Tina's body felt heavy and warm but sleep darted away each time she tried to catch it. The boy under the table didn't even have a blanket. He didn't have a pillow or some ragged old toy that he had been dragging around since he was a baby.

'He's not Tim,' Tina said aloud in the dark room.

Tim had carried a ratty old teddy bear everywhere when he was little. He named it Mr Lulu and insisted it was a boy. Even when he got too big for the toy it had still been on his bed. Then he got sick and Mr Lulu helped him get through the treatments and the long nights of pain. The thing had been vomited on more times than anyone could count but it survived every cycle in the washing machine.

Kids needed something to drag around with them. Some nights, when things looked completely dark, Tina longed for her old stuffed puppy dog. Of course she longed for a lot of things.

What did the kid under the table long for? Freedom? Death? Tim had longed for death at the end.

I'm so tired Tina, please just let me sleep okay? He didn't know what he meant, of course. He thought if he could just get enough rest he would be able to wake up again and get out of the special bed that went up and down with the touch of a button. Tina thought he should know, thought he would want to know, but her mother was adamant. They kept telling him he was going to get better.

God is the greatest healer, Christina, her mother said. Tina had looked at her and realised she had no clue who her mother was anymore.

Tim longed for sleep. He longed to rest his body. The boy under the table would not be able to rest if he was freezing. You could not rest if your body had to keep moving to stay warm.

Tina turned over in her sleeping bag and willed herself to close her eyes but the boy was the only picture she could see.

She grabbed a torch out of her backpack and switched it on, choosing one of the books she had read before. She would comfort herself with familiar words and wait for dawn and hopefully then she could sleep. Hopefully.

Sarah

On the day, on *that* day, the day they lost him, he had refused the breakfast at the restaurant.

The eggs weren't cooked properly. He liked his scrambled eggs dry and separated. The eggs on the plate in front of him oozed and clumped together. He had folded his arms and stared in horror.

Sarah had tried a minute of bargaining, offering Lockie a lamington as a treat if he ate his eggs before she heard Doug's irritated hiss of breath.

'He'll eat what's there or he can leave it. Eat your food, Sarah.' Doug wasn't one to send food back in a restaurant. He was out of his element and it showed. Sarah had listened, biting her lip—keeping the words inside. She hadn't wanted to make a scene. She hated to stand out for the wrong reasons.

As it was she could feel the stares. The country dust stuck to her no matter where she went now. Doug never looked like anything but what he was. Everyone in the restaurant could tell they were in the city for the Show. She could not remember the casual Sarah who needed her morning latte before she did anything else. She had willingly given that Sarah up, it was true, but when she was back in the city she yearned for the ease with which she used to walk in and out of coffee shops and giant shopping centres.

The irony of her situation was not lost on her now. The whole of Australia knew her name for some very wrong reasons.

Lockie had eaten toast with peanut butter instead and Doug had said, 'Leave him be, Sarah. We'll be eating all day at the Show.' Sarah had known that Doug was probably right. The excitement of the show would make the hours fly past and lunch would come soon enough. Lockie's choice of a corndog was already set firmly in his mind.

But Lockie was lost before lunch and he didn't get to have his corndog or his lamington.

The promised cake had occupied her mind completely at first. She should have given it to him before lunch. What difference would it have made? She spent so much time keeping to routine and saying no. Children needed routine. That's what all the books said. That's how her mother had done it; or, rather, how the nanny had done it. Routine and discipline made children feel secure.

What difference would the lamington have made? Perhaps the sweet chocolate taste would have been something for him to cling to wherever he was now. She imagined how he would have crammed the cake in his mouth, not pausing for breath or to chew properly. She saw the streaks of chocolate on his cheek. She saw his smile.

Sarah wondered what they—the 'they' who had taken her child; the 'they' or the 'him' or the 'her'—were feeding him.

Sometimes a fear dug at her until she acknowledged it: maybe they weren't feeding him at all.

Who would do that? Who would willingly starve a child? Who would hurt her baby? Who would take her baby? Who was this person and why were they allowed to exist?

And what would I do to that person if I got the chance?

There were days when she lay on the bed and concocted scenarios in her head. She would see herself finding Lockie. She was never really sure of the place. It would be a dark room in a dark house but the location wasn't important. She would see herself rescuing her child, folding him in her arms and saying his name. Then she would see the person who had taken him.

There was never a face, just a body with a blank head, but Sarah would see herself grow until she towered over the person and then she would hit and hit and hit until there was nothing left and all the time she would be screaming, 'How dare you take my child? How dare you take him?'

She had to find him. The desperate need to find him swirled around her body with everything she did. It ate into her soul and sometimes she had to hold on to the kitchen counter to stop herself running out into the road and screaming his name. She wanted to be looking for him all the time. She wanted to leave Sammy and Doug and just keep going until she got to the city and then she wanted to knock on every door across the whole of Sydney until she found her son. But maybe he wasn't even in Sydney anymore.

Maybe he wasn't even in Australia.

Where are you, Lockie? Where are you, where are you, where are you?

Each day she slashed through the date on her *Flowers of Australia* calendar with a red pen. One more day had passed and he wasn't home. Four months had passed and he wasn't home. Four months; one hundred and twenty-one days; two thousand, nine hundred and four hours and he still wasn't home.

On the days that she made it out of bed—and those were the bad days, because she was awake, and if she was awake she was thinking—she would clean the house and see him walking through the front door. She would make dinner and see him walking through the front door. She would bathe Sammy and see him walking through the front door.

What if he never walked through the front door again?

How would she go on?

So much time had passed, his return seemed at once impossible and just around the corner.

When he first went missing all she had felt was a slight impatience. For a few minutes it had been all about her triumph and she had wanted to celebrate it. She had wanted to celebrate being Sarah Williams—artist. She had won the blue ribbon and the prize money in the wedding-cake division. The money would be used for Christmas presents but the blue ribbon was a joy Sarah had never imagined for herself. She was in a kind of celebratory shock when she walked off the stage.

But when they couldn't find Lockie she had to slip back into mother mode. There were days when mother mode pulled her in kicking and screaming. That moment, just for one moment, she had wanted to remain separate. Just herself, whole and untethered.

As the minutes ticked by she felt her mind slowly growing blank. All she wanted was a chance to hold her boy again. Her prize was forgotten, everything drifted away and the only thing she could think was 'please'. 'Please, please, please.'

Even now she couldn't find the blue ribbon, although the money had helped fund the long days in Sydney. Her ribbon had been lost and not missed in those whirling hours she spent rocking and begging the universe.

Being a mother was all-consuming. There were so many mistakes you could make, so many ways to lose a child. The whole world was a threat. In the years after Lockie's birth she became addicted to those current-affair shows that inter-viewed parents who had made the one fatal mistake. They had let the blind cord dangle on the ground, they had left the pool gate unlocked, they had put the pot too close to the edge of the stove, they had just ducked into the shopping centre and left the child in the car. They had taken their eyes off the ball and that way lay tragedy and regret.

Sarah watched to see what mistake had been made and each time had been able to congratulate herself on never making any of those mistakes. But then she had made a mistake—one worthy of a current-affairs show.

She had looked away.

Doug had looked away.

They had lost Lockie.

Lockie had been lost.

It was so arbitrary. So cruel.

Everyone looked away at some point, didn't they? Why had she been the one to pay for so small a transgression?

Whenever she allowed herself to surface she acknowledged that she was being punished. She was being punished for her sin of pride. She had been so proud of the beautiful wedding cake that had taken six long weeks to create. The three tiers had to be covered in smooth white fondant icing before she could even begin to decorate them, and three times she'd had to start over when she'd failed to achieve the surface she needed. She had guiltily turned the damaged cake into lamingtons, aware of the money the fondant cost, aware of the waste—the terrible waste.

The cake was covered in fifty lilac and black fondant roses. Each rose had taken her twenty minutes to make, and each rose had been remade at least twice. The paste for colours and the fondant were only available in the city. Doug had smiled and waved her off on the train when she went up for a couple of days. He had given her the money when she knew there was none. Sarah knew that he was relieved she had found something to curb her restless soul. She knew he watched for signs she would leave for good. On the train she had been ashamed of herself for not telling him more often that she wasn't going anywhere. She had accepted the money and kept quiet about a truth only she knew, but she had been ashamed. The prize had swept that shame away.

She had returned from the city excited with her supplies and full of ideas for the cake. Doug had watched her work for a few nights, but she found his presence suffocating. She felt she was proving her worth with every flower. Each small tendril was drawn separately and then placed on the cake. The tiniest of details were the most important. Small, glistening drops of sugar lay on some of the petals, inspired by the rain and the smell of renewal that wafted through the house when it began.

She had begun decorating cakes with nothing more than a spatula and an icing bag, but for her birthday Doug had presented her with a collection of everything she could possibly use to create her cakes. Another wife would have seen the gift of domestic tools as an insult but Sarah knew that the specialist icing tools had to be sent away for and she had hugged them to her chest, grateful for Doug's understanding of her need to do something else and occasionally be somewhere else. The idea for the wedding cake had begun with a faintly remembered dream of her own wedding.

She worked late into the night with only her own thoughts for company. She worked in the easy silence of a house at the end of a long day.

She worked through the heat of the summer and then she had worked as the rain began to fall. The beautiful, wonderful, needed rain.

Doug and the children had been asleep and she had worked on the cake. Well, the children had been asleep. She had known that Doug was awake when the rain came, listening to the drops and working out how much and how long.

She had watched her own hands produce the beautiful flowers and admired her ability to do such a thing. She had not been able to believe the beauty of the cake when it was completed. For the two days before they left for the Show the house was filled with friends and neighbours. They came to admire and to congratulate and to wish her luck.

The drive up had been nerve-racking and she had made Doug pull over numerous times so she could check that the cake was safe in its layers of tissue and cardboard and wood. It wasn't until she placed it on her stand that she had relaxed and embraced the idea of some time away from the farm.

And then to win the prize had been incredible. She felt like she was being seen, actually being seen, for the first time in the endless years of being a mother and a wife.

She had committed the sin of pride.

Her mother had almost said as much. Alison had no idea what Sarah's cake decorating meant to her, and what it meant to go to the Show. Her mother thought a trip to the Show should only be about the children.

'You mind those little ones, Sarah,' her mother had cautioned.

'Of course, Mum—but don't you want to meet us and spend the day with us? The children would love it.'

'Will Douglas be accompanying you?'

'Of course, Mum, you know he will.'

'I have my bridge game, dear. I can't miss the game. How will they get a fourth?'

Sarah had called her mother to tell of her failure to protect Lockie and even on the phone she could sense Alison thinning her lips.

'Well I have to say, Sarah, I never took my eyes off you or your sister when we went to the Show. Mothers have to have eyes in the back of their heads. Do you want me to come?'

'No, Mum, I'll keep you posted, I'll . . .' And Sarah had put down the phone. She would not have been able to stand her mother's presence. Sarah had considered calling her sister but she had no idea what to say. Caitlyn was living in Dubai while her husband worked a five-year contract with one of the big oil companies. The sisters were worlds away from each other. When Caitlyn called Sarah refused to speak to her. She didn't want to talk and she didn't want anyone else in her house. She felt a desperate desire to be alone with her thoughts of her son.

As it was her skin crawled when Sammy climbed on her or Doug asked her what she wanted to eat.

She felt like she needed to sit very still until Lockie came back. She could not eat or drink or move until he came back.

Sarah had not expected comfort or reassurance from her mother. The time for that sort of mother–daughter relationship was long past. She had in fact called for confirmation that Lockie going missing was her fault. She had known it was, and once her mother had spoken Sarah had unleashed the full fury of her guilt upon herself.

It was her fault Lockie was lost.

It was her fault someone had taken Lockie.

Mea culpa, mea culpa, mea culpa.

Sarah spoke to her mother less with each passing week. Her mother had not been overly attached to the children. She had only met Lockie a few times. She had found him too boisterous, too tanned by the country sun and too casual in his manners. Her mother had dreamed of a daughter who married a professional man and occasionally dropped by for tea with perfectly groomed children who could discuss the weather. She had worked hard to turn Sarah into that kind of child and she had almost succeeded.

The night she had met Doug, Sarah had been contemplating a proposal from Edward, an accountant whose parents were close friends of the family.

Sarah had been pleased with the match, pleased with how pleased her mother would be. She had seen herself fitting right into the four-wheel-drive school zone at the little school she herself had attended. And then she had met Doug. Beautiful Doug with his blue eyes and blond hair and shoulders that could hold the world.

For the first few years she had known him Sarah had assumed that beneath the quiet exterior lay a deep river churning with emotions, an idea gleaned from the romance novels of her youth. But there was only the surface with Doug.

There was a simplicity to him that Sarah found a relief. After so many years of being tutored in the importance of hiding the horrors of a real self from the world, she sighed and took a deep joyful breath at being with someone who hid nothing. If he was angry he said so and if he wanted to be alone he told her so. She never had to wonder about him and even now, in the depths of this terrible nightmare, she could read everything he was feeling. He knew that she blamed him and he was right. But the blame she threw his way was nothing compared to her own culpability.

It didn't seem possible at first.

Doug kept saying that he had only looked away for sixty seconds.

The head of security kept telling them that they'd never lost a kid at the Show.

The room had felt so full of love when they had been applauding her triumph. Everyone was smiling. They were happy for her. Who among those people could have taken her child? Who could have taken him and what had they done to him?

If only she'd been tougher on him when he'd wandered away in the beginning. He had kept racing ahead of them but he was always easy to spot with his golden curls covered in a red Bulldogs cap. She should have yelled and threatened but it was such a special day for all of them. She wanted it to be a memory that the children held on to forever.

So she had smiled and warned him lightly, had mentioned possible danger, but Lockie hadn't really listened.

Lockie had always thrust himself head first into life. As a toddler he was covered in bumps and bruises because he could not understand that he needed to get walking right before he ran. He climbed and jumped and laughed his way through endless scrapes and cuts. He had exhausted her.

Sometimes she caught Sammy looking at her when she was involved in a task. Not looking—staring. She was letting Sammy down now as she had let Lockie down at the Show.

'Rubbish,' Margie said on the days when she came over to watch Sammy. 'You're a wonderful mother, Sarah. You didn't let anyone down. Someone took our boy and you know we'll not rest until we get him back. But someone took him. Lockie let go of the stroller and someone took him. It wasn't your fault.'

'Doug shouldn't have looked away. I shouldn't have looked away.'

'It happened, Sarah. God willing we will get him back, but you have to try and get out of bed, luv. Sammy needs you and Doug barely says a word to anyone these days. My heart breaks for you, it breaks for all of you, but Lockie wouldn't have wanted you to do this to yourself.'

Sarah had to bite back the retort that Margie was not a mother. Only another mother could understand.

She had gone into town to buy winter pyjamas and, even though she had seen all the other mothers looking, had heard the whispers wafting through the air like bad smells, she had still bought a pair for Lockie. She had chosen the Ben 10 flannel pyjamas in a size ten because Lockie liked his pyjamas loose and he was a big kid.

She had taken two pairs and placed them defiantly on the counter in front of all the other mothers who had not lost their children, who had not fucked up so horribly.

The whole town would have coffee over this, she knew they would. They would lay their pity on the table, each more distressed than the other. They were good people and they were hurting for her, Sarah knew that, but as time wore on she could not see them as anything other than tragedy vultures circling over the ruins of her life.

She took the pyjamas home and put them in Lockie's cupboard and when his birthday came she spent money they didn't have filling the cupboard with gifts. Doug had held his tongue. He had kept the words to himself and she was grateful for that.

Dr Samuels suggested talking to someone. He suggested it every time he saw her but Sarah couldn't see the point. What would a psychologist say?

'It's not your fault.'

'You have to forgive yourself.'

'You have to think of Samantha and the rest of the family.'

Sarah repeated the same things to herself over and over but she couldn't make herself believe them.

Some days she made up her mind to let go. She would start putting her life back together, she would bake and cook and clean and take care of Sammy and the farm. But it never happened.

Every morning she pulled open the curtains in his room and she couldn't go on from there.

She had watched the news reports in horror two years ago when that little girl was taken from her hotel room. She had never been found despite the whole world looking. Despite the whole world looking for her, she had never been found.

Never been found.

Sarah had seen the mother on television. She looked completely broken, like her soul was damaged.

How do you recover from that? she had thought, and she had been determined that she would never make such a silly mistake. She would never go out with friends to laugh and drink and leave her children unprotected in a hotel room, even if you could see the room.

Evil was everywhere. It was the most astonishing thing to realise but it was true. Most people could not really conceive of someone truly wicked. It was on television and in books, but how could such a person actually exist?

They didn't exist in Cootamundra. The whole town was filled with people just getting through the day, getting through the drought, getting through the work. She had never let Lockie and Sammy roam around town but other parents did and their kids were fine. It wasn't fair. Not fair. Not fucking fair. She knew how the woman on the television felt now. You never got over such a thing. You never got on with your life, you never recovered, you never . . . you never anything.

In her darker moments she thought that it would be easier if Lockie had died. At least then they would know where he

was. They would know that he would never return. And they
would have to try and pick up the pieces of their lives.

You couldn't pick up the pieces when your child was lost.
You had to leave them on the ground, waiting for the missing
piece. Her puzzle was shattered.

There was Sammy to worry about. Sammy, who had
completed the family. Sammy, the golden girl to go with
Lockie, the golden boy. Sammy, who had been left behind.
Her big eyes watched her parents and she waited for everything to be all right again. Sammy, who had been let down by
her parents when they lost her brother and was now being let
down every day by her mother.

When Sarah couldn't get out of bed for days or when she
had no interest in Sammy's prattling or when she was too tired
to read a story or play a game or smile at a picture from school
she was failing her child. She was losing Sammy just like she'd
lost Lockie only she was doing it by degrees, and for the life of
her she didn't know how to change it. She did not know how
to smile at Sammy when she was so broken.

She had felt the cracks appearing and growing larger day
after day as they sat in the motel room in Sydney waiting
for news. They hadn't wanted to watch television. The room
that had been such an exciting treat at the beginning of the
trip had morphed into a prison by the end of the month.
They could not leave in case there was news, in case Lockie
somehow found his way back, in case they needed to go to the
police station and identify . . . Just in case.

Despite the long empty hours spent in that hated room,
they couldn't switch on the TV until Sammy was asleep.
Lockie's face was all over the news and they hadn't wanted

Sammy to see. As the days passed their story moved further and further back in each news report. The city moved on and the world moved on. Celebrities tore up hotel rooms and politicians cheated on their wives and their taxes.

Now Lockie wasn't mentioned anymore, not unless some other child went missing, and even then it was just a little note at the end, as if to say, 'Oh and by the way, in case you were wondering, Lachlan Williams is still missing.'

In case anyone was wondering.

The world moved on and the news left the front page and here they were, her sad little family, still waiting for the missing piece. And her greatest fear was that she would never really be anyone other than that woman whose child was taken from the Show.

That she would now and forever be that poor, poor woman.

Tina

Tina read until her eyes burned. Her cheap watch told her it was four in the morning. In the other room she heard the soft snores of Mark and the other boys. One of them, she wasn't sure who, cried out in his sleep—an appeal for 'mum'. She often heard this cry from the other room. The voice was always muffled by sleep so she never knew who was dreaming of his mother, but she never asked about it. You couldn't escape your past in dreams and Tina was sure that there must have been times when she called for Tim or even her mother. The dream searches for the lost were never discussed. There were too many secrets to reveal. 'Mum' came the call again and then 'Mum please' and then silence.

Tina saw the boy under the table. She had managed to lose the image as she read about love in another era, but now it came back with such clarity she could have been staring at the child right in front of her. The boy under the table would call for his mother in his sleep. He was only eight, or maybe nine, and Tina knew that he would call for his mother if he managed to stop shivering long enough to dream.

'There's nothing I can do about it,' Tina whispered to the cold air.

You couldn't have saved him, her mother had said.

We should have done more. I should have done more.

You're just a kid, Christina. There was nothing more anyone could do.

Tina sat up in her sleeping bag and then pulled herself out. There was no light at all in the place but she knew her way around in the dark. She put her shoes on, pulled the backpack over her shoulder and tiptoed through to the front door.

'Where are you going?' whispered Mark.

Tina bit her lip. Mark would be good if he had just scored but fuck-all help if he was on his way down.

'Did you get some stuff tonight?' she asked.

'Yeah, all good. Where are you going?'

'Have you still got your knife?'

'Yeah—what the fuck is going on, Teen? Where are you going?'

'I'm going to ... Fuck, I'm going to rescue some sad little kid and you can come with if you want but you can't stop me.'

Mark got up out of his sleeping bag.

'Anything for a laugh,' he said and Tina smiled. Mark was almost a good guy.

Almost.

Once they were back out on the streets of the Cross, Tina explained about the boy under the kitchen table.

'Tina, you're fucked in the head if you think you can help this kid. Let's just go to the police. Tell them where the house is, and they'll get the kid out.'

'Remember when we told the police about Ruby?'

They had knocked on Ruby's door for ages. They had called her phone and they had even tried to break the door down. They knew she needed them so they braved the police station. When they walked into the station they felt like they had targets on their backs. But they had needed help.

Mark was quiet. He looked at the flashing lights of a stripclub.

The police knew she needed them but they just looked right through her. The body was rotting by the time they found it. Maybe they could have saved her. Well, not saved, but helped at least.

That's two people I couldn't save. The words were a stray thought that tormented her while she stood on the street watching the cars go by. The universe had a weird sense of humour. *Two people I couldn't save.*

'No one believes people like us, Mark. We're the scum of the earth.'

'Speak for yourself.'

'I am speaking for myself. I can't just leave that kid there. He only looks half alive now. I have to get him out.'

'Why do you care? It's not your kid.'

'Why don't you care? He's someone's kid. I don't want to discuss it. In or out?'

'Fine,' Mark sighed, 'but you know the bloke probably has a gun or something. You could get us both killed.'

Tina hadn't thought about the possibility of a gun. A security guard could have a gun. A security guard *would* have a gun.

She shrugged. 'It's not like I've never seen a gun before. You stay outside. If you hear a shot, call the police.'

'Yeah, that's a good time to call the police.'

'Shut up, you wanker. Let's just go.' Tina was using her teacher voice again. 'Make sure your phone is on and don't fall asleep on me.' They kept their mobiles working. Tina went to the gym to charge hers and sometimes she went without food rather than run out of credit.

Mark nodded like he understood and suddenly he looked ten years old instead of the sixteen he was.

What the fuck am I doing? Tina asked herself as they walked along the road in the cold.

The rain had stopped but she could feel it preparing for a return.

If the rain stays away and if the guy is a heavy sleeper and if the window really is broken and if it moves without making a noise and if the kid doesn't scream or cry and if I can climb out quickly and if no one sees us . . . If, if, if.

See what you can do, universe.

It took fifteen minutes to find the house. The streets had that eerie silence that three o'clock in the morning always brought with it. The wind had died down but the cold wrapped itself around their bodies. Mark blew warm breath rings in the air.

Tina spotted the window immediately. From the outside it was higher off the ground than it seemed inside. She was glad she had Mark along to help.

'Give me the knife.'

'What's it for?'

'Cutting some rope.'

'I hope it's not too thick. The knife's basically a piece of crap.'

'It'll have to do.'

Tina felt a flash of disbelief at what she was about to attempt. She stomped hard on the feeling. There were a lot of things she did now that she would never have believed possible. Tonight she was going to steal a boy from an animal. Tomorrow—who knew?

Tina stood on Mark's shoulders and tried the window. It moved. Relief flooded her body. She inched it up slowly and quietly just the way Mark had taught her to do when she had been out with him on a job. She had only gone out a couple of times. She didn't enjoy the adrenalin rush and the fear. Sometimes the boys made enough to stop working for a week or so but they always went back to it. Food was cheap but the blissful warmth that came through a needle was expensive. They did what they had to do. Tina had never even taken a step down the path of oblivion, however tempting it sometimes seemed. She held on to her books and the stories in her head. She lost herself in words. It would have made things so much easier to let the warmth in, but it also would have made anything but a life in the Cross almost impossible. She didn't think about the future but sometimes it crossed her mind that one day she might be somewhere else. She knew it would be better if she managed to hold on to a little of the person she had been, just in case she needed her again.

She held on to that and a regular shower.

The window slipped up easily enough.

The man would be the kind of person who kept every hinge oiled. If Tina hadn't been looking for an escape route she would never have noticed the one thing the man had missed. The window looked perfect if you didn't look too closely. From the outside, no one would know the window was broken. From the outside, no one would know what was going on inside the house.

Tina took a deep breath. It had been almost too easy.

Mark lifted his hands and made a cradle for Tina's feet. Tina stepped on them and swung herself inside. She knew there was a counter under the window and she landed as quietly as she could, tensing all her muscles.

The counter was completely clear. Nothing out of place.

The streetlight helped her see her way around. She waited on the counter, letting her eyes adjust to the dim light. Everything was just the way it had been, but there was a faint whiff of food in the air. It was mostly covered by the smell that was coming off the boy, but Tina also detected a hint of tomato sauce. She didn't know how the man could bear to cook or eat in the kitchen with that stench. Would he have given the boy some food or would he have looked into that gaunt little face and deliberately ignored the kid's obvious hunger? Did he cook his food and take it into another room and forget that there was a child under the table? How could he eat and not care about the starving child? Tina worked hard to cut herself off from everything, but she did not know how a person could cut themselves off from a child starving under their very own kitchen table. Most people would find it hard to cut themselves off from a dog starving under their kitchen table.

It occurred to Tina that she had no real idea what she was dealing with. She had come through this window determined to grab the child but the clean man was like nothing she had ever encountered.

She had met men who were drunk and looking to end their night with a bang, and men who were angry about their wives or their ex-wives. She had been with men who wanted her to tell them she was twelve and boys who were looking for a way to begin their sex lives. She had a couple of men hit her and a few who stole from her but she had never seen anything like this. The calculated way he had brought her into the house and let her see the child indicated someone with no fear of repercussions. Without fear. If he caught her here tonight, doing this, he would surely kill her.

Tina looked around the room from the top of the counter.

The boy was still under the table, shivering in the icy air. Whatever was going to happen, there was no way she was going to leave him here. It was too late now to turn back. He was so tiny and skinny Tina stopped to breathe in and out before approaching him. He looked breakable.

Her body relaxed in the silence and she thought how easy it would be just to climb back out the window and go to the police. She could shout and scream until they came. She could . . . but she was here now and this was where she was supposed to be.

She slipped off the counter and got down on her hands and knees. She crawled over to where the boy was, almost sliding

along the polished floor. When she got close to him she saw his
body tense. He was awake and he was waiting for something.
He had probably been listening since she slid the window up.
Before he could make any noise she pushed her hand across
his mouth.

He sat up instantly, already terrified and struggling, but
when he saw Tina he became still. He had not been expecting
Tina.

For a moment he just stared at her and waited. Tina could
see him thinking it through. Here was something new and he
would wait before going crazy at her.

Tina pushed her finger up against her lips and the boy
nodded. She took the knife out of her pocket and began
sawing at the rope that was tied around his leg.

He sat stiffly for a moment and then he leaned forward
and pulled the rope a little to make it easier for Tina to get
to. His fingers brushed against her. They were ice-cold. Tina
resisted the urge to grab his hand and blow warm breath on
his fingers.

It was heavy-going. The knife was a simple flick knife and it
wasn't in the best shape. Tina knew there was probably a much
better knife somewhere in the house, but if the man had any
intelligence he would have taken them all out of the kitchen.

Finally the rope around the boy's leg loosened and broke.
The skin underneath looked wrong even in the dim light
coming from the street. Like it had chafed and healed many
times.

Tina was sweating. She took off her heavy coat and
draped it around the boy. He sighed quietly as he sank into
her leftover warmth. But then she had to take it off his

shoulders so she could get at the rope on his neck. He didn't protest but she saw him bite his lip.

He was motionless and noiseless. If she looked at his face he lowered his eyes. Even the fiercest of animals can understand when they are being helped.

Tina was terrified of hurting or cutting him so she went very slowly. Her hands were starting to cramp.

She put the knife down on the floor and opened and closed her hands a few times until the cramp went away.

Then she sighed and picked up the knife again.

All she could hear was her ragged breath and the boy's whistling one. He wiped his nose on his T-shirt every few minutes.

Jesus, Tim, get a bloody tissue, will you?

I don't need one.

Yes you do. Come here. Blow.

The boy's head lifted a little and he turned as though he was listening to something. Tina stopped sawing at the rope and listened too. They both held their breaths.

Right here, right now, in this cold kitchen they were just animals. They only had their senses and their instincts to rely on so Tina cocked her head like a cat and tried to hear what the boy was hearing.

In the stillness of the kitchen they could hear something other than the air moving in and out of their lungs.

Tina moved closer to the boy and crouched next to him to wait until she could work out what the noise was. She made herself small and felt his cold arm against her. She stilled herself. Something, someone was coming. There were footsteps. Slow, creeping footsteps.

Light flooded the kitchen.

'What the fuck?' said the man, lunging for Tina.

Tina scooted to one side, bumping her head and shoulder, and dropped the knife. She slipped out from under the table between the man's legs and stood on the other side of the kitchen.

'What the fuck do you think you're doing, girlie?' said the man. He had a slight smile on his face. He was ready to play.

Tina knew there was no reason to say anything.

'You don't want to be playing the hero here, luv. You belong on your knees and maybe if you're a good girl, I'll let you live.'

Tina held her tongue. He sounded like he was reading his speech off a cue card. He sounded like some stupid horror-movie villain. He sounded like the arsehole he was. Tina knew that what she should be feeling was fear but all she could feel was the churning anger in her stomach leaping and growing.

Some people should not be allowed to exist.

The man started towards her. He moved slowly as if she might not figure out what he was trying to do.

The boy under the table was curled up and small again. He was covered in Tina's coat.

Clever kid, thought Tina.

She looked towards the door to the lounge room and in that moment she knew that she had been planning what to do all along. It hadn't been a concrete idea, just an image somewhere in her mind. She had seen herself with her hands on the poker that stood next to the large fireplace. She had not known what her hands would do with the poker but she had seen them holding it, white-knuckled and tight.

The man started towards her and she darted through the door and into the lounge room. A small lamp was on, giving her enough light to see.

Thank you, universe.

She went straight for the fire and didn't even think about it. She picked up the poker and as she felt the man's hand on her shoulder, she turned around and swung it, letting her anger and her fear give her the strength.

It connected with his hip and he stepped back and then she swung again and this time it connected with his nose. Blood gushed everywhere.

'Jesus, fuck,' said the man, stumbling backwards across the room and onto a chair. He held one hand protectively over his nose.

'You little cunt, you fucking slut,' he said. The words came out hollow and slurred but Tina heard them.

The man stood up and came back towards her and she swung the poker again. This time it connected with the side of his head and he went down.

He lay on the ground with one hand over his nose and the other on the side of his head. Tina felt like she had been in the house forever but she knew it had only been minutes.

She stood over the man with the poker at the ready. In the place of thoughts there was only a buzzing in her head.

'Don't, please,' the man moaned. 'Just stop, okay? Please, I'm begging you—I'm really hurt. My wallet's in the bedroom on the chest of drawers. Please just take the money and leave. I won't say anything to the police, I promise—just don't hit me again, okay?'

As the man's voice changed from aggression to fear Tina felt her stomach loosen. He wasn't so tough. He looked big and scary but he was just like anyone else. Not many people could stand up to a poker in the face.

The desire to hurt the man rose up and bubbled in her throat. She wanted to hurt him for what he had done to the boy and for what he had made her do.

Tina stared down at the man. Her body was fizzing with the power to end this man's life. She felt her strength as she let the poker hover just above his head. The man had not said anything about the boy. He thought she was after his money and maybe she would just take it. It could buy her a few more meals and maybe a book or two. She could take his money but she would take the boy as well. The man did not see the possibility that she was only here for the boy. He deserved to die just for that. For thinking that the child had no worth to anyone other than himself to do god knows what with. She lifted the poker again and looked at his frightened, bloody face. He was still a man, still a person.

She sighed. It would be better to just leave. If she saved the kid she could take him to the police and then they could deal with the man. The police might not believe her but they would believe the boy. There is some shit that kids just don't make up.

She stepped back to put the poker down when the man grabbed for her ankle and pulled her off her feet.

Stupid girl, thought Tina as she hit her head against the fireplace. She kicked out at him hard, connecting with his nose and making him curl up in pain again.

He let go of her ankle and Tina scrambled, hitting her back on a corner of the brick fireplace. The pain sliced through her body.

The man was on his knees, getting up. He looked around the room and his eyes focused on a desk on the opposite side of the room.

The gun, thought Tina.

She took a step forward and grabbed the poker again. This time she would not let go. She swung the poker down onto the back of the man's head. She swung it like it was a golf club and a hammer and a cricket bat. She swung it like a girl, like a boy, like a monster. She swung it and she knew what it would do and she was glad.

The man dropped back onto the floor again.

This time he went quiet. Blood was everywhere but Tina swung the poker again and again and then again.

Her face felt wet and she thought it must be spatters of blood but then she realised she was crying. She swung the poker again hitting the body, the man's body, with a soft dull thud.

She could almost feel his death enter the room.

It was a ringing silence that stopped time.

He went wherever he was going. Down probably.

Suddenly she was alone.

Tina is a sweet, lovely student. She is generous and kind to all her friends and we are delighted with her progress this term.

Tina stopped swinging the poker and leaned against the fireplace to catch her breath. Sweat poured down her face and neck. Killing someone was hard work. She saw some movement and looked up. The possibility that someone else was in the house clenched her stomach.

The boy was standing in the lounge room holding the knife. He had sawed the rope from his neck.

His eyes were black holes. His whistling breath filled the silence.

'Is he dead?' he asked. His voice was rough and low as though he hadn't spoken for a long time.

Tina nodded and for a moment she and the boy just stared at each other.

She is generous and kind to all her friends.

Tina took a deep breath and then she stepped towards the boy. He stumbled backwards, but stopped moving when she held out the poker. Half of it was covered in blood. In the dim light there was no colour, just a wet sheen.

Tina didn't know if the boy would take it, didn't know if it was fair to offer it. There was no need to include the boy in what she had done. But, if she had been the boy she would have wanted to feel the poker in her hand. If she had been the one tied up under the table she would have *needed* to feel the poker in her hand. So she held it out to the boy and for a moment they just stared at each other. Then the boy nodded slightly and stepped forward and took the poker out of her hand. He looked too weak even to hold the thing, but once he had his hand around it he swung it backwards and connected with the man's body with all the strength he had left.

The poker went up and down three times before the boy collapsed on the floor. He was not crying. His face was a blank mask and Tina did not want to know what he was thinking.

They shared a look and Tina nodded.

'Let's get you out of here,' she said.

The boy nodded.

Tina took the poker. Mark would get rid of it for her.

Before they went out the window she wiped down the sill with one of the tea towels from the kitchen. The wallet was tempting but the more time she spent in the house the more exposed she became.

She tried to wipe everything she had touched. She took the tea towel with her. She grabbed her coat, which the boy had left lying on the floor, and looked quickly around the kitchen for evidence of what had happened in the house. Everything was still in its place. Only the broken pieces of rope under the table told a different story.

She helped the boy climb through the window, whispering that Mark would catch him.

Mark was awake and waiting and he did catch the boy. He had not let Tina down.

It occurred to her that the boy had no idea if she was there to help or if she had some other terrible motivation.

His unquestioning acceptance and willingness to go with her made it clear he thought that whatever he was going to could not possibly be more terrible than where he had been.

Pete

Pete forced himself to call only once a week now. He knew they would call him if they found anything, anything at all, but he called them anyway. He needed to know they were still thinking of Lockie.

They had one of the juniors talk to him these days. She was barely out of the Academy but they had struck up a kind of friendship. Lisa was never too busy.

'Nothing yet, Pete, I'm afraid,' she would say.

'I know, but I thought—you know . . .'

'Yeah, I know. But, Pete, you have to believe me when I say that Lockie is still on our radar. We haven't closed the case. It's still on the top of our lists.'

Everyone called him Lockie now, like they knew him. It was a technique used by the police so that the victim became real, even after years on the job. He had become Lockie to everyone on about day four.

'So there's been no word, even dead ends?'

Lisa sighed. 'Pete, you and I both know that if anything ever happens—bad news or good—we'll call you.'

'I know, it's just . . . the parents are friends, close friends.'

'Yeah, you've said. We're dealing with another missing child at the moment. Six-year-old girl. Cute mop of curls with green eyes, name of Kelly.'

Pete knew what Lisa was doing. In the kindest way possible she was letting him know that Lockie wasn't the only kid in trouble. He wasn't the only child who was now part of some nightmarish reality that no kid should ever have to contemplate. She was changing the subject before he worked himself up, asking questions that had no answers. She was playing to his instinct as a cop, to the cop's desire get the whole story. Lisa would go far. She had the touch.

Pete obligingly took the bait. 'You are?'

'Yeah, but no link I'm afraid. The parents say she was taken from her bed.'

'They say that, do they?'

'That's what they claim.'

'So you like them for it?'

'Well, I shouldn't say, but you're one of us so, yeah, we do. DOCS have known about the family for years. Personally, I think the mother will turn on the stepfather.'

'Nice people!'

'Oh, you know. They did their kid in so, yeah, the best kind of people. I have to go now, Pete. Stay in touch, okay?'

'Okay. Thanks, Lisa.'

He wouldn't tell Margie about the missing girl. Margie took every child-abuse case really badly. She took them as a personal affront. The way she saw it, God had decided she couldn't have kids but gave them where they were not wanted.

He had been part of the police force for forty years and he had never dealt with a missing child before. Kids went missing in his town but only when they were older, and then they were always found. They would have run away to the city or passed out on a couch at a friend's farm. He wasn't stupid, he knew this sort of stuff went on. He knew there were people for whom children were things to be used and abused. They weren't spared the horrors of bad parenting in a small town. There had been that family a year ago who had been the only topic of conversation at the pub for a while. Eventually the kids were taken away and the parents moved on. But stealing another person's child was not something he'd ever come across. He knew about it from stories in the newspaper and American cop shows. His colleagues from the city kept the horror stories filed away in their heads. On nights when the day had been too long and a few drinks loosened their tongues they took out the stories, hoping that they could release them into the air and be free from the distressing details.

Pete always listened when he was up for a visit and shook his head at what men and women could do to those who were meant to be precious and protected. He never discussed the stories with Margie. She flew into a rage whenever she heard about some mother who had allowed her boyfriend to batter her child. 'It's not fair,' she would wail and Pete's heart would break.

They had tried everything. Who knew why some people got to have as many kids as they wanted and then beat the crap out of them?

'That's just the way it goes, son,' his father would have said. 'No one said anything about fair.'

They were too old for adoption by the time they gave up on science so Margie adopted everyone else's kids.

He knew about the darkness inside some people but he never thought he would have to know and think about it because one of the local kids had gone missing. He felt like he had to protect all the kids in town and Margie felt the same way.

He had not known what to do when the news about Lockie's disappearance came through.

It seemed like the whole town had turned up at the station, frantic for information.

'Oh god, Pete, is it true? Is Lockie really missing?'

'Poor Doug and Sarah, they must be beside themselves with worry.'

'How could it have happened, Pete? Who takes someone's child?'

'When will they find him, Pete?'

Pete never had any answers. The only thing anyone knew for sure was that someone had taken Lockie. No one disappeared so completely unless someone made them disappear.

He had gone up to Sydney to help but it wasn't long before he felt out of his depth. He had arrived with a carload of presents for Lockie and Sammy. Everyone had wanted him to take something once they knew he was going and he had walked into the situation like Father fucking Christmas. Sammy had gone mad for the toys and Doug and Sarah had just watched her, speechless and desperate. They put the toys for Lockie away in a cupboard in the motel room. They still had them now, Pete knew. Trains and books and cowboy hats all stacked up in his room, waiting to be claimed by their owner.

The police up in the city had endless files filled with people who were so malevolent it was almost impossible to believe they were real. People for whom children were toys. When they were broken they were simply replaced.

The internet helped these people connect. Helped them find the pictures to feed the habit, and then it helped them find what they wanted. Everything was available for a price. The fucking animals went online and ordered themselves a child to play with. They went online and found some other sicko who thought the same way they did and all of a sudden they weren't deranged or evil—they were just part of a special club. Pete could actually feel the blood in his arms heat up just thinking about it.

The city cops brought in a man named Robert who was in charge of searching for the worst sites and tracking the bastards down. Robert had dead eyes and hunched shoulders. Pete didn't want to believe that Lockie had been taken by one of the men Robert watched. He never said anything to Doug and Sarah. If they had found something he would have told them, but otherwise what good would it do to plant the horrifying images in their minds? They both looked like a good wind would blow them right off the edge. There was a reason the police kept some things quiet.

After a week of looking for Lockie he had returned to a town bewildered by what could happen to a nice family.

Sarah had gone up to the Show to enter the cake competition. She was famous for her cake decorating. The wedding cake with its beautiful icing flowers had been front-page news in the local paper. Lockie had been so excited he had barely been able to get the story out, leaping up and down as he told Pete about his first visit to the Easter Show.

'And they have rides there, Pete, big ones, not like the small stuff we have here. I'm gonna go on a rollercoaster, a real rollercoaster. Mum says maybe not but Dad says we'll see— but Sammy can't go 'cos she's too little. There's like a trillion people at the Show and there's loads of stuff to eat and drink and everything. I'm gonna do everything after the contest. And Dad says Mum should win the prize 'cos her cake is the best. Don't you think it's the best, Pete? Mum says we can't eat it but I don't like the icing, it's a bit yuck but Mum makes the best lamingtons. Do you want a lamington, Pete? Will you come to the show with us, Pete? It's gonna be awesome.'

'Slow down, mate. I'm sure you'll have a great time but remember to help your folks with Sammy. You be a good big brother.'

Afterwards Pete had wondered whether, if he had told Lockie to stay with his parents all the time, he would be safe at home telling wonderful tales of his adventure. If he had just said the words, 'Don't leave your parents, Lockie, and if they walk away for a minute don't move,' would it have made a difference? If he had told him of the dreadful possibilities in the big city would Lockie have waited by the stroller and then screamed if someone came near?

But his parents had said the words.

Doug kept repeating to anyone who came near him, 'I told him not to move. I told him to stay where he was and hold on to the stroller. I was only gone for sixty seconds.'

Sixty seconds can change your life.

Pete and Doug had formed a quiet friendship after Doug's father died. Pete had taken over for his lost mate and watched over Doug and the farm.

The boy had struggled in the beginning but farming was in his blood and eventually he and the land got to know each other. They would make proper money this year and Pete was happy for them. Doug had worked until he couldn't stand. Not that money would be any good now.

He was really stoked when Doug and Sarah got together. Everyone had been a little wary of Sarah at first. She spoke like she came from money and she looked like she belonged in the city. But Sarah had slid right into farm life. Even at its worst Pete could see that Sarah had become part of the land. She needed some time away every now and again, but she would always come back.

The arrival of Lockie was good news for the town. Every baby was a bonus, but Lockie was Pete's favourite. He grew up talking fast and running when he should have walked. He was a kid filled with ideas about the world. He was smart and funny and Doug knew that he wouldn't be staying on the farm. Lockie loved the farm but Doug could see the spark inside him—a spark that needed the whole world to shine in.

The whole town seemed a little faded now.

'It's not fair,' was all Pete would hear as he walked through the streets.

No one said anything about fair.

People still stopped him and asked about Lockie. Everyone who went to Sydney kept their eyes and ears open. One of the local lads knew a few of the bikie boys and even they were looking for the little boy.

But there wasn't even a trace of him. It was like the universe had opened up a hole and dragged Lockie down into it.

When the family had finally returned home after a month in Sydney there was nothing anyone could say.

They were broken. Heartbroken and soul-broken.

Sarah had folded up inside herself. Nothing would comfort her. The pills made her numb, but every time he visited Pete could see her punishing herself. There was nothing left of her now. And to think she and Margie used to exchange diet tips.

When Pete went over for a drink on Saturday nights he could feel the despair wrapping itself tighter around the house with each passing week.

It was the not-knowing that killed them.

Sarah looked after Sammy and the house on automatic. Some days the switch was off and she stayed in bed. Margie went over then and did her best.

Pete had quietly suggested counselling to Doug but the younger man had just given his head a shake.

'She's not ready, Pete. None of us are. We have to give up first, and I don't know how to give up. I haven't given up on this farm all through the years of drought. I've watched the sheep die and I've seen the land burn but I didn't give up. How can I give up on my boy?'

Sometimes Sarah would be up and about and when she saw Pete she would let something slip.

He would walk into the kitchen to say hello and she would say, 'Do you think whoever has him knows that he likes to read about space? Do you think they know he loves pasta but hates corn?'

They were random questions. Pete tried to answer at first but then he realised that Sarah wasn't really talking to him. She was simply voicing out loud the questions that went through her head every day, all day, tormenting her.

'Do they know he likes Vegemite toast for breakfast?'

'Do they know how he likes his scrambled eggs?'

'Are they making sure he has his milk every day?'

'Are they keeping him warm?'

'Are they being kind to him?'

'Is he going to school?'

'Do they know he hates to be tickled?'

'Are they hurting him? Are they hurting my little boy?'

What could he say to that?

Pete said nothing. He hung his head and waited for her to stop asking questions.

They were questions about the smallest of things but everyone knew that in the end it was the little things that got you. It was the little things that tore you down and made you give up. The little things were worse than the big stuff. They poked at you day in and day out, forcing you to think.

Pete tried to keep his mind off the little things but he couldn't tell Sarah to do the same. It seemed to him that mothering was all about the little things anyway.

In all his years as a cop he had never felt this helpless, as though he had one hand tied behind his back. He had always been able to sort everything out. People came to him the same way they went to Father Andrew.

Now he was watching this family, his family, die a little every day and there was nothing he could do to save them. Some days he powered around in a rage, yelling at Margie and giving speeding tickets and even throwing a few drunks in jail, but mostly he just felt so unbelievably sad. Sadder than he had ever been about the babies he and Margie never managed to have. Those were the days he phoned Sydney and talked to Lisa. She was only young but Pete had a feeling she had seen more than he had.

The worst thoughts of all came in the middle of the night. He would wake from a sound sleep with his heart racing and just knew that wherever Lockie was he was suffering. He was suffering and he was probably just waiting for Pete to come and save him the way the teacher told all the kids every year.

Every year he went into every classroom—even the ones with the older kids—and told them that he was there to help, no matter what. Every year he promised them that he could solve whatever problem they had, even if they didn't like the solution. He promised them every year and in Lockie's class they had all smiled and nodded like they were absolutely sure that was the truth.

They had smiled and nodded and promised to trust a policeman so what had gone wrong? Who had taken Lockie? Who had he gone with and where was he now?

Where was he now?

Tina

Tina dragged her coat through the window again. She landed on the ground with a small thud. Pain streaked through her ankle but she moved it a bit and the pain settled down. Her head was aching and her back was throbbing but she had managed to get the kid out of the house. Her breath darted shakily in and out of her lungs. It could have gone the other way. She could have been the one lying on the floor covered in blood. She could have landed up tied to the table leg with the kid. Jesus, Jesus, Jesus. It could have gone the other way.

She had to leave the window open. Mark was holding the boy. His face was scrunched with disgust. The kid stank worse than the stairs in their squat.

Mark put him gently onto the ground and wordlessly took the poker that was now wrapped in the tea towel. He lifted it up and down feeling its weight. The boy sat on the ground in the icy air. He didn't look like he could move. Slowly he pulled his legs towards himself and folded up into a ball.

'Pick him up, Mark. He can't walk and he's got no shoes.' Tina spoke slowly so she could keep her voice under control. The urge to cry and scream and run crept up her spine but she held still.

Wordlessly Mark handed the poker back to her and lifted the boy lightly into his arms. Tina took her coat and wrapped him in it, like she had wrapped Tim when he was an infant. The boy just stared.

'What the fuck happened in there?'

'Not worth talking about.'

'Why have you brought this? Why is it wet?'

'It's blood.'

'Jesus, Tina, what the fuck did you do?'

'Something that needed to be done. We have to get rid of it.'

'Fuck, Tina, I don't need this.'

'Are you going to help me, or what? Because if you aren't just leave now and let me deal with this myself.'

'Calm the fuck down. I'll help you.'

'Let's get this kid to a police station.'

'No,' said the boy in his gritty voice. 'No uniforms.'

'These are the good guys, kid, they'll help you. They'll make sure you get home.'

'No uniforms,' said the boy. His voice was climbing. His body was stiff and he started to move around in Mark's arms, trying to get down, to get away.

'Look, kid—you need to relax. I just rescued you. I don't want to hurt you. I'll only take you somewhere where they can help you.'

'No uniforms, no uniforms, no uniforms, please, please, please,' begged the boy, and Tina could feel the fear radiating off his battered body.

She remembered the uniform hanging in front of the shower.

A uniform had taken him. A uniform had starved him. Who knew what else the uniform had done to him.

If they dumped him at the front of the police station he might run or he might just give up. If they took him into the police station then they would be inside, where there would be questions and assumptions. She was not prepared for questions from the cops. She had no answers. The man was dead and police liked to close the case and put someone in a cell. There were things you did not do when you were of 'no fixed address'. The most important thing was not to draw attention to yourself.

She hadn't really thought further than getting the kid out of the house but she had not seen herself walking him into a police station either. She wanted to stand outside and watch him go in and congratulate herself on a job well done.

'This wasn't part of the plan,' she said to Mark.

'Let's just take him home, Teen,' said Mark. 'We can deal with it later.'

'Can you carry him all the way?'

'Yeah, he's like nothing. Maybe we need to feed him?'

Tina calculated how much money it would take to feed the kid. He looked like he hadn't eaten in months.

It would have been so easy to drop him off at the police station. So easy to just drop him on the step and pat herself on the back. But if she wanted to help him she would have to put herself out in the open. No way was he walking inside alone. Tina could see the fear in his eyes—even in the half light from the street. It was deep and powerful and the kid was not going to just go where they told him like a good little boy. Tina could see that in his face. He had learned a hard lesson, but he had learned it well. Stay away from the uniforms.

Tina sighed. 'Okay, let's go to Maccas.'

She looked at the boy. Anyone seeing him would be horrified at the state he was in. He stank and his skin was grey with dirt. Tina worried for her coat, hoping it wouldn't absorb too much of the smell. The air was frigid and Tina missed her coat more with every step. She swung the poker back and forth in the cold air, feeling its weight.

She tried not to think about the body she had left in the house. She had never hurt anyone before. Even when Tim really could have used a good smack she didn't see the point in hurting him. The man had turned the boy into his dog and she'd turned the man into a thing. Round and round it went. She would not worry about who he had been, about the pain he might have felt. She would look at the skinny dirty boy and let the man be a thing, a uniform with an evil darkness inside him. The sort of thing that deserved to die. She really hoped that she had actually killed him. If he was still alive and if he came after her he would kill her. There was no doubt about that.

Along the way they found a garden with a tap right on the edge. Tina rinsed the poker and then they cut across a park. Tina threw the poker into the pond. The water closed over it as if it had never existed. She threw the tea towel in after it. It took a few minutes to absorb the water and then it too disappeared from sight.

'Let's go,' said Mark after standing in silence while the water closed over Tina's guilt.

'Yeah,' said Tina. 'Let's go.'

It was warm inside the McDonald's and the greasy smell of comfort filled the air. Arik was serving behind the counter. His staff had a habit of turning up whenever they liked. He'd offered Tina a job once but there were too many questions to answer on the application form.

He gave the trio the once-over. He scrunched up his nose.

'My little brother,' said Tina without thinking. 'He ran away from home. I'm going to take him back in the morning.'

'He ran away without shoes?' said Arik.

Two small blue feet hung below the hem of the coat. Tina stood in front of the blue feet so Arik would not notice the chafed ring around the boy's ankle. She chose silence as an answer. She could see Arik working his way through the problem. Arik had worked in the Cross for years. He once told Tina that he hadn't been hired to be night manager in the Cross because he had experience or because he was studying law. He had been hired because he had completed a first-aid certificate and had a black belt in karate.

Tina wished she could think of something to say to Arik, something that would explain the boy's presence but she knew that nothing would be good enough. Arik was a father and she knew he was looking at the boy in the way a father, a good father, might. If she asked him he would get involved, Tina knew he would. But Arik had a class to get to and a wife and kids to go home to. Tina didn't want to be just one more responsibility he had to deal with. Arik shook his head and Tina could see him asking his God what he was supposed to do.

In the end he simply said, 'What will you have?'

Tina looked at the boy. Mark had set him on the floor. Tina's coat covered him completely.

He was obviously starving. He should have been demanding everything on the menu but he wasn't asking for a thing. He was looking everywhere but at the menu board.

What the fuck happened to you? Tina wondered.

'We'll have four Big Macs and four large fries and four large Cokes,' said Tina.

Mark looked at her. 'I'm skint.'

'That's okay.' She pulled out her precious fifteen dollars and hoped it would cover the food. She felt a pull in her chest as she handed over the money. It had only lasted one day.

Once, a long time ago, fifteen dollars would have meant a movie ticket and junk food. Easy come, easy go. Such a long time ago. Tina wanted to put the money back in her pocket and bolt for the door but the kid needed her right now. No one had needed her for a while.

'That's all you got,' stated Arik.

Tina nodded and swallowed.

'You've ordered a lot of food,' he said.

Tina nodded again. 'We're all hungry.'

Arik sighed and ran his hands through his hair. He looked over his shoulder to the kitchen at the back.

Tina still held the money in her hand.

'Tell you what,' he said. 'Why don't you go ahead and keep that?'

Tina felt her eyes get hot. 'Thanks, Arik, you're a mate.'

'It's almost time for the breakfast crew anyway. You can finish up what I've got left.' Arik waved them away and they seated themselves at one of the back tables. The stink coming off the kid was intense.

Tina rolled up the sleeves of the coat so the boy could use his hands. He had tucked his cold blue feet under his body.

The boy was wide-eyed and watchful. Tina could see he was smart. He was biding his time, waiting to see what would happen next. She wanted to ask him about the man but she could see he would have nothing to say. There were a lot of people wandering around the Cross with nothing to say.

No one would ever know the truth of what had happened to the boy. The man was dead and he would never be forced to explain what he had done and why he had done it.

Tina wondered if it was better to know your tormentor was dead or in prison. If it was her she would choose dead every time. In prison the man would have been able to tell others the story of his life. Whatever reason he had for taking the boy it would have been turned into some bullshit sob story. 'Boo-hoo, my mum didn't love me, my dad was mean and I had no friends.'

It didn't justify anything. It didn't excuse anything. Everyone had a story to tell, but not everyone spread the pain around in such a big circle.

Once Tina had seen a program about paedophiles where they had interviewed the animals and asked them why. It had been a whole lot of sitting in a circle and crying about their childhoods. Tina had switched it off in disgust.

She would choose dead every time.

Arik came over with a tray loaded up with food. He was followed by one of the counter staff holding a tray of drinks.

'No noise, you guys, okay? And I leave in an hour so you'd best be gone by then. The day guy doesn't like night-time leftovers.'

'You're a proper mate, Arik, you really are,' said Mark.

Arik looked at the small boy. 'Yeah, whatever.'

Arik had brought out at least ten burgers and as many cartons of chips. They all just stared at the bounty. The boy's eyes widened but he didn't move. Tina leaned forward and took a burger. She opened it up and took a bite. The boy watched her mouth move.

'Come on,' she said, indicating the food.

The boy's hand, with its long black-rimmed fingernails, moved towards one of the drinks.

'Wait,' said Mark, and the boy's hand dropped instantly back into his lap. Something flicked across his face. Resignation. He had known the food wasn't for him.

'What the fuck, Mark?'

'Listen, Tina, he might not have eaten for a while. I know what that's like. Take small sips, kid. Small sips and small bites. Take it slow or you'll just chuck it up before it gets a chance to go down.'

Tina put down her burger and said to the boy, 'Mark is probably right. Take it slow. We've got time and if we get kicked out we'll take it home with us. I'm not picking up my food until you pick up yours, okay?'

Mark put his burger down as well and they both waited for the boy's answer.

The boy nodded and his hand moved towards the food again. He closed it around a handful of chips and shoved them into his mouth, chewing and swallowing with epic speed.

'Slow down,' Tina said in her teacher voice.

The boy nodded again and breathed in before taking a small sip of Coke. He looked up at Tina to see if he'd done the right thing.

'Good, that's good,' she said.

The boy ate for about forty minutes. He took small bites and small sips of Coke and only made his way through two small burgers, but Tina could see his cheeks colour slightly. Tina and Mark just watched him without speaking. He was in his own private world. A world of sensations. Taste and smell and satisfaction. He ate with his eyes closed.

Tina wondered if each bite would change his memory of being starved. Would he be able to remember what it felt like? Or was it like eating a big meal and never being able to imagine being hungry again, but then wanting something else only minutes later?

Why would the man have starved him? Was it for reward and punishment? Was it to keep him weak? Was it just for kicks?

Tina shook the thoughts away. She would definitely choose dead. Every time.

Finally the boy gave an impressive burp and his eyes drooped a little.

'You had enough?' said Tina.

The boy nodded. And then he looked frantically at the food. Who knew when he would be able to eat again?

'We'll take it home. You can eat it later. I promise, okay?' A Maccas burger could last forever, especially in this weather.

The boy nodded and his whole body seemed to subside.

Tina wondered how long he had been on alert for. How long he had been terrified and panicked, waiting for the next dreadful experience.

'What's your name, kid?' said Mark

'Lachlan . . . but they call me Lockie,' said the boy. His voice sounded a little lighter.

'I'm Christina, but they call me Tina.'

'I'm Mark. They, whoever they are, call me Mark.'

Tina and Mark laughed and Lockie gave them a small smile.

Who are you? Where do you come from? What happened to you? Where are your parents? Tina wanted to ask, but she kept her questions to herself.

'Tired?' she said instead.

Lockie nodded.

Tim had been like that. A good dinner and he was practically asleep on his feet.

'I'll take the food. Mark, you carry him.'

The trio wandered through the Cross in the breaking light. The strip clubs looked pathetic, winking their promises in the cold dawn. Patches of vomit littered the streets and some young boys from the suburbs slept off their big night on the benches. The Cross looked like an old hooker in the weak rays of sun. Broken and filled with despair.

Tina didn't think about what she did for a living and what she would look like one day. She closed her eyes to the seediness surrounding her and walked. Her head hummed and there was no more room for thought.

The boy was asleep in Mark's arms. Children understood a lot more than most people gave them credit for. The kid—Lockie—had known she was there to help him and now he was asleep in Mark's arms because he knew she would take care of him. It should always be like that. Kids should grow up assuming that everyone was basically a good guy who would help them.

Tina barely noticed the filth on the streets and the junkies dozing in the alleys. The street sweepers and the cops would be along soon, cleaning up the debris. It was a good time to get off the streets.

When they got back home Tina opened her sleeping bag and covered both of them. They lay close together on the mattress. The smell coming off the kid filled the whole room. He was so fast asleep she had checked he was still breathing. She let the kid stay wrapped in the coat even though she was cold under the open sleeping bag.

It took her a while to get to sleep, but at last she drifted off to the sounds of the snores coming from the other room.

In her dreams there was blood everywhere and an iron poker.

Margie

Margie got herself ready to go out to Doug and Sarah's again, although the new romance novel and block of imported chocolate were calling to her. There were many ways to lose yourself, to avoid your life or to numb the pain, and a romance novel and expensive chocolate were not the worst things she could possibly do. Pete had his work and Doug had the farm and, right now, Sarah had sleep. Who would have thought that a body could be so tired?

Before taking the drive out to the farm she stopped at the bakery to get something for the kids. Kid.

Now, only Sammy would enjoy the chocolate-chip muffin. Lockie had loved them too. He would begin by picking out each precious chocolate chip and saving them for when the muffin was finished. He always made the most godawful mess but Sarah indulged him. She had always indulged him. She *had* indulged him. Would she ever get the chance to indulge him again?

'Stop thinking like that,' Margie told herself. Lockie still loved chocolate muffins. Lockie was still here. Lockie was somewhere. She refused to think of him as anything but lost. They would find him, they had to find him.

Well, that wasn't true really. They didn't have to find him. Just because the pain was intolerable didn't mean that it would end. Margie knew that better than anyone. The human spirit could not be defeated because it was impossible to believe that an end to your suffering wasn't just around the corner. All those years she had waited in the bathroom, all those months, all those cycles she was convinced that she had to get it right at least once. But the pain didn't always have an end. There was no universal law that said it would. But she couldn't get herself out of bed every day if she didn't believe Lockie was going to be found, even after all this time.

It was what she told Sarah every time she went out to the farm. She told her he would be found. She told her she was sure of it.

Today was Wednesday and there was fencing to be repaired so Doug would not be able to return home to throw on some washing and get Sammy lunch.

'I won't need the whole day—I did a fair bit when you were here last week,' Doug had said. Margie was happy to help.

In the bakery Susan greeted her with a smile. 'On the way out to Doug and Sarah's?' she said when Margie ordered the chocolate-chip muffin and some grain bread.

'Yes, I thought I might drop in and see how they're doing,' said Margie, keeping her voice casual, unwilling to begin the conversation but knowing it was coming.

'How *are* they doing?' asked Susan.

Margie shrugged. 'Well, you know, Suze. As well as can be expected.'

Susan nodded gravely. 'That poor family.'

Margie winced inwardly. She knew what it was like to be 'poor Margie'. Sometimes, when she was still the right age, she would catch a few words drifting on the air around the supermarket.

'Five IVF attempts, poor girl.'

'Breaks my heart just to look at her.'

'Too old for adoption.'

'That one terrible miscarriage.'

'Poor Margie.'

If you weren't careful the anger could consume you and then every time you saw one of the kindly souls who felt so sorry for you, you would have to bite back the desire to spit. Margie was good at biting her lip. Some days she literally made her mouth bleed rather than scream across the supermarket, 'I don't need your pity, you smug bitch.' She was grateful now that she had kept quiet, of course. It didn't do to make enemies in a small town. People were still a little careful with her when the talk of grandchildren came up, but then she had Lockie and Sammy to boast about and everyone just accepted her status as de facto grandmother.

Truth be told she wanted to climb into bed alongside Sarah and wait until Lockie came walking through the door, but she couldn't succumb to grief. Her job was to take care of the family when they needed help and to field all the whispered questions.

Margie knew she shouldn't resent the questions. Everyone meant well. They just wanted Sarah and Doug to know they cared.

Sarah never came into town anymore except to drop Sammy off at school and then pick her up. And even that she did rarely.

She would stand at the school gates wearing a baseball cap and dark glasses and stare at some distant point. The other mothers had tried to talk to her at first but she would smile vaguely at their enquiries and then just walk away. She walked away and she faded away. Sarah was so thin now that Dr Samuels was dropping in once a week just for a chat.

Margie understood a little of her reluctance to talk. She had no new information to dispense. Lockie was still missing. Her heart was still broken and she still did not know how she would manage to force herself out of bed every morning.

The kind glances filled with sympathy could make your skin jump with rage eventually. Margie knew that. The one time she had managed to perform the basic female function of getting pregnant they had spotted it before she had even allowed herself to be aware.

'Oh goodness, I can see it in your eyes,' Edna at the pharmacy had said. And then she was surrounded by a cluster of women and she was forced into the discussion when she had been trying to pretend it was not happening. Trying to pretend that she was not pregnant in the hopes that the universe or God or whoever was watching her would let their attention drift somewhere else and allow the small cluster of cells inside her to grow into a living being.

The desperate desire to have a child of her own had never really left her, and each time her body had failed her there had been those kind looks filled with sympathy. She had to stop herself from screaming at them, from letting her white-hot rage at the unfairness of it leak out all over the nice people who only felt sorry for her.

Even now when the hot flushes burned her up on the coldest winter nights she still yearned for a child of her own.

Doug and Sarah had been generous enough to share.

Sarah had needed the help when Lockie was born—her mother had absolutely no interest in her own grandchild. It made Margie want to hiss with bitterness. People were never grateful for things that came too easily.

Margie had loved those long hours holding a wide-awake Lockie while Sarah got enough sleep to get her through the next long night. For a little while Margie felt as though her arms were finally full.

'You know, new families sometimes need a little space to get used to things and whatnot,' Pete had said one evening when she had come in late full of stories of Lockie's first smile. He had said the words gently and quietly, without looking up from the newspaper.

Margie had instantly felt the truth of the words sting. She had breathed in, trying to dislodge the spike placed by her husband. He was not being cruel. He didn't have the ability to be anything but kind and concerned, but she had wanted, just for a moment, to scratch his eyes out.

'I'm just helping her through the first few weeks,' Margie had said. 'She doesn't have a mother—or at least not one who's interested. She's all alone.'

'I know, my love,' Pete had said. 'I was just thinking that it may be time to pull back a little. You know, to see how she does on her own.'

Margie had nodded dumbly and taken herself off for a bath armed with her chocolates and a new romance set in the sixteenth century.

She couldn't bear to watch television or read the newspaper. Children were dispensable in the real world. They were less important than drugs and alcohol and new husbands. Children were hurt in so many ways. They were beaten and tortured and starved.They were stuffed into suitcases and buried in the backyard.

Margie would watch, open-mouthed and despairing, as yet another story of neglect filtered into her living room. There would be articles in the newspaper and discussion panels and people shaking their heads about the system, but nothing ever changed.

In the bath, the water so hot she had to steel herself against the sting on her skin, she felt the real pain loosen. Pete was right. She should pull back.

For a few days she had heard nothing from Sarah, but then the young woman had called for help and Margie had returned. She was the official babysitter and it was a role she was happy to accept. When Sammy arrived she had to force herself to give the family space but Sarah always called again.

Now she went out there whenever Doug called. He never asked. That wasn't Doug's way. Instead he would ask how things were in town.

'Everything is good here, Doug. What about Sarah and Samantha? How are they doing?'

'Yeah, well, you know, Marge. They're okay. Sarah ate some breakfast this morning, so that's good, isn't it?'

'Yes, Doug,' she would say, her heart breaking at his awkwardness and his fear of his whole world falling apart.

'Yes,' he would echo.

'I was thinking of coming out this week,' she would say. 'What day is best?'

She would hear the relief in his voice when he said, 'Well, Wednesday would be really good. I have to be away all day and it might be good company for Sarah. You could come when you liked and, you know, spend some time.'

'How early do you want me, Doug?'

He would sigh and she would want to die for him. Even though they were so close it took everything Doug had to ask for help.

'Around seven in the morning, Marge, so you can get Sammy ready for school.'

'No worries, Doug, I'll be there.'

Today she was only going over after lunch. Winter school holidays were proving a bit of a problem for Sammy. She could only be outside for a few hours before it got too cold and her mother, who had been the best at craft and playing dolls and games, barely managed to get out of bed these days.

Margie had thought, everyone had thought, that eventually Sarah would rally a little and manage to get on with things, and she did try, but still with each passing month she seemed thinner and more removed.

The presence of Sammy did little to help. Sarah would not take her anywhere and nor would she let anyone else take her out. She had been into the big wide world and she had lost her boy. She had no plans to go out there again.

Mostly Margie listened while she knitted and played Monopoly with Sammy. Every now and again she tried to talk sense, but mostly she listened. It was what she would have wanted from a friend when the feelings of loss and failure were almost too much to bear, and so she listened and lied to Sarah when she asked if Lockie was ever coming back. Because she would have wanted to be lied to as well, if only until she felt strong enough to deal with the truth.

On the journey out to the farm Margie admired the green that was carpeting the land. It was a beauty she had imagined she might never see again but here was the rain, despite all the dour predictions of the whole planet drying up. She knew that now the floods would come as well. Australia was a harsh country but everyone she knew was devoted to the land. They called it 'the lucky country', and most of the time it really felt that way. She and Pete had seen the best and the worst the country had to offer but nothing could have prepared them for the sinister violence that only came from man.

When she arrived at the farm Sammy was playing outside on the swing set. Doug had obviously only just left because she was soaring into the sky on a push that only strong hands could give.

Sammy dragged her feet on the ground and came to say hello with a series of jumps.

'Margimum, Margimum,' she shouted, warming Margie's heart with the name both children used for her.

'Hello, my love. How are you today?'

'I was on the swing. Daddy pushed me high in the sky.'

'Yes, I saw that you were very high.'

'I almost touched the moon, only it's the day.'

'I'm sure you did. Is Mum in the kitchen?'

'Not today,' said Sammy, and Margie could hear Doug's words come out of the little mouth. 'Today's not a good day.'

'Oh well, love, we'll just have to make Mum a cup of tea and then we can play a game.'

'Yay!' said Sammy, jumping into the house.

It was so easy to make the child happy.

So very easy.

Tina

Tina woke to a thin beam of afternoon sun. She lay still for a moment, revisiting, reliving, trying to get comfortable with the events of the night before. The sound of rustling paper got her up and the smell assaulted her again. Lockie was eating a burger, trying for slow, but failing.

He had his back to her as he perched in a corner, secretively stuffing his mouth.

'Hey, Lockie,' said Tina.

Lockie turned, wild-eyed and fearful. He stopped mid-chew and pushed his tongue through his teeth to spit the gooey mess out.

'Gross, kid, just swallow for fuck's sake.'

'Sorry,' he mumbled. 'Sorry for touching, sorry for eating, sorry for being a bad boy.'

'You're not being a bad boy,' Tina said. She hated how pathetic the kid sounded. 'The food is for you, do you understand? It's all for you.'

Lockie stared. He was still and silent, as if waiting for what would happen next. Tina hated the idea that he was afraid of her, that he would have to be afraid of everyone he ever met from now on.

'Say it, kid. Say, "It's all for me." Go on, say it.'

Lockie stared.

'Say it, Lockie.'

'It's all . . .' He faltered.

'"It's all for me." Say it, I mean it.'

'It's all for me.'

'Say it again, Lockie.'

'It's all for me. All for me, all for me.'

'Okay, kid, you can shut up now. Get back to your break-fast. I might have a cigarette.'

'The food is all for me,' said Lockie. His voice was deter-mined. He was telling her, but mostly he was telling himself.

'That's right, kid, it's all for you.'

'But you can share it with me,' he said, and he gave Tina a small smile.

Someone had taught Lockie all the right rules. Someone who didn't even know if he was alive right now.

'I bet you've got the best mum and dad somewhere.'

Lockie nodded and chewed. 'I bet I do.' He didn't talk anymore after that. The memory of his parents had obviously been put somewhere far away so thoughts of them wouldn't hurt. He wasn't ready to take them out again.

Tina had tried to put Tim somewhere so she could get to the part where memories of him made her smile. Jack had given her a book on grief and even though she had acted like she thought it was a piece of shit she had read some parts.

It had mostly been about giving yourself and your grief up to
God. It had mentioned God so many times Tina thought she
was listening to a lecture from Jack. He kept asking her if she
had read the book and if she would be willing to pray with
him so she could find closure. He asked again and again and
finally Tina said, 'I didn't read it and I'm not going to.' But she
had read it. She read some pages two or three times. It detailed
the stages of grief and they stuck in her mind.

If you managed to make it past the denial, anger, bargaining and depression you got to the part where you accepted
what had happened and could move on with your life.

Tina had watched as her mother zipped through the stages
like she was passing some sort of test. But Tina wasn't moving
on. She had been at stage two for so long it felt like that was
who she was.

She wondered what stage Lockie's mother would be at right
now. Was she still looking for her kid or had she given up and
moved on?

Tina pushed her way through the broken balcony door and
lit up. It was already three in the afternoon.

The boys were gone, probably getting some food and something to help them sail through the night ahead. She still had
fifteen dollars. The kid needed some clothes and he needed a
shower—really needed a shower.

It would be a good idea to wait until six and then she could
sneak him in with the after-work rush at the gym. He would
have to wear her coat. St Vinnie's would be good for clothes
and shoes, and if Maureen was on she might be happy to give
Tina a bit of a discount. Maureen wore her purple hair in
curlers and didn't ask questions. People who had lived in the

Cross all their lives got pretty good at not wanting to know the full story. Except the do-gooders. They wanted you to pour out your misery in a nice big puddle so they could tell you how to clean it up.

Tina went back inside. Lockie was sitting on the mattress waiting. Just waiting.

'You need the loo, kid?'

'May I go, please?'

'Fuck, kid, you don't have to ask. I'll take you to the toilets by the park. Nothing works in here. Can you hold it?'

Lockie nodded vigorously and held onto himself.

Do you need to go, Tim?

No, I don't have a wee.

You're jumping about like you do, Tim. Go on, go to the toilet. We can stop the game. I'll wait.

You come with me.

You're a big boy now. Time to go alone.

No, Tina, you come with me.

Okay, little man, let's go.

They made it to the bathroom just in time. Tina took Lockie into the ladies. She made him hang the coat on a hook before he went.

She made him wash his hands twice. The dirt sluiced down the plughole, leaving clean pink little-boy hands at the end of grimy arms.

'Let's get you some stuff to wear.'

'For real?'

'Yeah, kid, for real.'

Tina kept her head down and pulled Lockie out into the street. She hoped he would manage to avoid standing on anything. His bare feet were already filthy but the streets of the Cross held the worst bits of human detritus. Tina didn't want to have to deal with a piece of glass in Lockie's foot, or worse. He was walking on tiptoe and more than one adult stopped to look at them. Tina moved quickly, getting Lockie out of sight before the questions had time to form. People tended to ask a lot more questions in the daytime. They saw things more clearly. Tina preferred the dark, where it was easy to hide.

She had no idea what she was going to do with the kid after the new clothes and a shower. Maybe if he was warm and fed he would agree to walk into the police station and tell his story. Maybe he just needed a little time. He looked like a thinker. It was possible that she was really fucking up by keeping him. She had no idea what his body had been through. He could drop dead right now or have some kind of psycho meltdown.

He looked at the ground as he walked. He held her hand and she guided him around the obstacles. He would not look up.

He was locked up inside himself. His body was doing what it needed to do and maybe somewhere in his mind he was trying to find a key. If she got him to go to the police they would bring in a counsellor. Someone with a box of dolls and a soft voice. She had seen a movie about it. Lockie would be able to point to the doll and tell everyone exactly how his childhood had been taken. But would that help? Tina hoped he would be ready to talk to the police soon. If he wasn't she was really screwed.

Maureen was at the counter in the Vinnie's store.

She was smoking a cigarette and jumped when she saw Tina walk in.

'Fuck, Tina, you gave me a right scare—you nearly killed me.'

'You shouldn't be smoking in here, Maureen.'

'I shouldn't do a lot of things, Tina, but I always have and I always will.'

Maureen's voice had the rough edge of a lifetime smoker. She laughed at her joke and then coughed until she could breathe again.

'You should give up now, Tina, while you've still got your lungs.'

'You could give up as well if you wanted to.'

'Too late for me, girlie. Too late for anything except death. Might as well enjoy the last few years.'

Maureen had been one of the first people Tina had met in the Cross. Running away in summer was a stupid idea. You couldn't imagine the weather changing. Maureen had given her the coat for practically nothing.

'You look like I did when I was your age. Such pretty green eyes. I could have been anything you know ... anything. Try to stay off the streets, luv, there's nowhere for an old whore to go except behind the counter at the Vinnie's store. It's not like there's a pension plan.'

Tina had nodded, grateful for the long black wool coat that looked almost new. Grateful for any kindness and surprised that there were so many people willing to give when they had so little.

'Some people have no idea what to do with their money. I bet that coat cost a few bob when it was new. I would've kept it meself except I'm way too fat.' Maureen kept her large body settled on a stool all day long in the store. Sometimes she charged for the clothes, sometimes she just lost the stuff. 'Those little girls who come in here because they think it's ever so chic to dress like they got no money get charged double sometimes, but I always look after me mates,' she had told Tina when they met.

Ruby had introduced them. Ruby was a subject both Maureen and Tina left alone. Ruby was a worst-case scenario because she had been taken by disease. The Disease.

There were so many ways to die doing what Ruby did, but she had gone the worst way. It crept up on her while she was just trying to survive. She should have been okay, she could have been okay. There were so many drugs to treat AIDS now but you had to take the pills and visit the doctors. Ruby had other ideas. Nobody told Ruby what to do, not even her sick body.

'So,' said Maureen, squinting at Lockie through the smoke, 'who's your little friend?'

'My brother actually,' said Tina.

Maureen gave her a long look but accepted the lie. 'Well, let's see the size of him. Take off the coat.' She wrinkled her nose. 'He needs a bath or something.'

'I know, I'm going to take him to the gym, but the thing is he ran away from home in his summer clothes. I need to get him some warm stuff.'

'He must have run away a long time ago then.'

'He . . . I need to get him some warm stuff.'

Tina watched as Maureen looked Lockie over, taking in his skinny arms and blue feet, the torn T-shirt and filthy shorts. She knew Maureen wouldn't miss the mark around his neck or the one on his ankle.

'Ya know, Tina, I always thought you were one of the good ones. One of the smart ones. I'm not wrong am I, Tina?'

'You're not wrong, Maureen, not wrong at all.'

Maureen shook her head and gave Lockie another long look.

Lockie dropped his head under the scrutiny and Tina wrapped her coat around him again. She felt bad for exposing him to someone else's gaze.

'Pretty stupid to run away without shoes,' said Maureen, and Tina could see that she had made her decision. She would help them and she would keep quiet about it.

'Yeah, but I'm taking care of him now. I'll make sure he gets home. I'll keep him safe.' Tina needed Maureen to know that the boy's state had nothing to do with her.

'You do that, Tina,' said Maureen softly.

She heaved herself off the stool and wandered around the shop, picking stuff up.

A few minutes later there was a pile of clothes in front of Lockie.

A pair of jeans, a skivvy that had once been white, a top with a picture of some sort of robot on it and a hoodie lined with wool. Maureen also found a scuffed pair of sneakers and some socks.

'That should do him fine, but I'd get him cleaned up before you let him put on the new gear'.

Lockie stared at the pile in front of him. He mumbled something.

'What, Lockie?' said Tina. She leaned down so she could hear.

He whispered the words and Tina could feel his humiliation. 'Undies, I need some undies.'

'Oh right,' said Tina, looking past Maureen. 'You got any undies?'

Maureen took a few more minutes and came back with two pairs of undies.

Both were blue but both were clearly for girls. 'It's not exactly something people donate, luv. Got to take what you can get, eh?'

Tina nodded. 'Okay, Lockie?'

Lockie nodded and Tina saw him swipe at his eyes. Tears, finally tears, and over having to wear girl's undies. Human beings were strange.

Tina felt her stomach roll at the sadness of the tears but it was better than the stare and the polite requests to be allowed to eat, or go to the bathroom or even to exist.

'No one will know, Lockie,' she said and he gave a long sniff.

'I don't have much, Maureen, and I don't know when I'm going to be able to work again.'

'How much have you got?'

Tina swallowed. It would be smarter to lie but Maureen could spot bullshit from a mile away.

'Fifteen dollars.'

'Well, I reckon that'll cover this lot.'

Tina felt her throat tighten. There would be nothing left for food and the hamburgers were nearly gone.

''Course, there is the discount.'

'Discount?'

'Yep, you know me, Tina; I look after me mates. I reckon with the discount this lot comes to two dollars.'

Tina laughed with relief. 'That's a good discount, Maureen.'

Maureen shrugged and lit another cigarette.

Tina bagged the stuff herself and Maureen gave her the change. Tina wanted to say something, something that would let Maureen know how much the gift meant, but that wasn't the way you did things. Maureen knew what it felt like to have only the change in your pocket to get you through the next few days. She knew and she would know how much she had helped.

'See ya,' said Tina as she pushed Lockie out of the store.

'Yeah,' said Maureen. 'See ya.'

The two-dollar shop across the road yielded a pack containing shampoo, conditioner, shower gel, a sponge, a toothbrush and toothpaste.

'You've got to love a two-dollar shop, Lockie.'

Eleven dollars left.

'Okay, we've only got a short walk to the gym and then we can get you a nice shower. I wonder what this stuff smells like, eh? Doesn't matter—anything will be all right. My old shampoo smelled like strawberries. Do you like the smell of strawberries? Most people do. I'm really looking forward to a shower. It's so fucking . . . it's so cold.'

Tina didn't let the fact that the boy was so silent stop her from talking. Towards the end Tim had got quieter with each passing day. Just breathing took it all out of him, but Tina kept talking. She told him what was on TV and what was in the comics and what she could see outside the hospital window. She talked until she ran out of voice and then she came back the next day and did it again. Tim was listening; she knew he was listening.

Tina and Lockie arrived at the gym with its imposing black glass doors. The sleek modern building looked out of place, but Tina could see that one day it would be the norm. The ugly truth of the Cross would move underground.

Nothing stopped the developers from moving in. Above the gym was a really fancy new block of flats with a valet to park your car when you came home. The residents drove in through a giant metal garage door and handed their keys over. They didn't have to see where they lived until they got to the tenth floor and then they could watch the winking city lights and pretend there wasn't a room one block away filled with people intent on wiping out their thoughts.

'Okay, Lockie, this is it—time for a shower. You take the bag with the clothes.' Tina took her backpack off her back and slung it over one shoulder. *Just going to the gym, you know. It's not like I have my whole fucking life in here.* Lockie looked downright weird in the long coat but that was nothing compared to what he would look like without it.

She took a deep breath and pushed the heavy door open.

Doug

Doug returned to the house around five. Things were back in order. The dishwasher had been emptied and the house cleaned. There was something good cooking in the oven.

It was possible that Sarah had been up all day and had only just gone for a lie-down. It was possible.

Margie was sitting on the couch knitting another of her countless scarves. Half the town were walking around in Margie's scarves.

'Everything okay?' he asked quietly, bracing himself for the answer.

'She didn't make it up today, Doug,' said Margie, smiling sadly.

Doug dropped into the old leather armchair. The chair had belonged to his father and his grandfather. Sarah hated it but she knew she couldn't throw it out. There wasn't much he was stubborn about. He didn't care what she did with the house when there was money available but the chair had to stay. It was something he kept to himself, but when Doug sat in it he hoped for the accumulated wisdom of his father and grand-father. Neither man had spoken very much about anything other than the land.

The farm was all-consuming. The way his father saw it, if he could teach Doug everything he needed to know to run the farm he had done right by him. Doug had never been able to argue with that logic but Sarah wanted him to talk to the kids about other things.

'Ask them how they feel, Doug. Ask them what they think. They're people too, you know.'

Sometimes it was easier just to nod when Sarah said something.

He would have liked to have his father around to sit and talk to. Or, more importantly, not talk to. Sometimes silence was all you needed. Of course, neither his father nor his grandfather would have known how to deal with something like this.

His father had lost a brother. His grandparents had lost a child.

His name was Lachlan and Lockie had been named for him. Lachlan had been twelve years old when he got in the way of a tractor. He knew better but he was distracted or careless or something and there was nothing they could do to save him. His father had only spoken of the incident once and then he had made the healing sound swift and sure.

'Mum took to her bed for a couple of weeks but then it was time to shear the sheep and she got up and got on with things. The men needed to be fed.' Things needed to be done and the world kept going. That was it. Doug wondered if it would ever be possible for Sarah to get up and get on with things.

Maybe it was easier if you knew your child was dead. It was a thought that stopped him in his tracks sometimes but he knew that it was the truth. If the child was dead then you had to figure out a way forward. It was being locked in this permanent state of limbo that was keeping Sarah in bed.

One night he had come home from the day with a story of one of the young lads sliding through some fairly big cow pats. The boy had landed on his butt and there had been laughter all round. Restrained laughter but, still, it was funny. He had sat on the edge of the bed and related the story to Sarah and she had smiled and then released a small giggle. Immediately he could see her regret it and he had watched her bite down hard on her lip. Hard enough to draw some blood. 'It's okay, Sarah,' he had said gently. 'It's okay to laugh.'

'Bullshit, Doug,' she had spat back at him. 'How can you laugh if he's not laughing? How can I laugh knowing that he may be suffering?'

'I . . . I . . .' Doug had started, then he had left the room.

If a child died did it end this struggle? Could you put your faith in God and heaven and know he was in a better place, laughing with other children? Was that how you were able to move on?

Doug covered his eyes with his hands and wiped away some of the tears. Margie's knitting needles clicked and the heater warmed the room. The answers would not come tonight.

It was unlikely that there were any answers anyway.

Tina

Tina swiped her card and the turnstile moved. The gym was packed. The beautiful people from the city had descended. Trendy sneakers and tight butts were everywhere. Rock videos competed with televisions showing the news. The treadmills went round and round with people working off their long lunches.

Tina felt like she had entered a different universe. She felt it every time she came to the gym. The people worrying about bulges and muscle strength would not be able to believe her life. Unless they saw it on television. Television made everything real.

She looked down at Lockie but his eyes were on the floor. Tina understood. There was too much noise and too many people to deal with after his solitary time under the kitchen table.

Alex, the up-himself personal trainer, gave her a look. Tina had never spoken to him but his name bounced off the walls of the gym. He was physical perfection itself and he wasn't shy about showing it.

He looked at Lockie and then back at her again. The question mark in his head had gone off. Ding, ding, ding. He wasn't exactly a rapid-fire thinker. Kids weren't allowed in the gym. Alex knew the rules. Tina knew the rules too. She was just hoping that everyone would be too preoccupied with themselves to remember the rules.

When Alex started to move towards her Tina squeezed Lockie's hand. She tensed her body and got ready to run. She felt him do the same. One day on the street and the kid knew a problem when he saw one.

Alex only got halfway across the floor before some blonde with huge tits said, 'Hi!' and then he had other things to do.

Tina breathed in and out slowly.

She moved Lockie through the gym to the back, where the showers were, at a kind of running walk. Not so fast as to draw attention but fast enough that by the time someone saw them they were gone.

She hid him in a cubicle and told him to wait.

In the change room she hovered by the bin where the clean people deposited their wet towels. She studied her nails and thought about buying a latte. Ha ha.

If you wanted a dry towel you had to sign for it.

That screwed up rule number one of living in the Cross.

When no one was looking Tina grabbed two damp towels out of the bin and then locked herself and Lockie in the shower cubicle.

'Okay, kid, you go first.' Tina opened the pack of soap and shampoo.

Lockie just stood in front of her.

'Jesus, kid, let's get this done. I need a shower as well.'

'My mum helps me.'

'Helps you do what?'

'She helps me,' said Lockie.

Tina felt her jaw clench. She had had enough of all of this. She should have been getting ready to go out and earn some money but here she was playing Mummy to a fucked-up kid.

'My mum helps me,' said Lockie, and he swiped his hands over his cheeks.

'Jesus. Okay, kid, don't cry. I'll help you.'

The kid was turning into a faucet.

Lockie had probably been able to shower himself before . . . before the uniform. He had probably insisted that he could do it himself. Who knew why he was going backwards?

Tim had been able to shower himself by the time he was seven, but she still remembered the drill.

'Arms up,' she said.

He lifted his arms slowly above his head as though he had aged while standing in the cubicle. Tina grabbed the filthy torn T-shirt and pulled it roughly over his head. Then she looked at him and regretted her impatience.

Lockie's body was one massive bruise. Some parts were black and some were the faded yellow of an old punch. *Poor little boy*, thought Tina. *Poor, poor little boy*.

That's what Lockie was—a little boy.

It could do your head in if you thought too much about the cruelty that one person could inflict on another. It was best not to think about it, but here in front of Tina stood an example of the worst cruelty in the world.

There was a large bump on one of his ribs. Tina knew what a bone that had healed itself looked like; Mark and the boys were always getting themselves into trouble.

It was too much to think about. Too much to try and imagine the pain Lockie must have been in. Too much to imagine him crying for his mother and father. He was so small, so defenceless.

'How . . . how old are you Lockie?' Tina asked.

Lockie looked up at her and then he held up five fingers on one hand and three on the other. When Tim was three he used to hold up three fingers. He might have done it once or twice at four but after that he would tell anyone who asked his age:

I am five years, three months and twelve days old.

Lockie wasn't ready to be a big boy right now. Tina nodded, accepting his eight upheld fingers in lieu of words.

Suddenly she wished she'd hit the man harder. The churning anger in her stomach roared into life and she felt her throat constrict. She felt the poker in her hands again and felt a surge of adrenalin. Some people deserved to die. That was a fact. Whatever the God-botherers said, whatever the politicians said, some people just deserved to die.

'Shit, what an arsehole.' The words were out of her mouth before she could censor them. She had been trying to keep her language under control, just like she had done when she was with Tim.

Lockie looked up at her.

'Not you, kid—the uniform. Did he hit you all the time?'

Lockie clenched his fists and said nothing. That was okay with Tina.

'No one's going to hurt you again, Lockie,' she said, borrowing from books and movies, knowing that she didn't have the right to promise such a thing. 'No one is going to hurt you while you're with me,' she amended.

Lockie nodded at his feet and his fists unclenched.

She took down the shorts and let him step out of them. His underwear was stiff with dried urine, and there was something else as well. Blood.

How the fuck am I supposed to deal with this? went round and round in her head. The kid should have been in hospital. He should have been surrounded by doctors and counsellors and his parents.

She turned on the shower and got it to the right temperature. She washed him twice and got him to do his bum and penis himself. No way was she going to freak him out by touching anything. He touched himself gingerly, carefully, fearfully. But he kept washing himself, washing and washing as if the dirt would never truly be washed away. Then he stood under the warm water for a few minutes, just standing with his eyes closed. Tina didn't rush him. Everyone else could wait.

Dirt and dried blood swirled down the plughole.

She washed his hair twice as well. His ribs were a xylophone waiting for the music to start.

When he was clean she wrapped him in a towel and sat him on the small bench. He looked sleepy, like baby Tim had been after a bath and a massage.

'I'm going to shower now. You look at the door, okay?'

Lockie nodded and turned to face the door.

Tina soaped herself, glancing at him every now and again, but he was always resolutely facing the door.

Kids should do stuff they were told not to. That was how it should be.

She washed her short black hair. The colour was nearly out again. She hated having to dye it; it made such a fucking mess. Ruby had done it for her the first time. 'It'll bring out your green eyes,' she had said.

She loved the feeling of being clean. She wished she could thank Ruby again for giving her the card for the gym.

As far as the people at the gym were concerned, her name was Ruby Jenkins. Ruby had just known something was up. Colds didn't last that long. Small cuts usually healed after a few days. Ruby had known and she had given everything away before she disappeared. They knew where she was but Ruby had no interest in sharing the last gory details. She had no interest in the doctors either. They could have helped, but Ruby was tired. Really tired. She was only twenty but she was already done with life.

'Don't cry for me, kid,' Ruby had said. 'Just try not to fuck things up like I did.'

Lockie looked almost normal when he was dressed. The clothes hid the bruises and his too-skinny body. He could be any ordinary boy. He could be any ordinary boy, but he wasn't.

His gums bled when he brushed his teeth so she made him brush them again. Brushing them was the only way to fix things. He didn't whine or cry, though it must have hurt. He just did what he was told.

Tina tried to picture him as he might have been, just some naughty little kid exploring the world. She hoped he would be that way again, but she knew it was probably unlikely.

She cut his nails with her nail scissors and rinsed them under hot water.

'How come he didn't let you shower?'

'Who?' asked Lockie, although Tina knew he was bluffing.

She whispered her words again. 'Him, the uniform. How come he didn't let you shower? His house was so clean, he was so clean.'

Lockie shook his head and looked down at his feet.

Tina shrugged. She hadn't really expected an answer.

The clean ladies at the gym chattered about dinner and who said what. They whined about a shifty boss and a wanker boyfriend. They had no fucking clue really, but that was okay. Tina felt better knowing that for some people what to wear to work the next day was a real dilemma. It was the same way she felt good about knowing that there were people out there saving the whales. If she couldn't do it she was glad someone was. And right now, if she couldn't live an average life she was happy to watch others do it. That way she might not forget how to be ordinary.

Tina did her makeup, aware that the black liner would only be smudged tomorrow and she was not going out to work anyway. Just as she was getting ready to leave, Lockie said something. She leaned closer.

'He said I was a dirty boy,' whispered Lockie. 'I was a dirty boy and that was why he did stuff to me, because I was dirty. It was my fault.'

'Bullshit!' Tina shouted and half the locker room turned around. Tina grabbed Lockie's hand and they didn't stop moving until they were out on the street. The cold was a shock after the warmth of the gym but she kept him walking fast until they got back home.

'It wasn't your fault, Lockie. It's never the kid's fault. The uniform was an evil piece of shit and nothing he said to you was true.'

'It was my fault—it was,' whined Lockie.

'Why? Why was it your fault?'

'I was supposed to stand by the stroller. I was supposed to hold on and not move while Mum got the prize. Dad had to carry the cake. I was supposed to stand by the stroller and not move. It was my fault.'

Lockie's tears burst like a dam. His small shoulders heaved and his sleeve became a tissue.

Tina leaned down and grabbed him by the shoulders. 'Look at me, Lockie.'

He did as he was told.

'This wasn't your fault. Kids do stuff like that all the time. I have no idea what you're talking about but I can tell you that my little brother wandered off every chance he got. It wasn't your fault, Lockie; you were just being a kid.'

'Have you really got a little brother?' His interest stopped his tears.

'I don't want to talk about it, okay? Jesus, you're tiring. I think we need to figure out how to get you home.'

'Home?'

'Yeah. Where is home?'

'Cootamundra.'

'Where is that?'

Lockie shrugged. 'We came in the ute.'

'You came where in the ute? What does that mean?'

'We came in the ute to Sydney.'

'Your parents drove you here in the ute?'

'Yeah. Me and Sammy sat in the back. Mum and Dad were in the front. Mum was worried about the cake.'

'What cake?'

'The cake. The wedding cake. It had black and purple roses all over it. Roses made from icing and other flowers and green stuff.'

'What was the cake for Lockie? A wedding? Did you come to Sydney for a wedding?'

'The Easter Show—Mum made a cake and she won a prize,' said Lockie patiently, as though he was explaining things to an idiot. 'She said I couldn't have a piece of the cake but if I stood still and held the stroller I would get my corndog and my lamington. We came for the Easter Show.'

'The Easter Show? Jesus, that was four months ago.'

'Four months,' said Lockie. His eyes widened in disbelief. Four months. He took a step back from her and sat down on the stained carpet. 'Four months,' he said quietly.

'Yeah, Lockie, I know it was a long time ago, but you're with me now. It'll be . . . it'll be okay.'

'How many days is four months?'

Tina counted in her head. 'I don't know . . . about a hundred and twenty or something like that.'

'I tried to keep counting but sometimes I forgot. I tried, but sometimes . . .'

'It doesn't matter anymore, Lockie. It's over and soon you'll be with your mum and dad. If we could just go to the police they would—'

'The uniform said they didn't want me anymore,' interrupted Lockie. Tina could hear some anger underneath his

faltering words. 'He said they weren't even looking for me.'
The words were said quietly and there was a question in them.
Kids thought their parents were superheroes. Surely if they
had been looking for him, they would have found him?

Tina knew better. Parents were just kids with more responsibility. They couldn't control the world any more than an
eight-year-old kid could.

'Don't quote that evil fuck at me, Lockie. Of course they
were looking for you—but four months? Jesus. They must
think you're dead.'

'I'm not dead . . . I'm not dead,' said Lockie, his voice rising
in panic.

''Course you're not. Calm down, for god's sake.'

'I'm not dead.'

'Jesus, kid, I can see that. You eat too much. Where is Cootamundra?'

Lockie shrugged again.

'How long did it take you to get to Sydney?'

Lockie looked down at his feet but she could see him
working through something. 'I went to the toilet twice and
we stopped to eat our sandwiches. Then we stopped for ice
cream. I had a sleep and so did Sammy.'

'That doesn't exactly help, kid.'

'Sorry, Tina.' He wiped his face with his sleeve.

'It's okay, Lockie, don't cry. I'll figure it out.'

'You'll figure it out.'

'Yeah, I'll figure it out,' Tina said, more to herself than to
him. Maybe this *was* one she could figure out. She couldn't
figure out how to help Tim or Ruby, but maybe, just maybe,
she could figure this one out.

Sarah

Sarah dreamed of the beach. As a child it had simply been part of every summer holiday.

She had known she would miss the beach most of all. At first the land with its unending colours was enough to keep the longing for the blue and white of the sea at bay. But as the drought took hold and the only things to see were the patches of cracked brown dirt, she missed her home. Her head had filled with dust and she longed for a sea breeze to clear it away.

The year that Lockie was six she felt the dirt eating its way inside her. She drank litres of water trying to release its hold. Everything in the house was covered in a fine brown powder that caught in her throat. Lockie would cough all night and Sammy's nose ran constantly.

'We need to get away for a while,' she said to Doug.

'Yes,' agreed Doug. 'We do.'

'So?'

'So there's no money, Sarah. The bank doesn't take kindly to me using their money to have a little holiday. We can't afford to go anywhere.'

'We have to go, Doug. You don't understand. I'm going insane.'

'Oh Sarah,' he had sighed. 'I do understand. Whenever I find a dead sheep I understand. Whenever I lift the brown crap that passes for soil these days I understand. This is my land, Sarah, and I can't grow a fucking blade of grass on it. I can't keep my stock alive and I can't make the rivers run. I can't do anything except look to the skies like every other farmer in this godforsaken land. I understand more than you think and we can't go away.'

She had not pushed him. Doug could become a brick wall when he needed to. Instead she had called her mother. She had swallowed her pride and called her mother. She had stamped on her anger and called her mother.

She could picture her mother's thin lips and the slightly triumphant smirk as she said, 'Yes, well, farming is not exactly conducive to the kind of lifestyle you grew up with.' She emphasised the word *farming* with obvious distaste. But she had come through with the money and a house at the beach that belonged to a friend of a friend of a friend.

Doug's anger had been written all over his face when she told him. He chewed over his mother-in-law's supposed generosity, knowing what it had cost Sarah. His pride had told her he would not go. It was the way you had to be in the country. Sometimes pride was the only thing the drought left you with.

Sarah had told him they were going and she had not asked for his permission or his company.

'We need to have some time away from here. The children have to breathe some different air. I know you hate how I got the money but I really can't think about that now. You can come if you like—and you know that's what I want—but if you have to stay here that's okay as well.'

She had clenched her fists as she spoke, dragging the courage from inside.

In the end he had joined them for one week and she and the children had stayed for two.

Lockie and Sammy were like different children. Lockie's freckles blossomed on his face despite the sun block. The coughing stopped and Sammy learned to swim. The children ran around from dawn till dusk without getting bored or wanting anything else. On the days when Doug was there he and Sarah drank wine at sunset and watched the waves. The whole holiday was a dream. Sarah had seen the possibility of a life that was not dictated by the land, but she had made her choice. Doug would never leave the farm, regardless of how bad things got, and she had made her choice.

In her dream she was watching Lockie trying to stand up on his boogie board. The determination on the boy's face was so like Doug that even he couldn't help but laugh. In her dream she saw the blue sky and smelled the green sea as the waves leaped onto the beach. In her dream her family was whole again. She could taste the sharp, cold wine and she felt healed. Sleep was a balm; sleep was the life she wanted to live. Sleep was all she needed.

When they had first returned home from Sydney, Sarah had not been able to imagine achieving the miracle of sleep ever again.

When Dr Samuels had given her the pills she had asked doubtfully, 'Do you really think I can ever close my eyes again?'

'Try them,' he had said, and he touched her cheek as though she was his child. Dr Samuels had hitched up his grey trousers and sat drinking his tea in silence. He was like that with all his patients. He would listen for as long as they needed to talk and if they only wanted to sit and just be in his presence, that was okay as well. He had come down from Sydney as a locum. There were rumours of a failed marriage but he never invited questions about his private life. He had only meant to spend a few months in town before taking a long holiday overseas but they so desperately needed a doctor he ended up staying. He had never married again but there was talk of a son in the city. Dr Samuels went up to Sydney to take exams and attend lectures. He belonged in a major hospital but he preferred the quiet of the town.

He had said to take one pill but she had taken two, defiant in her belief that they would not work. She had switched off the light and stared at the shadows on the ceiling, seeing only images of her child calling for her.

And then, without her realising it, the pills had dragged her into oblivion. And what a sweet nothingness it had been. She had been shocked to wake up to a sun high in the sky. She had never imagined that something as wonderful as the pills existed and that first afternoon all she had been able to think of was how long she had to wait until she could take the pills

again. The pills and Lockie, Lockie and the pills chased each
other around in her head.

Now she took the pills and, just before she closed her eyes,
she summoned Lockie and his smile, and then the dreams
would come.

In her dream her golden boy tries again and again and again
to stand up on the boogie board until he manages to remain
upright for at least a minute.

Sarah experiences again the joyful pride in her boy and the
pleasure she takes in him being just like his father. Together
she and Doug applaud his shout of triumph.

Sarah dreams of Lockie jumping the waves and Sammy
building sandcastles. She dreams of those perfect moments.

The pictures from the holiday were pored over by the kids.
It had been one of those magical times that make a family
believe in itself again.

In her dream Sarah can feel the tears on her cheeks.

Her golden boy was lost and she was too.

She tried to dream that they found each other again but she
couldn't control her dreams any more than she could control
her nightmares.

Right now the nightmares were in her waking hours so she
needed to stay asleep.

When she dragged herself out of bed one day she caught
a glimpse of herself in the mirror and she'd had to go back
and look again. She could understand the gauntness that now
possessed her body but it was her eyes that drew her. There was
something there that she recognised. After a few minutes she
realised what she was looking at. Her eyes were like the other
woman's eyes: the woman on the television whose child had

been taken from the hotel room. Sarah had never been able to imagine what that woman's life was like but here she was, staring at the same eyes. She was just like the woman on the television. She was broken. Shattered. Devastated. Crushed. There was nothing left of the woman she had been.

She could see it in her eyes.

When she was awake she had to acknowledge her brokenness. She had to admit to herself that she might never be fixed.

It was too much to think about. Her boy had to come back and, until he did, she needed to stay in her dreams.

Tina

Work would be impossible. There was no way she was leaving the kid by himself and an eight-year-old boy would not exactly be good for business. Oh, there would be some who liked the idea. The world was full of freaky wankers.

They divided the last of the food, Tina giving Lockie the lion's share. When it was time for bed he snuggled right up to her just like she was the mother koala. She rested her arm over him even though she knew she shouldn't think about him as anything except a burden.

It felt strange to be going to sleep so early, but Tina was exhausted. She didn't hear Mark and the boys come in.

There were no dreams that night. Tina fell asleep to the feeling of Lockie's ribs moving up and down. It felt strange to be touched by another person. She had not been touched by anyone for two years. Well, she had been touched, but those were the touches that burned your skin and made it crawl.

Tim had been a big one for cuddles. He liked to sit on her lap and rest his head on her shoulder. When he was a baby and he couldn't sleep she would walk up and down holding him so her mother could get some rest.

In his sleep Lockie pushed himself further against her and grabbed her hand. Tina felt her eyes sting with the sweetness of it. She sighed into the air and brushed the thought away. She had to get this sorted out so she could get back to her life. She had to.

Lockie was up early. It was just beginning to get light. Tina hadn't seen the sunrise for a good couple of years. Lockie was working his way methodically through the empty McDonald's bags, looking for anything he might have missed.

Tina sighed. She had forgotten that kids needed to eat all the time. All she wanted to do was roll over and wait for sleep again but the kid was obviously starving.

'Okay, kid, let's get you to the bathroom.'

'Can we get some food?' he asked hopefully.

'I don't want to spend any more money so we may have to . . . wait a second, I know where we can go.'

'Where?'

'The Chapel. They serve breakfast. I used to eat there when I first got here.'

When I first got here. When I was starving and terrified and excited all the time. When I had no idea what the fuck I was doing, at least I could count on breakfast at the Chapel. In those days I could count on Ruby, but now there's just me. Just me and some screwed-up little kid who is counting on me. How did that happen?

How did I become this person?

Once she had entered the Cross she had been determined to leave everything she had been behind.

She had phoned home only once.

After the first time. *The First Time.*

The twenty dollars had been warm in her pocket. Ruby had cheered and clapped like she had won some sort of prize. Mark had just touched her lightly on the shoulder.

Tina had almost backed out. The guy Ruby had found for her had taken down his pants and Tina had been so completely revolted that her stomach had cramped and she knew she was about to throw up. She wanted to get up off her knees and run until she was home again and safe in her own bedroom. She could imagine how horrified her mother would be if she told her what she was about to do. And Jack? Jack would tell her it was a terrible sin, a sin that would be punished. Jack's God was big on punishing you for your sins. Tina had looked up at the pathetic man with his pants around his ankles and known that nothing could be worse than losing Tim. So how exactly could she be punished for this 'service'? She had cleared her mind and got on with it.

It wasn't a step she had taken easily. She had tried at first to find a regular job, any job. But no one wanted someone without references. They wanted an address and a home phone number. They wanted to know where and what and why, and Tina had come to the Cross to get away from the questions and the discussion. She did get one job, waiting tables at a café staffed by backpackers, but everyone wanted to be friends. They wanted to drink and laugh and visit the bloody beach. Tina couldn't stand it. Her anger kept rearing up and forcing words out of her mouth. They fired her for yelling at a man who gave his kid a quick smack on the leg. Tina was not fit for normal people. She knew that. When she watched people milling around the Cross talking and shopping and eating they seemed strange and foreign. How could they not know about Tim?

How come they weren't hurting when the world had lost such an amazing little soul? Didn't they know?

Logically she understood that everyone had something they were hiding, some hurt they kept deep inside, some reason why they were not really normal either, but she didn't understand how they functioned. She didn't understand how they got out of bed every morning or breathed in and out without the hurt weighing down their lungs.

Ruby had waited patiently until she was ready. Until she had exhausted all her other options. Until she was desperate enough to join the others who were not fit for normal people.

She couldn't quite believe she had become one of them. Her life had been so very different from theirs. She had never experienced the fear that Mark alluded to, that she saw flare behind his eyes in moments when he thought no one was watching, in the moments before he managed to cloud it all over with nothingness. She had never been mistreated in the way that the others had been mistreated.

Before she had walked out the door and out of her life she had spent hours on the computer haunting the chat rooms of the grief-stricken. One piece of advice stuck fast. A woman who had lost her young husband had written: *You may find yourself behaving in strange ways and doing strange things.*

Tina couldn't think of a stranger place to be or of a stranger thing to do.

This was not who she was supposed to be. Despite everything that had happened, this was not who she was supposed to be. And yet she could not change it. There was always the choice to go home, but Tina could not see how to make it happen. Her feet would not walk in that direction. The anger kept her stuck where she was. The anger and the grief and the impossibility of ever feeling normal again.

When she called after the first time her mother had answered the phone and the words had stuck in Tina's throat. How could she explain what she had just done and what she would do again? Her mother lived in a different world now—not that she'd ever been in the same place as Tina.

Christina, is that you? Oh, please come home. Come home to me and Jack and God. Come home to us and we can help you embrace the Lord. We can help you heal. Please Christina, if you knew the glory of God you would be so much better. Please come home to us. You're only hurting yourself by being away. You need to come home and finish school. I've seen the truth now, Christina—Jack has shown me the truth and you need to come home. I want to share my life with you—we want to share our lives with you. Tim wouldn't have wanted you to shut us out of your life, Christina.

Tina had hung up the phone then. *How would you know what Tim would have wanted?*

They wanted her home but Tina never saw them in the Cross. If she was a mother it would have been the first place she would have looked. Maybe standing around and wringing your hands at your runaway daughter was easier than actually finding her. Her mother was free to start again. Tim was gone and now that she was gone her mother could take the same approach her father had. Family? What family?

'Okay,' said Lockie, breaking into her thoughts. Breaking in and breaking down.

Tina was pleased she had remembered about the Chapel. Getting food would be easy, although there was always the problem of questions. Everyone got suspicious when they saw a little kid. With enough makeup on she passed for much older than seventeen. Lockie could easily be her kid.

She made him brush his teeth again before breakfast and they made their way to the Chapel.

There was a line of people waiting for the doors to open. They stamped their feet in the cold. It wasn't the kind of line that people got chatty in. Mostly everyone looked at their feet. Funny how human beings stop looking at each other when they are ashamed of themselves.

The strong astringent smell of alcohol was in the air. It clashed with the smell of dirty clothes and dirty bodies.

Tina looked down the line at the shabbily dressed men and women. Everyone looked like they were wearing everything they owned. The older ones were fans of Jack Daniel's. The younger ones liked anything they could shoot, snort or swallow. There were some new ones as well now. Whole families who couldn't quite believe that they were in the Cross waiting for a free breakfast. You could almost see them wondering what the fuck had happened. *Where did my big TV go?* the GFC people whispered to one another but in the Cross there had always been a financial crisis. Whatever was happening on the stock market would never change that.

The first time she had come to the Chapel for breakfast Tina had known instantly that she did not belong with these people. There was no way she was going to turn into them. The free breakfast was just until she sorted herself out. When she thought back on it now she managed a smile at her arrogance. She had been fifteen. What exactly was she going to do? Open a shop?

The people in the line scratched and twitched and jumped depending on whether they were on their way up or down. They all wanted breakfast. The body was strange that way. Regardless of what you did to it, it wanted to keep running. Unless, of course, it turned on you.

In a fair world the people who set out to destroy themselves would be the ones to get the diseases and little kids would get to grow up without worrying. In a fair world ... but fuck-all in the world was fair.

The wait seemed to go on forever but eventually the doors opened and they were greeted by the smell of eggs and porridge. Tina's stomach turned. She was not used to eating breakfast.

Lockie stood quietly in the line but she could feel his body vibrating with impatience. For kids the whole world revolved around food. Their days were divided up by breakfast and then morning tea and then lunch and then afternoon tea and then dinner. It used to drive Tina mad when she was home alone with Tim. She would have just finished clearing up after lunch and he would be back asking what was coming next.

She wondered if Lockie had been a fussy eater before the uniform got to him. Tim was fussy as hell. He would only eat Vegemite toast for breakfast and then it had to be cut into perfect triangles. He hated the crust. At the end he even hated Vegemite.

Lockie made his way slowly through two bowls of porridge with milk and heaps of sugar, and then through two plates of eggs and toast. There was hot chocolate to drink and he had two cups of that as well. Tina hoped he wasn't going to throw up. The uniform must have known what he was doing. He had fed the kid just enough to keep him alive. Tina felt the heat rise in her body again as she thought of the man.

She was happy to watch Lockie eat while she worked on getting through some eggs. She felt the same way she did when Tim had managed to eat something she cooked for him. She sipped her coffee and longed for a cigarette. There was no smoking inside the Chapel. Passive smoking was dangerous. Ha ha.

There was a television on in the corner and Tina glanced at it, then looked again when she caught sight of the house. *The House.*

Her heart leaped around in her chest. How had they found him so soon? It had only been two days. Had someone seen them leaving the house? Did someone know? Were the police looking for her right now?

'Stay here, Lockie, okay? Don't move. I'm just going over there to see what's on television.'

Lockie stood up, still holding his toast. 'I'll come with you.'

'No, Lockie, I'm only going over there. Oh, Jesus. Okay.'

There was a lot of noise in the hall but Tina managed to catch a few words. 'Unknown assailant.' 'Respected by his colleagues.' 'Brutal beating.' Tina moved closer, straining to hear, and bumped against a woman shovelling oatmeal into her mouth.

'Careful there,' said the woman. She was large and dressed in so many layers she could barely move.

'Sorry,' said Tina.

'Careful there,' said the woman again, and Tina realised she was talking to herself.

There was a gap in the talk in the room and Tina heard the words the neat-looking blonde reporter was saying.

'Police were called by the victim's mother, who suffers from Alzheimer's disease. They did not respond at first because the victim had not been missing for twenty-four hours, but after repeated calls from his mother someone was sent to the house.'

The uniform's mother must have driven the police crazy. What a piece of work she must have been before her brain started dissolving. Who produced a son like that?

The house was cordoned off with police tape. A policeman with microphones shoved in his face was talking about 'investigating all avenues' and 'calling for witnesses'.

It meant they had fuck-all idea about what had happened. The reporters would be all over the place, digging up the nastiness.

Tina's picture had been in the paper for about a day. She had been leafing through an old copy left on the pavement when she came across her own face.

The article had contained every juicy detail of her family's life. The reporter seemed overjoyed to discover a dead younger brother and a divorce. Tina could almost feel him salivating over her exposed life. That night she had let Ruby convince her to dye her hair black.

She wondered if Lockie's face had been in the paper. She read the paper whenever she could but she couldn't remember Lockie. There was always some little kid missing.

There must have been a huge search on.

The police were always all over the missing-kids cases. Missing children made the community uncomfortable. It meant the castle walls had been breached. It meant that anything was possible. In a world where anything was possible the only real possibility was chaos.

Tina is a strong student of history and science. She has shown remarkable ability with essay structure. We hope that she will consider taking these subjects for the HSC.

If no one knew the man had Lockie, then no one knew who had been in the house. The television camera panned across the gold sedan. Someone could have seen her get in the car, but no one would say anything. It was hard to believe anything your average junkie said.

It was possible that one of the boys would talk if they were desperate enough. It was possible, but it probably wouldn't happen. Even the youngest kid in the Cross knew not to trust the police. Hopefully the police would look in the wrong direction. Hopefully.

The man's face flashed onto the television. Tina felt Lockie tense and hold his breath. His hand was sweaty and trembling in hers. His eyes were wide and disbelieving. The toast was forgotten.

'Stop staring, Lockie,' she whispered. 'People are watching us.'

'We killed him?' whispered Lockie.

'Quiet, it's time to go.'

Outside Lockie repeated the words again and again.

'We killed him, Tina. We killed him.'

Lockie had seemed to understand the word 'dead' in the house. He had asked her if the man was dead. But now Tina could see that he had not really understood that there was a human being on the floor and that he would never breathe again. Television fucked up kids' heads. You died one week and came back the next, and even though Lockie was smart it was still hard for him to see 'dead' as being real.

Tina sighed loudly. She was irritated that she had to deal with this and terrified that she had somehow been seen.

'Oh, for fuck's sake, kid, you didn't do anything. I killed him. You swung the poker a few times. You're just a little kid. You couldn't hurt a fly.'

Lockie looked at her with his big blue eyes. His lips moved around the words and he whispered to himself, 'Couldn't hurt a fly, couldn't hurt a fly.'

They started walking again and Tina could hear him repeating the words over and over. Finally he said aloud, 'That's what my mum always says.'

'What?'

'That I couldn't hurt a fly.'

'You're a good kid, Lockie. Don't ever think anything else.'

'I'm a good kid,' Lockie repeated, and then he went quiet. Tina looked over at him and his lips were moving, repeating the phrase again and again. She could see it becoming a habit, but what the fuck. He was dealing with all this shit the best way he knew how.

They walked along in silence for a few minutes. The cold air was almost refreshing after the fetid heat of the Chapel.

'Why did you kill him, Tina?'

'You ask a lot of questions, Lockie.'

'Sorry.'

'You don't have to be sorry, Lockie; you just have to know that some questions aren't meant to be asked.'

'Don't you know why?'

'I know why, Lockie, but I don't want to talk about it. I had to get you out of the house. End of story.'

'End of story,' said Lockie.

She took him back to the squat because she couldn't think of anything else to do with him.

They had to be quiet. Mark and the other boys were still sleeping. Tina knew they would probably sleep all day and then they would wake up in need of a hit and some food.

Lockie sat on the floor making paper aeroplanes out of McDonald's bags. Tina sat on the mattress and tried to figure things out. She watched his hands move but she knew his head was somewhere else. He was making the aeroplanes on automatic. Tina remembered the bed of newspapers he had been lying on under the table. There were things behind him, bits of paper, and now that she thought about it she had seen the shape of a boat and an aeroplane. Had he been making toys to play with? What had gone through his head while he was under that table?

He needed to be home, where he probably had a roomful of toys. Tina wondered if, after he was safe, he would ever make another paper aeroplane again.

'Look, Lockie, I know you don't like uniforms but you must know they're not all bad, right?'

'Pete's not bad.'

'Who's Pete?'

'He's the policeman at home. He has a beer with my dad on Saturday night.'

'There you go. And has Pete ever hurt you?'

Lockie considered this for a moment. 'He gave me a football for my birthday. When I turned seven. He gave me a book on trains when I turned eight.'

'Okay, so he's a good guy, yeah?'

'Yeah, Pete's a good guy.'

'Okay, so there are a lot of good guys who can help you. The police, the real police, are good guys.'

Tina tried hard to keep her voice light and high. She needed him to think she believed what she was saying.

'They probably know all about you. I bet your parents have told everyone that they're looking for you. The police will take you home. They'll take you back to your mum and dad. If we go right now you could probably be home by tonight, or at least tomorrow. Didn't they teach you at school that if you were lost you should find a policeman?'

'Yeah, they did. Mrs Watson said that you can always trust a policeman. And Pete came and told us too. Pete said he would always help. Always.'

'She was right, teachers are always right. Pete was right too, and I bet he's friends with the police in Sydney. I bet they would help you get home.'

'Teachers aren't always right. Not always. She was wrong about trusting the uniform.'

'Yeah, but she didn't know him so she wasn't wrong— she just didn't know.'

'I knew.'

'You knew? What do you mean you knew?'

'When he bent down to talk to me, I just knew.'

'Why didn't you run away? Why didn't you kick and scream or something?'

'I was lost and Mrs Watson said.'

'What exactly happened, Lockie? How did you get lost?'

Lockie sighed and smoothed out another empty bag. He concentrated on folding the edges, creating another aeroplane to join his fleet. He didn't speak while he worked.

Tina watched him for a while but she didn't ask the question again. Maybe Lockie was working out the story in his head.

Finally Tina lay down on the mattress and closed her eyes and that was when Lockie began to speak.

'I went to look at the rollercoaster. It looked so cool. I wanted to go fast like everyone else. I wanted to feel like I was flying. They were making speeches and it was so boring. Sammy was asleep and I had nothing to do. I went to look at the rollercoaster and then I got lost so I found a policeman.'

'Okay . . . but you found a bad guy. That happens some-times. You found a really bad guy wearing a uniform. He wasn't a real policeman, just a security guard. I'll take you to see some real policemen.'

'They'll be uniforms.'

Tina chewed her nail in frustration. 'I know, Lockie, but I've explained about that. The uniform you met was a bad guy.'

'The uniform said he would take me back to Mum and Dad. But he didn't.'

'I know, but he was a really, really bad guy. You know the difference between bad guys and good guys, right?'

'Sometimes . . .' He paused.

'Sometimes what, Lockie?' Tina worked to stay calm. It was a frustrating conversation.

'Sometimes the bad guys look like good guys.'

'Oh Christ, Lockie, I know that but . . . look, if you want to get home you're going to have to go into the police station. If you don't go to the police, you can't go home.'

'You could take me home,' he said quietly.

'Me? No, Lockie, I have to stay here. I can't go rushing across the country to take you home.'

'Why?'

Tina almost said, 'Because I said so,' but she knew that wouldn't satisfy the kid. It had never been the right answer for Tim either.

Instead of saying anything, she chewed on a piece of skin on her thumb. Why couldn't she take him home? It wasn't like her diary was full. *They won't miss me at work*, she thought with grim humour.

Well, she had no money for a start. She also had no idea where it was that he actually lived and fuck-all idea of how to get there. It was a stupid idea. She needed to take him to the police station and just shove him through the door. But she couldn't go in with him. She couldn't keep all the lies straight and the police would figure it out and then she would be in jail for the rest of her miserable life. No. There was no way she could take the kid into a police station. But what if he ran away and some other weirdo found him?

She hated having this fucking responsibility. She should have just left well enough alone. After Tim she swore she would never have kids, never get attached to anything that could die. No kids and no pets. Now here she was right back there again and without even thinking about it she knew it was all going to end badly. Everything always did.

They stayed in the squat all day.

When the afternoon sun disappeared Mark woke up. He looked into the room.

Lockie had fallen asleep on the floor. He hadn't complained about being hungry and he hadn't said he was bored. It was like having a robot kid.

'How come he's still here?' said Mark.

'He won't go into the police station. I'd take him, but . . .'

'Yeah, but . . .'

'I don't know what I'm going to do with him, Mark.'

'Should have thought of that before you turned into a superhero.'

'Shut the fuck up, Mark. I couldn't just leave him there.'

'You're all heart, Teen.'

'Yeah, I'm a fucking angel.'

'I wouldn't go that far.'

Tina laughed. It felt good to laugh. Lockie didn't even smile properly. Tina rubbed her eyes. She was tired. Taking care of someone else was draining.

'I think I have to take him home.'

'Where does he live?'

'Some hick town called Cootamundra. Heard of it?'

'Nah, but then I've never been out of Sydney.'

'I have, but I wasn't exactly paying attention.'

'Patrick might know.'

'Why would he know anything?'

'He's from Young.'

'Where's that?'

'Dunno, but he's from there.'

'Is he up?'

'Yeah, getting there.'

'Is he okay?'

'Not brilliant, but he'll talk to you.'

'All right.'

Mark went out of the room and came back a moment later with Patrick. Patrick looked like he belonged on a surfboard on some beach. Even in winter he looked tanned, although that was probably because of some nasty disease eating him alive. His blond hair stood straight up in spikes. The men loved him. He looked like everyone's idea of a beautiful surfer. Once Patrick had let slip that his dad thought he was beautiful too. Any evil fuck could have a kid.

'Yeah, what's up?' he said. His eyes darted around the room, landed on a sleeping Lockie and kept moving. Tina knew he wasn't looking for anything. He just couldn't keep still. He scratched at his favourite spot on his wrist. There was only a small amount of blood but it was disturbing to watch him open up the scab. Tina was glad that Lockie was asleep.

'Do you know where Cootamundra is?'

'Yeah, 'bout forty k from Young. Nothing much happening there. Don Bradman was born there but.'

'Do you know how I could get there?'

'What the fuck you wanna go there for? Piece-of-shit boring town.'

'I want to take this kid home.'

'What kid?'

'This kid, Patrick,' said Tina. Christ, he was nearly over the edge.

'Fucked if I know, Tina. I s'pose you could catch a train.'

'All the way there?'

'Yeah, you know, a country train. I don't know. Ask the bloke at the station.'

'Okay, thanks, Pat.'

'Yeah, whatever.'

'Do you want to come out tonight? One of us could watch the kid while you work,' said Mark.

'Nah, thanks. I'll just get him some dinner and get some sleep. Might go past the train station and see what's what.'

Mark's offer was real but Tina knew that there was no way he would live up to it. A short attention span was just the smallest side effect of his habit. There was also no telling what he would do for enough money. Lockie could turn into a commodity. She waited until the boys had left and then counted out her money again. It was still only eleven dollars no matter which way she looked at it.

'Up you get, Lockie,' she said, touching his shoulder, trying not to stroke his hair but failing.

He sat up rubbing his eyes and yawning. His face had that pink-cheeked glow little kids get after they sleep.

For some reason the glow made Tina proud, like she had made it happen.

'Can we go to the bathroom?'

'Yeah and then we have to go to the train station and figure out how to get you home.'

'Are you going to take me home?'

Tina sighed. 'Yeah, Lockie, I'm going to take you home—at least I'm going to try, but if I can't figure it out then you have to go to the police station, okay?'

'You'll figure it out,' said Lockie in a small determined voice. 'You'll figure it out.'

Are you listening, universe? Tina asked. *Are you listening?*

———

The man at the station was not in a good mood. Tina understood the man's attitude. He was wedged in his life with no way out. Tina didn't think she would love the idea of sitting in a booth all day either.

'Yeah, what?' he said, giving his large belly a scratch. The buttons on his grey shirt hung on for dear life. It amazed Tina that people seemed to know automatically how to treat her. The man would fawn and smile at other people but he seemed to know that Tina would just take any crap. The Cross stuck to her.

'I need to know how to get to Cootamundra.'

'Where?'

'Cootamundra. It's in the country.'

'I'll have to look it up,' said the man, eyeing Lockie and then giving her the once-over as well. He didn't move.

Tina felt her body grow tight. Stupid arsehole prick.

'Could you please look it up? We need to go home.'

The man took a sip of his Coke, belched loudly, and then went to work on his computer.

'You can catch a train from Central to Cootamundra.'

'How long does it take?'

The man rolled his eyes and looked back at his computer screen.

'Takes about five hours. It leaves at seven forty-two in the morning. How many are travelling?'

'Just me and the boy.'

'You an adult?'

Tina nodded without even thinking about it. It wasn't like she had any sort of card to say she was a student, and everything would just be easier if she was an adult. Easier and more expensive.

'How old is the kid?'

'Eight,' said Tina.

'I assume you want economy class,' said the man, giving Tina a yellow-toothed grin.

Tina nodded.

'That'll be sixty-four dollars and sixty-nine cents, luv.'

'Jesus, that's a lot.'

'Travel ain't cheap.'

Tina looked at the man. 'I'll have to go to the bank. I'll be back tomorrow.'

'I'll be here,' leered the man.

She pulled Lockie away from the window.

'Why didn't you buy the tickets, Tina? Aren't we going home?'

I'm never going home, thought Tina.

'Tickets cost money, Lockie—money we don't have.'

'My dad has money. You could call my dad.'

'Oh yeah, that would work out real well,' muttered Tina. 'Probably give the man a heart attack.' Lockie's father would send the police after them so fast Tina wouldn't even have time to hang up the phone. And then everything would be chaos. No one would give her a chance to explain. Maybe if she got the kid home then they would take the time to listen. Maybe.

'How are we going to get some money, Tina?'

'I don't know, okay? Just shut up now. You talk too much.'

'Sorry, Tina,' he said and swiped furiously at his cheeks.

'Ah, fuck, Lockie, I didn't mean to shout. Look, don't worry about it, okay? I'll figure it out.'

'Yeah, you'll figure it out,' he said, and then, almost to himself, 'Tina will figure it out.'

Jesus, the weight of his trust was heavy.

'I have trains at home,' said Lockie after a few minutes of silence.

'Yeah, what, like Thomas the Tank Engine?'

'No,' said Lockie fiercely. 'Not Thomas. I'm not a baby. Real trains. They go over mountains and under tunnels. My dad built a big table for them. There are people on the trains. My mum made me a train cake once. She made a station out of icing. She made people out of icing. I got to eat the conductor. Sammy wanted the conductor but Dad said no because it was my birthday. Now I have real trains. They're small but they're real.'

Tina waited until Lockie ran out of stuff to say.

'That sounds pretty cool.'

'I got them for my birthday when I turned eight.'

'Yeah,' said Tina. She was not really listening, not really thinking. Small kids were easy to tune out.

'When is your birthday?' she asked and then immediately cursed herself. Lockie was not some ordinary kid. Who knew what a birthday meant to him now?

'On the nineteenth of June,' said Lockie.

'Oh,' said Tina, completely lost for words.

'What month is it now?'

'August.'

'Yeah, I'm already nine. I'm nine now.' The words were said without emotion. This terrible fact was just another one to add to the list Lockie must have in his head.

Tina remembered the anticipation of a birthday ahead. She just knew that in Lockie's house it would be a really big deal. Kids waited the whole year for their birthdays. Tim had crossed days off the calendar for two months before. The night before his birthday he had always been almost psycho with excitement. The whole family had to get up at the crack of dawn to open presents and sing to him. She must have done the same thing when she was a kid but she couldn't remember it. Her mother always baked a cake and bought as many presents as she could afford.

'I bet they've got presents for you,' she said to the silent Lockie.

'Who?'

'Your mum and dad. I bet they bought you presents and they kept them for when you get home. When you get home you can open them.'

'For real?' said Lockie.

'Yeah,' said Tina, hoping it was true. 'For real.'

She relaxed a little at having figured out a way to move Lockie on. He was still looking at his feet but she could see him considering what could be waiting for him when he got home. Presents made the possibility of getting home seem real. He didn't understand the dilemma of no money—not really. Tina hadn't really understood it either. Even when things were really bad there was always food in the fridge at home. There was always money for stuff she really needed. Only after a few days in the Cross did she realise that it was possible to go hungry. It was a scary thought. One that she didn't want to contemplate right now. She needed help from somewhere but there was nowhere to go and no one who could help.

'I could really use a cigarette,' said Tina to the world in general.

'Here you go,' said a man in front of them. He turned around and offered Tina a lit cigarette.

Tina backed away. 'No thanks, I mean . . . no.'

'Go on, take it. I'm trying to give up. I light them and give them away.'

The man was wearing a suit. An expensive suit. His hair was perfect and his brown eyes had that healthy glow which meant he ate well and generally lived an upstanding life.

He could have had any nasty disease hiding in his mouth but Tina put her hand out and took the cigarette.

'Thanks,' said the man and disappeared into the crowd.

'Thanks,' said Tina to the universe. You never knew who was listening.

She savoured the cigarette until there was nothing left.

She kept Lockie moving towards Martin Place, where the vans would be dispensing food to the homeless. The streetlights came on and the temperature dropped even further. Lockie pulled his hood up over his ears. She held his hand in her pocket, keeping both of them warm.

He didn't protest at the long walk. He just put one foot in front of the other. Tim used to just sit down. He didn't care where he was—on an escalator, in the park, or in the middle of the road—he would just sit down when he got tired. Tina would have to pick him up. Even when he was already too big to be carried he liked being picked up. Tina smiled, remembering how she used to yell at him. He didn't care. He knew she would take care of him. He had absolute faith in her.

Tina stopped moving as a thought hit her like a punch in the stomach. She had thought of Tim and she had smiled. Actually smiled. How had that happened?

She looked down at Lockie's bent head. He had stopped as well without even asking why.

She had smiled when she thought of Tim. She had never imagined it would be possible. She had tried in those first few months after his death to work her way through the pain and the anger towards accepting what had happened. She had even prayed a little in her own way. The pain was so overwhelming that she didn't think she would survive it. Sometimes she thought she had a handle on it but then she would be standing in the shower and crying without even knowing. Running away had seemed to be the solution to the pain but you can't run very far from yourself. Lots of people in the Cross were angry and in pain. It was so easy just to join them and rage at the world. She had raged with the best of them. For two years the anger had kept her company, kept her warm, kept her moving and doing what she had to do.

But today, walking the cold streets with Lockie, she had smiled.

Everything was the same but everything was different. It felt like she had climbed some sort of mountain and now here she was, looking at the view. She felt the air going in and out of her lungs and it felt lighter. It was easier to breathe. She had thought of Tim and she had smiled. After two and a half long, terrible years she had smiled. The anger was still there at the bottom of her stomach but it felt small and hard like a stone.

Not like a volcano about to erupt. She started walking again. She wouldn't think about it too much. She had smiled and that would have to be enough for today.

She turned her mind back to the problem of getting Lockie home.

Lockie knew she would take care of him as well.

Tina was disturbed by how much he trusted her. Little kids were so stupid. She couldn't ever remember being so stupid, but she must have been. Before her whole world fell apart she must have thought that there was nothing more terrible than rain on a summer's day or some such other shit.

She needed seventy dollars to get Lockie home. She needed seventy dollars and she had eleven.

'*I wanna be a billionaire so frickin' bad,*' she sang softly.

Seventy dollars was not a lot of money but it might as well have been a million. She couldn't work and she was no good at stealing. She was up shit creek.

In Martin place they blended in with the crowds who would pay way more than seventy dollars for dinner. It was still early so they sat together in a doorway waiting for the vans to arrive.

The first one came with sandwiches. Tina looked around the square. Along the sides were all the folks who needed a free meal. They were hidden in doorways and sitting on the cold flagstones with their backs against the buildings. They needed food but if she dragged Lockie over to the van there would be raised eyebrows and questions.

'You have to stay here, Lockie, while I get some food.'

'I'll come with you.'

'Lockie, I'll only be over there. Nothing will happen to you. I promise, okay? If I take you to the van they'll want to know all about you.'

'I'll come with you,' said Lockie again. His body was stiff, determined.

'Lockie, they'll take you to the uniforms,' said Tina.

Jesus, I'm a bitch, she thought. And then, *What else can I do?*

Lockie stepped back further into the doorway. He pushed himself into a corner.

'I'll stay here,' he said.

'I'll be quick,' she said.

The van was run by a priest. He'd brought along some schoolboys to help. The boys were obviously on some required excursion. They all had earphones in their ears and they tried really hard to look everywhere but at Tina.

'I need a few,' she said to the priest. 'I have to take some for my friend.'

'Why don't you get your friend to come over here?' said the priest.

Tina sighed. He only wanted to help, she knew that, but she felt the anger at having to deal with this heat up her body. If not for the kid she wouldn't be here, begging for food.

'Please,' she said, looking straight at the priest.

He smiled and lifted his hands, sensing her desperation. She kept glancing over at the doorway.

'Okay, sure, don't worry. How many do you need? What kind?'

'Anything's good. About six? And something to drink?'

The priest moved to the back of the van and gathered some things together. He found an old plastic shopping bag and filled it. Tina kept her eye on the doorway. The schoolboys in the van were pointing and smirking at the slow movements towards the van. Once Tina herself would have laughed at the sad rabble drifting towards the van. Once she would have done a lot of things.

She thanked the priest, took the bag and turned around. Then she saw a big man with a beard move into the doorway where Lockie was standing.

Her feet barely touched the ground.

'What the fuck are you doing?' was already out of her mouth before she reached them.

The man, startled, moved out of the doorway. Lockie was crouched on the ground, making himself into a ball.

'Nothing . . . I just . . . nothing . . . Don't panic, okay? I just wanted to say hello to the kid. I just . . .'

The man was drunk, homeless, harmless.

'Get the fuck out of here before I beat the shit out of you,' yelled Tina. She was enraged but she was also crying.

'Sorry . . . sorry . . . Don't panic, okay? Sorry.' The man backed away into the middle of the square then took off at a slow run. He didn't look back. He was afraid of her.

Tina felt her heart slow. She would have roared if she could have.

She put the bag of food down on the ground and crawled over to Lockie. He was not moving at all. He was a statue, a ghost, a piece of the wall. He wasn't there.

'Sorry, Lockie. Did he touch you?'

Lockie kept his head buried in his knees.

'Please, Lockie, I'm sorry. I shouldn't have left you. Please, Lockie, are you okay?' She had done exactly what his parents had done. She had left him, and who knew what might have happened? She stopped talking and sat down next to him. There was no point in going on at the kid. She had fucked up. She had fucked up but she was all he had right now. Lockie wasn't a stupid kid. He would understand that.

Tina took off her backpack and worked her way through it. One lonely, crushed cigarette presented itself. She didn't have a light and even though she could see the glow of cigarettes all across the square there was no way she was moving away from Lockie. She sighed and pushed the cigarette back into the empty box.

Two more vans entered the square. One was giving out hot food, but still Tina didn't budge.

Lockie moved a little and there were some muffled words.

'What, Lockie?'

'I wet my pants,' he said, lifting his head and looking her straight in the face. His nose was running again and his eyes were red.

'Oh fuck, Lockie,' she said. God, she was tired.

'Look, don't worry about it, okay? We've got a spare pair of undies and there's an all-night laundromat near where I sleep. We'll get it sorted and hopefully we can get the money together for tomorrow so we can catch a train and get you home.'

Lockie nodded and stood up. It was time to walk again. There was not enough money for a bus, there wasn't enough money for anything, and now she had to use some to clean the kid's clothes. She couldn't let him be dirty. She knew that.

They made their way to the laundromat and Tina draped him in her coat again. Four precious dollars went on the washing machine and tumble dryer.

They ate their sandwiches and leafed through old maga-
zines. It was warm and it was quiet. The man at the back barely
looked up from his newspaper.

After Lockie had eaten two sandwiches he fell asleep. He
had wanted one more but Tina knew they would need it the
next day. If they did manage to get on the train they would
need some food. She had sneaked onto trains before. She
could always make a quick getaway if she was caught, but she
had the feeling that a country train was different and there
was no way she could go anywhere quickly with Lockie in tow.
It was nearly midnight and the train left from Central at seven
forty-two.

Tina rubbed her eyes. It was completely impossible. There
was absolutely no hope at all. There was nothing worse than
feeling there was no hope. She'd felt it when Tim was at the
end and she tried to stop feeling it every day since. People
went on because they clung to hope. If you didn't have that
you basically had fuck-all.

Tina woke Lockie up when his clothes were dry. She dressed
him and they made their way back to the squat. The longer he
was with her the more babyish he became. He let her dress
him and hold his hand and at every opportunity he would
sidle up next to her.

The constant touching was making Tina's skin crawl. It was
too much. She kept telling herself that they were the touches
of a child but it had been a long time since she had been
so physically close to anyone. It took everything she had
not to shake him off. She needed her space but Lockie
needed his mother. Right now what Lockie needed was more
important.

He needed help to process what had happened to him. He needed to feel safe and cared for. He needed to be with people who understood how to deal with kids who had been through shit like this. She was barely qualified to take care of herself. Tina wondered if, in the end, she would have to walk into the police station and just confess so she could get the kid some help. It was a thought she didn't allow to develop. Instead she kept the facts moving around in her head, trying to come up with an idea.

Lockie stumbled along with his eyes down. He was half asleep.

Suddenly he stopped and pulled at her hand.

'Fuck, Lockie, I'm freezing—let's go.'

'Look,' said Lockie.

'I don't want to look, Lockie; I want to get some sleep.'

Tim had been like that. The world was full of interesting objects. He was always looking at the ground, searching for treasure. He had kept a collection of bits of glass and stones on his bookshelf. He wanted to be an explorer when he grew up. When he grew up.

'Look!' said Lockie again.

'Fuck.' Tina turned around and looked at the ground where Lockie was pointing. People moved around them.

On the ground, in the gutter, partly covered by a piece of meat pie, was a ten-dollar note.

Tina just stared at it for a moment. It was probably fake, something that had belonged to a kid. It was probably just a piece of paper. She reached down and picked it up. It was a ten-dollar note. She wiped it on the pavement and then on her coat. It was still a ten-dollar note.

It wasn't like she had never found money on the street before. The whole city thought that the Cross was a cool place to have a drink. They stumbled in from the city with their pockets full of cash and a big night on their minds.

Drunk people tended to drop things a lot, but tonight the money felt like a gift. Tonight the money *was* a gift. Tonight the money was a little slice of hope. Tina smiled at Lockie. 'We've got seventeen dollars, Lockie. We're almost there.'

'Almost there,' said Lockie and he gave her another one of his small smiles. Almost there, but actually so far away the idea was just a dream. Tina shoved the ten dollars down to the bottom of her backpack. As she brought her hand out of the bag it brushed against the warm metal. She tried not to touch it just as she tried not to think about it. Not ever.

Oh God, not that, please not that. But the universe would not be swayed. It had given her the answer.

Reluctantly, unwillingly, Tina took the locket out of her bag.

It was all she had taken when she left. She hadn't even been clever enough to think about the cold months ahead or to empty her mother's purse. She had just wanted out. She couldn't take deep breaths, she couldn't get enough air into her lungs. It felt like only she could feel the grief in the house. It coated everything thickly like grease and she couldn't bear to be in the space. She couldn't bear to be with her mother and Jack and their endless conversations about God. She had known she had to leave, but she had stayed because Tim was still there. In his room, in his toys and clothes he was still there.

Tim's door was always closed but his bedroom was exactly as it had been before his last stay in hospital. Mr Lulu slept on his pillow, waiting for . . . for what? She'd wanted to take something that had belonged to him but when she opened the door to the bedroom she couldn't go inside. Her mother wanted to clear the room out. She wanted to give as much as she could away and keep only a few things to remind her of Tim. But the first time she tried Tina had gone completely crazy.

What the fuck do you think you're doing? she had said when she found her mother in Tim's room with a garbage bag.

Please, Christina, don't use that language—and you can see what I'm doing. I just thought it was time.

It's only been a few months. You can't wait any longer? What do you need the room for? Do you need a home gym or an office? Will it be better if there's nothing to remind you that he ever existed? Do you need to throw out everything so we can all forget? Didn't you love him? Don't you miss him? Who the fuck are you with all your future plans? Tim is dead and there is no future. Not for any of us. Why can't you get that? Why do you keep trying to pretend he never existed?

Tina was crying and screaming. She was out of control and the anger was in charge.

Okay, Christina, her mother had said, backing out of the room as though away from a wild animal. *We'll leave it a bit longer. Don't get upset, Christina, please. I'll leave it as long as you want. You tell me when you're ready.*

How come you're ready? Tina had shouted. *How come you're ready? You're his mother. You are never supposed to be ready. And I'll never be ready either. Leave it all alone. Just leave it alone.*

That night she heard the whispering as her mother told her side of the story. She heard the word 'doctor' drift through the walls.

They wanted to fix her. They wanted someone to say the right words or give her the right pills so they could all move on with their lives.

They thought she was crazy. They were right but there were no words that could lighten the weight of her grief and there was no way she was going to gloss over Tim with some fucking pill. And she had seen, very clearly, that one day without warning she would come home and everything that was Tim, everything that had touched Tim, would just be gone and all that would be left was Jack and her mother and their God.

The next day she had left.

She'd just wanted out, but she had taken the locket.

The locket was eighteen-carat gold and opened to reveal a picture of her aged ten and a picture of Tim aged three. Tim and Tina together forever.

The locket had belonged to her mother. It had belonged to her grandmother. Now it was hers.

In those first lonely, hungry days she had taken it to the local pawn shop and the thin man with thick glasses had priced it.

'This is a beautiful piece, dear, but there's not much call for lockets, I'm afraid. I can give you one hundred dollars for it.' Tina knew she could have taken the man a tree that grew its own money and he would say, 'Not much call for money trees, I'm afraid.'

Business was business. Just about everyone who ever walked through the door of a pawn shop had a sad story to tell, especially in the Cross. Tina knew the man had to keep his head above the misery. He had to build a wall to hold back the gush of other people's problems. Tina understood. Her own wall was pretty crap after Tim but with each day in the Cross it got stronger and higher. Now that she had it just right Lockie was busy pushing through. The sooner she got him home the sooner she could go back to strengthening her defences.

The thin man's voice had been kind but the gun under the counter was there for all to see. When she'd looked around properly Tina had lost the nerve to sell the locket. The shop was filled with reminders of better times. A signed guitar hung on the wall and even though she couldn't make out the signature it had obviously meant a lot to someone. There were rings under the glass counter that told the stories of broken hearts and broken lives and some slim laptops that told of broken dreams. People didn't start out wanting to stand on street corners and obliterate their mind any way they could. At some stage everyone had dreams.

Tina hated the idea that her locket would join the debris of so many other lives. She would keep the memory for herself. She would wait until the hunger was too much and then she would think again.

'Save it for a rainy day,' said the thin man with a thin-lipped smile.

Hello, thought Tina looking at the locket. *Hello, hello, it's fucking pouring down here.*

So what now?

She could keep the pictures. Did the oval locket engraved with flowers really matter? She held the locket in her hand. Even in the freezing air of one in the morning the gold felt warm. It was her last connection to home. Her last piece of the boring, predictable life she would never get back.

What was it worth to get Lockie home?

You're just a kid, Christina. You couldn't have done anything.

'Come on, Lockie, we've got one more stop to make.'

If only saving Tim could have been so simple.

She walked on through the streets. Lockie stumbled after her. He was almost asleep on his feet but of course he didn't protest. Finally she got tired of pulling him along so she hung the backpack on her front. She lifted him onto her back and felt his head drop onto her shoulder. He stayed awake for a while, reading street signs and talking to her.

She was pleased to feel that he was a little heavier than he had been when she found him. At least she had done that right.

On William Street there was a twenty-four-hour pawn-broker. Tina had walked the streets enough to know that the shop really was always open. There were times when money was needed right then and there, and just like there would always be dealers willing to get you high there would always be people willing to provide the money. It was all just business. The exchange of drugs and money and bodily fluids—all just business.

'I'm doing my bit to keep the economy going,' Ruby had laughed, but she hadn't been able to keep herself going.

Tina never had the full story from Ruby, but one night, just before she knew what she had, Ruby talked about a dinner with her parents and grandparents.

'It was a proper banquet,' she said. 'Mum cooked for days and all my aunties came as well. It was to celebrate the New Year. The food was so good, Tina, you wouldn't believe it. Not like the restaurant crap—it was the real thing. We ate and ate and ate but after a while I looked around and I couldn't recognise anyone. They didn't know what I knew about the men in my family. They didn't know fuck-all. It was like I was sitting at the table with a whole lot of strangers, know what I mean?'

Tina nodded. She knew exactly what her friend meant.

'Poor Ruby.'

'Who's Ruby?'

Lockie had been so silent Tina had thought he was asleep.

'What? Oh, no one. Well, not no one. She was a friend, a good friend of mine.'

'Maybe she could help us get some money.'

'No, Lockie, she can't.'

'Why can't she? My friend Tyler once gave me some money on tuckshop day. Mum forgot and Tyler had extra so he gave me some. I paid him back 'cos Mum said that's what friends do. We could pay Ruby back if she gave us some money.'

Tina laughed. 'Yeah, I suppose we could, but Ruby's gone away.'

'Where's she gone?'

'Remember what I said about asking too many questions?'

'My dad says questions are good. He says if you don't ask you'll never know.'

'I bet you ask your mum and dad lots of questions.'

'Yeah, I like to know stuff. Sometimes Mum looks up the answers on the internet.'

'She does?'

'Yeah. Mum likes the internet. It helped her learn to ice her cakes.'

'What's the best birthday cake your mum ever made you?'

Lockie was getting heavier with each block.

'When I turned eight she made a treasure chest. It had gold coins coming out of it but the coins were chocolate and we got to eat them. Tyler and me got to eat the pirate sign. It was made of black icing. It looked like it would be yuck but it was good.'

Tina listened to Lockie talk. His voice was a little boy's voice again. Light and high and she knew he was using the memories to push the other thoughts away. Lockie's memories were good for that. Tina had used thoughts to push the memories away. Now she listened to Lockie. She walked in the cold, listening to Lockie and she didn't think about anything else.

Tina set Lockie down in front of the shop. He leaned against the wall and closed his eyes. In the yellow light he was ghost-like and frail.

She pressed the buzzer and after a few minutes the door was opened by a huge man with a gun at his side. They had obviously looked her over with a camera and decided she wasn't too great a threat. Lockie came up to her chest when he stood next to her. Tim had been big for eight but Tina had always been small.

'Yeah?' said the man. He was wearing a white shirt covered with grease stains and he smelled like fried chicken. He looked like he came from one of the islands and Tina could see where Ruby might have got the idea of Billy from.

'I want to sell this,' said Tina, holding up the memory.

The man picked his teeth with his little finger. 'Okay, come in. But your kid better not touch anything.'

'He won't.'

There was another man behind the counter. He had a long black beard and dark eyes. The remains of the fried chicken lay on a plate on the counter. It could have been dinner time instead of one in the morning. Tina wondered if someone else took over during the day or if the man was permanently awake, catching sleep when he could.

'Yeah?' he said.

'Not too big on conversation, you blokes,' said Tina.

Lockie sat down in an overstuffed chair.

No one smiled. The two men looked at her with statue faces.

Tina was not a big one for conversation either but she felt the need to connect to the men in the shop. She was going to give them the last piece of the old Tina she had left. She would have loved them to chat with her, to ask her questions and find out just how important the locket was, but it was easier to connect to the characters on television than it was for people to connect to each other.

Business was business.

Tina stopped wasting the man's time.

'I need to sell this.'

The man behind the counter got out his magnifying glass. He looked the locket over and then he burped.

'I can give you twenty dollars.'

Tina gasped. 'The man at the shop two streets from here offered me a hundred and that was two years ago.'

'Go there then.'

'I can't go there, I need the money now. It's an antique and its eighteen-carat gold.'

The man sighed and took a sip of some green-coloured tea. 'This is not a charity, you know.'

'Yeah I do fucking know. I'm not asking for charity. I'm just asking for what's fair.'

'Watch your language, girlie. I don't need to deal with your shit.' It was true. The man didn't have to deal with anything he didn't want to deal with. He had the money and the bodyguard. The power was all his.

Tina wondered what it would be like to feel that you were the one in control. She was in control of fuck-all but no one could make her sell the locket. Tina looked at her feet. They could wait one more day. The thought of giving away the locket for so little was too much to handle. It was just a thing and she knew that but she couldn't just throw it away. She would go to the other shop in the morning. The prospect of taking care of Lockie for another day, of keeping him fed and getting him to the toilet, of keeping him safe and stopping him from falling apart was exhausting, but they could wait one more day. She picked up the locket and turned to go.

'Forty dollars,' said the man.

'That's not even half what it's worth.'

'Take it or leave it. I don't care.'

Lockie was fast asleep in the chair. He should have been home in his own bed sleeping on cowboy sheets or whatever it was little boys slept on these days. *Why is it my problem?*

Just because. Just because. Just because.

'I'll take it.'

The man smiled and took the locket back. He opened it and grabbed a small screwdriver to pry the pictures out.

'I don't want them,' said Tina.

The man lifted his dark eyebrows at her. 'Sure? I'm just going to throw them away.'

'Sure,' said Tina. She wasn't any better than her mother really. It was hard work holding on to your grief.

Tim wasn't three anymore and she wasn't ten. She could barely remember being ten. She could barely remember being a child. Why hang on to the pictures? The memories only hurt.

Tina put the money in her backpack and lifted Lockie up into her arms. He was heavy to carry that way. She stepped back a little as she adjusted to his weight. His head lolled on her small shoulder but he refused to wake up.

Good for you, kid, thought Tina.

She staggered to the shop door. Lockie was a dead weight but she couldn't put him down. In more ways than one.

Fifty-seven dollars.

They needed sixty-five.

She would have to ask Mark for the rest.

The man in the white shirt opened the door for her and she walked out into the cold. The wind blew in circles around her head and she felt the exhaustion begin to take over. She had only walked a few steps when she heard a shout.

'Hey, lady!'

Tina stopped and then tensed. The shout was probably not directed at her but it was best not to find out. She started to run but Lockie got heavier with each step and she didn't get very far before she felt a hand on her shoulder. She turned around, prepared to fight.

The big man in the white shirt was standing in front of her. He was panting.

'Fuck . . . what . . . did . . . you . . . run for?'

'Sorry,' said Tina.

'Here,' said the man. He handed her a small plastic bag with the two photographs inside. 'You should keep them. That shit is important. You should keep them.'

Tina shifted Lockie to one side and took the plastic bag.

'Thanks,' she said.

The man nodded and turned around to walk back to the shop. Tina felt a surge of warmth in her body. The man was right. She should keep the pictures. She was grateful he had run after her. It wasn't something she would have expected.

She had to put Lockie down then. She couldn't carry him one more step. She shook him a little and he stumbled on, holding her hand.

Back at the squat she put Lockie on the mattress and covered him with a sleeping bag. She would wait up for Mark. Maybe he could lend her the money—and by the time he needed it back again she would be on a train to Cootamundra.

She felt bad for thinking that way; Mark was her friend. But Lockie was her responsibility. There was a huge difference.

———

Mark came in at four in the morning. Tina was dozing when she heard the door slam.

'Hey,' she said when Mark looked into the room. She had one candle dying on a saucer on the floor.

'Hey, you still got that kid?'

'Yeah. I found out about the train.'

'Yeah?'

'It leaves at seven forty-two in the morning from Central. I have to wake the kid up soon so I can get there and get tickets.'

The numbers repeated themselves in her head. Seven, four, two; seven, four, two. They were her anchor. They held her fast to her choice. Seven, four, two was all she needed to concentrate on.

'Okay.'

'The thing is . . .'

'Yeah?'

'I need another eight dollars.'

'That's a lot.'

'I know, but the tickets are sixty-five dollars. I need to get him home. Do you think you can help?'

'That's a lot of money, Tina. There's no one on the street. I need to keep some for myself.'

'I know, and I know it's a lot to ask, but I'm desperate. Maybe you could ask the other guys. If everyone gave a little . . .'

'You should have let us watch him. You could have worked.'

'He's my responsibility, Mark. I have to take care of him. I'll pay you back, but I have to get him home first.'

Mark ran his hands through his tight curls. 'You won't be coming back.'

'Why do you say that?'

'I just know. You won't. You don't really belong here.'

'No one belongs here.'

'Yeah, but especially not you. You should be at uni or . . . or somewhere else. I don't know.'

Tina couldn't see Mark properly in the dim light but she could hear something in his voice. He didn't really want her to come back. He wanted her to move out and move on. Tina could do it for him, too. She knew Mark was certain he would never escape the Cross. Maybe it helped to see a mate get out.

'Maybe you should go home.'

'Home is a big word, Mark.'

'Yeah, I know.'

'Maybe I could give the best blow jobs in Cootamundra?'

They both laughed at that. Hard sad laughter that made the stomach tense and took your breath away.

'I'll see what I can do,' said Mark when they were quiet again. 'What time do you have to go?'

'I should go to the station at about six. I don't want to miss the train.'

'Okay.' Mark nodded and then he left. Tina had no reason to believe he would come back but there was nothing wrong with an hour's worth of hope. There was nothing else she could do anyway. She handed the problem up to the universe. *Show me what you got universe. I'm waiting.*

It was a dangerous way of thinking. People liked to be in control. Tina liked to be in control. If you handed something up to the universe you had to let go. Tina knew how hard she was hanging on to everything. Before Lockie she had held on tight to her pain and her loss and her isolation. Now she had to hold on to her responsibility for a child that wasn't hers.

Somewhere inside her she held tight and she stood still. If she moved just a little everything would unravel. But sometimes she was just so weary. She liked that word—weary. It described the exhaustion of body and mind perfectly.

She had been a good student. Straight As, even when Tim was at the end. The books were somewhere to go. She could control the work. She could mould it and shape it and make it turn out exactly the way she wanted it to. Shame about the rest of her life.

Tina lay back down in the dark room and stared into the smooth blackness. Mark didn't think she was coming back. He imagined a different life for her. Sometimes Tina did the same thing. She would close her eyes and see herself at university being clever and witty. She would see herself in a power suit telling everyone else what to think and what to do. It was possible. Anything was possible when her eyes were closed. But when she opened her eyes even getting through the day was like trying to shift a mountain. Now the mountain had shifted her.

Half an hour later Mark was back. He emptied his pockets onto the floor. Five one-dollar coins fell out. Two dollars and seventy cents short, but she wouldn't tell him.

'Where did you get that?'

'Does it matter?'

'Nah. Thanks, mate. I really mean that. Thank you.'

Mark gave her a smile. He was proud of himself. He had done what he'd said he would do. The boy behind the mask peeped out for a moment and made Tina feel incredibly sad.

She wondered if anyone had ever told him they were proud of him in his whole life. Kids shouldn't have to be scared of the ones who were supposed to love them. It wasn't fair but then Tina knew better than anyone: fuck-all was fair.

'You're a good guy, Mark. You know that, don't you?'

'You're a good girl, too, Tina. You're more than good, you're ... you're ... I don't know. There's something in your eyes. You look like you're always thinking. You're not like the rest of us. None of us would have given a shit about that kid.'

'You're just kids yourselves. We're all just kids really. I don't know why but I can't let him down.'

Mark scratched at his skin. It was nearly time for another hit. Tina savoured the last glimpse of the real Mark before something else took over.

'The needles are what stop you thinking, Mark. You know that, don't you?'

'Fuck, Tina, I stopped thinking long before I took my first hit. Thinking puts you somewhere you don't want to be.'

'Maybe—but maybe it also helps you figure things out.'

'There's nothing to figure out, Teen. Not for me anyway. I'm so beyond fucked.'

'You could do something else, you know. Change your life. There are people who can help.' Tina said the words but they didn't mean anything. Change for Mark was almost impossible. His only relief would be death. Like Ruby. Tina felt her eyes grow hot as she thought of Ruby in her red high heels. Ruby was never going to change.

'There are all those numbers on the walls where you get yourself sorted. There are clinics and people who really want to help. You're so young, Mark; maybe you should give them a call. They could help you.'

'Yeah, but first they want to climb up inside your head and get you to explain why you want to suck men's cocks for a living and stick needles in your arms.'

'You don't have to tell them.'

'Fuck, no; I don't have to tell anyone.'

'You could tell me if you wanted to.'

Mark gave Tina a long look. 'This kid's making you soft, Tina. You'd better get him home as soon as you can.'

He stood up. 'I've got to get something to eat. Do you want anything?'

'Nah thanks, I'm good.'

'Okay, I'll see you.'

'Okay,' said Tina, and Mark left.

And that was it. No big goodbye, no emotional scene. Nothing. Every time they left the unit it could be the last time they saw each other. Why make a big deal now?

They had known each other for almost two years but they didn't really know each other at all. Mark didn't know about Tim or about what her life had been like before the divorce, and Tina had no idea what Mark was running from. Their friendship had formed over a mutual acceptance of their pasts being separate worlds. She couldn't imagine taking down the wall she had built around the subject of Tim. At least, not when it came to Mark.

Lockie was a different story. Each time she looked at him she saw Tim. Little boys were all the same. Little boys who were suffering were all the same. Lockie was making chinks in the wall. No matter how hard she tried to stop it happening, he was making small holes and letting the light through.

Tim and Lockie might have been friends. She could see them up in the tree house at the back of the garden. The wood was shonky and there were nails sticking out all over the place but Tim had loved the tree house. They would have been friends. They could have been pirates and cowboys together. They could have played video games and irritated her with calls for juice and biscuits. Tim was gone and he would never play anything again. Lockie was still here, but some part of Lockie was gone as well. Tina could see it when she looked at him and he was focused somewhere else. Part of Lockie was gone too. Where did all the missing bits of suffering children go? It was a sad thought.

She thought about the money instead. She nearly had enough to get herself and Lockie on that train. Mark was a good friend for helping. Mark had been her friend and Ruby had been her friend.

She would never see Mark again because he was right. Even though she had not thought about it at all, had not even considered her next move, Tina knew she wasn't coming back to the Cross. She just wasn't.

She was still short of what she needed but she set the alarm on her phone and slept for an hour. She would just have to hope it worked out.

Lockie was hard to wake up but Tina promised him that he could have two sandwiches when they were on the train. He stood up and held on to himself until they got to the train station. The toilets were filthy but at least they flushed. Tina didn't make Lockie brush his teeth again. Hopefully he would be home in a few hours and it wouldn't be her problem anymore. Right now, money was her problem. She was two dollars and seventy cents short.

She stood in the line at the ticket counter and tried to think of a solution but her mind went blank. All she could do was watch the early morning movements of the city.

The night people, people like her, had melted back into their hiding places. Now the city was ruled by the day people. The sun was only just beginning to light up the world but already there were busy bees everywhere. Buzz, buzz, buzz out of my way, I have a life to live. I am important. I am someone special. People need me. The world needs me. Buzz, buzz,

buzz. The people who had somewhere to go and something to do took brisk steps through the station. They walked with their elbows out, making sure no one got in their way. They were all talking into their phones, even at such an early hour. Making plans and exchanging ideas.

Tina had always laughed at the 'yuppie wankers' with Ruby, but she would have given anything to be dressed in a suit, swinging a briefcase and watching a scruffy young girl holding a little boy's hand, instead of being that young girl.

The fat man wasn't in the ticket booth. Instead he'd been replaced by a blonde girl who still looked young enough to be enjoying her job because every morning she managed to convince herself that a better job and a better life was just around the corner.

'Two tickets to Cootamundra, please,' she said to the woman. 'One adult and one child.'

'You'll have to change trains at Central,' said the woman, tap-tapping on her computer.

'Okay.'

'Return?'

Tina breathed in and out slowly. 'No,' she said softly. 'One way.'

'That'll be sixty-four dollars and sixty-nine cents,' said the woman with a smile. She had simply assumed Tina was Lockie's mother or older sister or whatever. Lockie hung onto Tina's arm and stared at nothing.

'Early for you to be up, isn't it?' said the woman, giving her blonde hair a flick and grinning at Lockie.

Lockie stared at his feet. Tina deposited all the cash on the counter, hoping, praying that the discrepancy of two dollars and seventy cents would somehow be missed. Though she'd been blank while waiting in the queue, now her mind went into overdrive with the story she would tell. She would cry a little and say she had to get home to her sick husband or mother or father. Or she could say that Lockie was sick and needed to be home for his medication. Or she could be aggressive and tell the woman the money was there. There were a lot of people in the queue. What would it take for the woman to just accept the loss?

I'm leaving this in your hands, universe. Sorry I've done that so much lately.

'You're short two dollars sixty-nine cents, luv.'

'Oh,' said Tina. Her mind blanked out again and all the stories she could have told refused to be put into words. She began scrabbling through her bag. 'I don't . . . I may have lost . . . I think . . .'

'For fuck's sake,' said a man standing behind her.

He was decked out in a fancy suit and holding a small laptop. His mobile phone was plugged into his ear.

Tina turned to look at him and then turned away. He had probably been talking into the phone. Behind her the line grew longer. She could hear the impatient shuffling and throat clearings of people who were being held up by someone else's stupidity. Buzz, buzz, buzz.

She continued to search her backpack, hoping to discover the change hiding somewhere. Hoping that the long line would force the woman to just push her through. But the woman seemed content to wait. She chewed her gum and twirled her hair.

Tina's cheeks were burning. She thought she had lost the art of being humiliated. She had sunk so low over the last two years that this moment should not have flustered her. Instead she felt naked in front of all the proper people.

'Hurry the fuck up,' said the man, and now Tina knew he was talking to her. She knew she looked like someone you could be rude to. Someone you could take liberties with.

'Perhaps I should serve someone else while you look,' said the woman.

Tina met her eyes. Kind eyes, but there was no way she could overlook the money. Tina started to pull her money back off the counter.

'Here,' said the man behind her, thrusting a five-dollar bill at the woman. Tina moved aside, thinking that he was buying his own ticket. 'Here, take the money out of this. Give her the tickets.'

The woman behind the counter took the money and tap-tapped on her computer. She handed Tina the tickets.

'I ... thank you ... thank you so much,' said Tina to the man. To her horror tears welled up in her eyes.

'Yeah, whatever,' said the man and he pushed forward to the counter. He bought his ticket and disappeared into the crowd. Five dollars was the price of a latte in the city. It was nothing to the man.

Whoever said money can't buy happiness?

Tina was left holding two dollars and thirty cents. He hadn't wanted his change. It was just bits of nothing to him. Something to pull down the pockets on his suit pants. The man had no idea what he had done and it struck Tina that through all the misery and shit there were some people who handed out bits of hope. Mostly without realising it.

'Come on, Lockie,' she said with a smile. 'Let's see what we can get for breakfast.' She added silently, *Thanks universe. I won't ask again, I promise.*

The doughnut shop had a special on. Two cinnamon doughnuts and a cup of coffee or tea for two dollars.

'Can I just get four doughnuts for two dollars?' asked Tina. It never hurt to ask.

The woman behind the counter focused her tired eyes on Tina while she worked it out in her head.

'Yeah, yeah,' shouted a man who was sitting at one of the tables reading a paper. 'Give her last night's doughnuts.'

He had looked Tina and Lockie over quickly and seen they would accept what others wouldn't.

Tina acted like she hadn't heard the man but she smiled at the woman. She nudged Lockie and he looked up at the woman as well. Tina could see her taking in his big eyes and angled face.

'Yeah, sure,' she sighed. 'Do youse want a drink as well?'

'Um, I've only got two dollars and thirty cents.'

The woman shook her head. Tina could see she had been on one side of this conversation a thousand times.

Tina dropped her eyes. She hated this feeling. She wished she could tell the woman that her life hadn't always been governed by this desperation. Once she had been a nice girl from the suburbs whose mother dropped her at the shops with friends and simply handed her twenty dollars for lunch. Once she had bought new clothes and seen the dentist every six months. Once she had thought that anyone living on the streets was obviously not trying hard enough. But once was a long time ago and the energy to try sometimes just ran out.

'It's okay,' said the woman, 'don't cry. I'll give youse some hot chocolate.'

Tina hadn't realised she was crying but she wiped her cheek and found it wet. 'Thanks,' she said. She lifted her head and met the woman's gaze. 'Thank you very much.'

The woman nodded and even attempted a smile.

I won't be here again, thought Tina, and it was the closest thing she could get to a vow to change things. *I won't be here ever again.*

The woman handed Tina two cups of hot chocolate and a bag filled with five doughnuts.

Serendipity, thought Tina. *That's what this is.*

Lockie ate four doughnuts. They were cold and slighty stale but neither of them cared. The hot chocolate was tongue-scaldingly hot with a slightly tinny taste. Tina blew on her cup theatrically so Lockie would do the same. It warmed them up and they sat for a few minutes in the sticky heat of the doughnut shop.

Tina felt like she could put her head down on the table and sleep forever. Lockie was watching the people walk by. He was quiet. Back in his own world, trying to make sense of things.

And then they were on the train to Central. Lockie watched the day form. There were no seats but Tina was happy to stand. She was carrying her backpack and her sleeping bag in case they got cold. She had left her books behind. Maybe the boys would read them but they were more likely to be used to make a fire.

She left them with a note for Mark and the boys: *Thanks. Love, Tina.* What else was there to say?

It took ten minutes of wandering through Central Station to find the right platform. Tina asked everyone she saw if she was in the right place. Lockie held on to her arm.

People were helpful. They smiled. They didn't know who she was. She might look like a young mother with her son. Away from the Cross she could be anybody. Anyone at all.

Finally they were on the train to Cootamundra. The blue fabric seats felt luxurious compared to other trains Tina had travelled on. The window was branded by the small handprint of another child on another journey. Lockie put his hand up to the smudged print comparing size and shape.

'Homeward bound, Lockie,' said Tina, feeling her heart lift with the miracle of having achieved it.

Lockie gave her one of his small smiles. 'Yeah,' he said. 'Homeward bound.'

Tina and Lockie both fell asleep as soon as the train started moving. It had been a very long couple of days.

Tina's sleep betrayed her. She was sucked into a dream she was too exhausted to escape.

The uniform chased her with a poker and Jack told her there wasn't anything she could do. Lockie was on the roller-coaster at the Easter Show. He went faster and faster. The ride was out of control and Tina was still trying to dodge the uniform with the poker. Lockie's face became Tim's face and her mother told her that she didn't know how hard it had been. The uniform and her mother were kissing and Tina's mouth was a silent scream.

She woke up when the uniform climbed onto the roller-coaster with giant spider legs to get to Lockie and she found herself glued to the ground.

She jerked upright and looked around the carriage.

Don't have to be too smart to work that one out, she thought.

Her head was filled with the bizarre images and she tried to clear them away by rubbing her eyes. You couldn't control your dreams no matter how hard you tried.

Lockie was awake and staring out the window. He was mouthing something to himself.

Tina leaned over to him and heard the whispered words, 'Homeward bound, homeward bound.'

Tina squeezed his shoulder. He turned to her and gave her a medium-sized smile.

Look how far we've come, she thought.

It was only then that she noticed the man sitting opposite them. He was large, with tightly curled black hair. He was sweating slightly in the warm carriage. He smiled and nodded at Tina.

'Your boy is beautiful.'

'Ah, thanks,' said Tina.

She felt her heart jump. Everything clicked sharply into focus. The patterned seats and smudged windows stood out while she felt her heart speed up. Who was he and why was he looking at Lockie?

Nowhere was safe. Nowhere.

Tina sat up straighter, tried to appear taller.

Nothing much could happen on a train to the country, could it? It was hard to imagine being faced with someone who wasn't a threat, who had no agenda and no motivation to speak to her other than simply to make contact with someone else. But the man's body was relaxed. He was just making conversation. Wasn't he?

'Thanks,' said Tina again, with a smile. Keep your friends close and all that.

Tina's phone told her they had been asleep for an hour. They had four hours to go. It seemed like a lifetime. There was nothing to do but stare out of the window.

The rhythm of the train was soothing and Tina felt her heartbeat slow down a little and take up the noise of the train. The man's arms were lying at his side. No signs of aggression. He was humming to himself and staring out of the window.

'Homeward bound, homeward bound,' sang Lockie softly in time to the clicks of the train on the tracks.

The trees and fields flashed by and Tina felt her mind clear of everything except Lockie's whispered singing.

She felt her muscles release as she relaxed. She was exhausted but she felt something else as well. She felt peaceful.

There was nowhere she could go right now and nothing she could do. For the next four hours she was trapped on this train. She did not have to find work and she did not have to find food. She did not have to keep herself from harm and she did not have to keep Lockie from harm. For the next four hours she could stop running and thinking about what to do next. It was a small space that had opened up after two years alone and two days with Lockie. She could not control the train and they were safe from the weather. There was no way they could be kicked off the train either. The tickets were tucked in her purse. They were safe. It was an odd feeling. Enclosed in the moving box, she was finally safe. It was a giddy feeling.

Lockie turned from the window and looked around the carriage. 'I'm hungry.'

'You always are,' Tina whispered to him, conscious of the smiling man sitting opposite.

He was beginning to give Tina the creeps. It was the way he smiled. He was not a threat—Tina was almost sure of it—but there was something else about him. Ruby used to divide the men into groups: fat ones, skinny ones, ones with mummy issues, ones with daddy issues, ones with ego problems, ones who were a little too into the idea of her being young. Tina didn't go for the grouping thing. She made their faces blank. Once she was done they didn't exist anymore. She wished them off the planet. What group did the man opposite her fall into? Or was he just a man getting through the day?

It took a lot of work to be suspicious of everyone you met. She was supposed to be safe here on this train.

Tina looked up and down the carriage. She and Lockie weren't exactly alone. There were two women who looked like they'd been to Sydney to do some serious shopping. They were surrounded by bags and they were constantly taking stuff in and out of the bags to compare and admire.

A boy of about seventeen was working on a laptop and plugged into his iPod. He was skinny but he looked pretty tall. He could probably help her fend the man off if needs be.

'I'm hungry,' said Lockie again.

'We have to save the food for a little bit. One more hour and you can have another sandwich. I promise.'

There was actually only one sandwich left. Tina knew there was no way it would satisfy Lockie, but if he could hold out for an hour then he could probably make it the rest of the way on one sandwich. She could go the rest of the day and maybe even another day without food. It wouldn't be the first time.

But whatever hunger she had ever felt it was nothing compared to the hunger that Lockie must have endured. He needed to eat. He was feeding more than just his body.

Lockie's hunger was catching. Tina had never really cared about where her next meal was coming from but Lockie's desperation about food was becoming part of her as well.

Not long now, she comforted herself. Lockie would be back home soon and then she would . . . Then she would what? She wasn't going back to the Cross but where was she going to go?

She could go to TAFE and do her HSC. She could start over, become someone else. It was possible but somehow not probable. You needed a place to live if you went to school, and you needed money. She could find some crappy job but she would have to work and go to school and the very thought of trying to do both was too much to seriously consider.

She sighed and looked out the window. She would worry about it all after Lockie was home. For now she would think of nothing but the fields and the rhythm of the train. That was enough.

The man opposite them filled a double seat. His flesh spread itself out, taking up the space. He smelled of something spicy and sweet at the same time. He looked like someone's fat uncle. He looked harmless but he was still looking at Lockie and Tina became aware of a feeling in the pit of her stomach.

Tina folded her arms and compressed her lips. *Just don't try one fucking thing, mister.* In her mind she saw her hands on the poker.

She looked at Lockie. He was kneading his stomach, pushing the hunger away. It must have been something he had learned to do.

She felt bad for Lockie but he could deal. He'd had months of practice. Tina knew the ache he felt now was the ache of a body that was being regularly fed. It was a good ache, and she was sure that on some level Lockie understood that. There was nothing she could do about it either. He had eaten enough for breakfast. He would survive for one more hour.

The man opened a leather bag at his feet and took out what looked like a foot-long sandwich. It emerged like the hatstand from Mary Poppins' bag.

Tim had loved that movie. Even when he had the choice of the new cartoons with the sophisticated graphics he still made Tina watch *Mary Poppins* over and over. He liked the part where they floated up to the ceiling because they were laughing so much.

One day I'm going to fly, Tina. Maybe I'll be a pilot or I could fly on one of those things that look like wings—what are they?

You mean a hang-glider?

Yeah, a hang-glider—and then I'm going to fly everywhere. I'm gonna be like a bird.

Oh yeah? Will you wave to me when you fly over our house?

Yeah, but you have to stand and wait till you see me, Tina. You have to stand in the backyard and wait.

Okay, little man, I'll wait for you.

Yeah, you'll wait until I fly over your head.

Yes, Tim, I'll wait.

The man took a serviette out of his bag and laid it on his lap. Then he balanced the sandwich on his lap and, with great care, unwrapped it.

Lockie and Tina stared and then Tina shoved Lockie a little. 'Look out the window, you might see a cow or something.'

Lockie swallowed hard and did as he was told.

'I've seen cows,' he said.

'Where have you seen a cow?'

'Duh, my dad has a farm. We have sheep but Mum has some cows for milk.'

'For real?'

'For real.'

'What else have you got?'

'You know, farm stuff,' said Lockie dismissively.

'Well what's that then?'

'Haven't you ever been on a farm?'

'Nah, I've never been anywhere really. We used to go on holiday to the beach but I've never actually been on a farm.'

'So, what? Do you, like, think milk comes from the super-market?'

'I'm not stupid, Lockie.'

'Didn't say you were. When we get home I'll show you how to milk a cow.'

'Okay.'

'Okay.'

Tina smiled to herself. For the first time since she had met him Lockie sounded like a nine-year-old boy. It was good to hear. She didn't kid herself that anything had really changed. The nine-year-old boy inside Lockie would have a lot of fighting to do to get out, but at least he was still in there.

Tina looked back at the man. He was cutting up the sandwich. He had a long sharp black-handled knife. No security on country trains then.

She felt her eyes follow the knife back and forth. He was just a man on a train cutting up a sandwich, but who was he really? What might he do with that knife?

Lockie was watching the knife as well. His hand found its way into Tina's. She gave it a squeeze.

Tina looked around for the quickest way out of the carriage. The man was huge; he wouldn't be able to move very fast.

The sandwich was filled with roasted vegetables. The eggplant glistened with oil. Tina could make out slices of capsicum and pieces of meatball as well. The tangy smell of vinegar filled the air. The bread looked crisp on the outside but soft and chewy inside.

She looked back out the window. The sooner the man was finished with the sandwich, the better. The sooner he put away the knife the sooner she could relax again. He really needed to put away the knife.

'On Tuesdays,' said Lockie to the passing fields, 'on Tuesdays we have spaghetti and meatballs. My mum makes the best spaghetti. I put cheese on top of mine but Sammy doesn't like cheese.'

'How old is Sammy?'

'She's . . . well if I'm nine now she's six. Her birthday is the twelfth of May.'

'Oh.'

'She wanted a Barbie house for her birthday. I hope she got it.'

'I'm sure she did, Lockie,' said Tina, giving the man a quick glance.

He was carefully sawing through the different layers of sandwich.

'Not long now, kid,' said Tina when she caught Lockie looking again. He nodded and turned back to the window.

Not long until you can eat whenever you want.

Not long until your parents will keep you safe from strangers.
Not long until this is all over.

They both focused on the passing fields.

'It's really green now,' said Lockie.

'What, you mean the land?'

'Yeah. Last year it was all brown but now the rains have come. Dad's been waiting for the rains. Everyone has.'

'Everyone?'

'Everyone who has a farm.'

'Oh,' said Tina.

Lockie rubbed at his stomach again.

''Ere,' said the man opposite.

Tina turned to look at him. He was holding out two large pieces of the sandwich.

''Ere, take it.'

Tina recognised the Italian accent. That explained the sandwich.

'Oh no, we couldn't,' said Tina. She held on to Lockie who was already leaning forward to accept the gift. Why the gift? What did the man want?

'Yes you can. Take it. Is too much for me.' The man laughed and gestured at his belly. 'I eat too much.'

'Oh, thank you, but we … I mean, we really couldn't …' Tina swallowed hard. Her mouth was watering.

'Take it,' said the man firmly. 'The boy, he is hungry. I don't like to see the little boy hungry. My grandson he is also hungry all the time. He need to grow. He need to eat to grow.'

Tina gave up the fight and reached out to take the offering. She handed the biggest piece to Lockie.

'Say thank you, Lockie,' she said.

'Thank you, mister,' said Lockie obediently.

Tina and the man smiled at each other.

'He is your boy?'

'He's my . . . my little brother.'

The man took a bite of the remaining piece of the sandwich. A piece of capsicum landed on his belly and he picked it up delicately with the yellow-stained fingers of a serious smoker.

'How come you don't know he live on farm?'

Tina shook her head and bit into her sandwich. She had known it was a stupid answer.

'It's all right,' said the man. 'I don't ask no more questions. My children they tell me I ask too many questions. You must not be so worried. I see you worry. No more questions.'

'Yeah,' said Tina vaguely.

'I like your food,' said Lockie. He had already finished his sandwich. Tina took one more bite of hers and gave the rest to him. It had been a taste sensation and Tina could have eaten the whole thing.

'He is hungry, your brother.'

'He's always hungry.'

'You have no money?'

'Oh no, we're okay. We'll meet my dad in Cootamundra. It's not long now.'

Lockie looked at Tina but kept his mouth busy with the sandwich.

The man nodded and smiled. Tina knew he didn't believe one word coming out of her mouth but he didn't seem concerned by the lies.

Tina rolled the words 'my dad' around in her head. How long since she'd said that?

Why didn't the man ask her more questions? Was he storing up the lies to use against her?

Tina shook her head. Get a grip, stupid girl.

'My son he is in Goulburn. He say is a nice town. I go visit today. My wife she is there five weeks with the grandchildren. Today I go for two days. I must work.'

'What work do you do?' asked Tina, watching the man wipe the knife with his serviette and put it away.

'You eat my work,' said the man.

Tina laughed. 'You own a sandwich shop?'

The man nodded.

'You make amazing sandwiches,' said Tina. She was gushing a little. It was the relief. He was just a man. A father and a grandfather. Just a man on a train who made sandwiches.

She felt her body relax against the seat.

Lockie leaned his head up against the window. His eyelids were drooping again. He seemed to be sleepy all the time, but maybe that was just the long night. She hoped it was just the long night. She opened up the sleeping bag and covered him, and then she tipped her head back and closed her eyes.

The man sighed. Tina opened her eyes and leaned forward. 'Thanks for the food, it was lovely. Thank you very much.'

'Ah,' said the man, 'is nothing. How old is the boy? Look like he eight?'

'Nine.'

'Ah. My boy was very naughty then. He liked to climb trees, but always he fall out and then he cry, "Mama, papa." I go to the hospital so many times they say when they see me, "Hello, Mr Accardo—did your boy fall out the tree again?"' The man laughed and Tina laughed with him. She could see the boy, a slim version of his father with dark curly hair climbing higher and higher in a tree and then letting go by mistake. She wondered if he had been scared as he fell or if he would have known that his mother and father would be there to help. Kids needed someone around when they fell or cut themselves or got hurt. Tim liked *Spiderman* bandaids when he was five and *Simpsons* bandaids when he was seven.

They should put Simpsons characters on IV bags, she thought.

The man tipped his head back and within minutes was asleep. His soft snores filled the space.

Tina felt her body go liquid. She curled herself up on the seat and let sleep drag her down. This time there were no dreams.

Pete

Pete was tapping keys on the computer and trying not to think about the call that had come from the city the previous day. But after a sleepless night he couldn't concentrate on anything else.

When he had heard it was Lisa on the phone his heart lifted a little at the possibility of good news; but then he had sat in silence and just listened to what Lisa was saying. He felt time stop and his hope sink. After Lisa said goodbye he realised she had been crying but he hadn't been able to think of anyone else. He had pushed the button to end the phone call and then stumbled over to his desk and put his head in his hands.

He hadn't wanted to cry. He knew someone could have walked in at any moment and it wouldn't look good if he had turned into a mess. Instead he breathed deeply, swallowing the pain. Margie, who came in to do some admin work a few days a week, was out shopping. He had been grateful for the empty station. He needed some time to get himself together.

Finally he had lifted his head and dialled Doug's mobile number. He wouldn't call the house. There was no way he could have spoken to Sarah.

He knew he should have gone round to the farm. That was what he should have done, but he could not deal with the look on Doug's face. There were some things that should be private. Grief was one of them. He and Doug were the kind of men who needed time alone to work through things. Doug would appreciate having some space to absorb the information. Pete had known Doug would not want to be looking at anyone when he got the news. He would not want to be looked at either. He would have to tell Sarah, of course, but Pete knew Doug would only relay the news after he had sorted through his thoughts alone in a field. He would only tell his wife what had probably happened to their boy, to Lockie, after he'd buried his grief in the rich soil of his farm. Only then would he be able to stand straight while the wind of his wife's grief tried to push him over.

Pete had waited for the mobile to be answered.

He wanted it to go to voicemail. He needed it to go to voicemail. But Doug said, 'G'day Pete' and Pete could hear he was somewhere out in the open doing what he did best.

'Hey, mate, how's it going?'

'Yeah, you know, much the same. It was great having Margie come over the other day. She's really good with Sammy and Sarah managed to get some extra rest.'

'That's good, Doug. Anytime you know. Margie loves to be there.'

'Yeah, I know. Thanks.'

'Where are the boys?'

'I've got them over at the other end. We're getting through all the fencing now.'

'That's good. Your dad always did the fences round about now.'

'I learned from the best.'

'Yeah, you did . . . he was one of the good ones. And Sammy?'

'Sammy is spending the day with a friend.'

Pete had felt the words sitting in his throat, but he couldn't get them to move out into the open.

'So . . . so why have you called, Pete? You're not one for a casual chat.'

'I . . . ah . . . look, Doug, the thing is . . .' Jesus, how did you say such a thing? How did you tell a father this news? How did you tell a friend? Jesus, Jesus, Jesus.

'Pete—you still with me, mate?'

'Yeah. Yeah, sorry, Doug, sorry, I . . .'

'You need to spit it out, Pete. Whatever it is you just need to say it so I can deal with it.' Doug's voice had been low and shot through with a sad awareness of what Pete might have to say.

'Look, nothing is for sure right now, it's all speculation, but the cops from Sydney wanted me to let you know so that you could get . . . get prepared.'

There had been silence on the other end of the phone. Pete had heard the wind chasing itself around the open field. He knew Doug was there; he just needed to wait until Doug was ready to hear what Pete had to say.

'Tell me,' said Doug.

'You need to listen, Doug, but I don't want you jumping to conclusions.'

'Just tell me Pete.'

'They found a dead guy in a house in Sydney. They think he was killed in a break-in gone wrong or something like that. They brought in the dogs and they found a whole lot of . . .'

'What? What did they find, Pete?'

'Fuck, Doug . . . I just don't know how to say this. They found a whole lot of skeletons buried in the backyard. It's only bones so they have to figure out ways to identify them.'

'Lockie . . .' breathed Doug.

'You need to know, Doug, that it doesn't mean that this guy had Lockie. He was some kind of lunatic but that doesn't mean he had Lockie.'

'Then why are you telling me about him?'

'The cops in Sydney just want you to know that they'll be checking things against your records and . . .'

'And what, Pete? Spit it out.'

'The guy was a guard at the Show. He was a security guard at the Easter Show.'

Pete had imagined Doug, out in the field, sinking to his knees next to a perfectly mended fence and resting his forehead in the dirt.

'I . . . I . . . What?'

'Doug, please, I don't want you to jump to any conclusions. This guy may have had nothing to do with Lockie. We don't know.'

'How long would a body have to be in the ground before it's just bones, Pete?'

'Fuck, Doug, you'd know that better than me.'

'A lot longer than four months, Pete, and it's only been four months.'

'Doug, you have to prepare yourself. You have to prepare Sarah. It won't be long before they have some answers. You have to get ready, Doug.'

'Jesus, Pete,' yelled Doug. 'Don't you think I've fucking been ready every day for the last four months? Every hour of every day for the last four months? I can't breathe in without being ready. I know all those statistics. They quoted them at me when they wanted me to go home. If a kid isn't found within the first twenty-four hours there's a chance he will never be found alive. I know that, Pete. Don't you think I fucking know that? Every time that fucking phone rings I can see Sarah's heart hit her feet. We're ready, Pete. We've been ready since the day we lost him. We're ready but we will never be ready. There is no way to be ready for this. No way . . .'

Doug had sunk into silence and all Pete had heard was his ragged desperate breathing on the other end of the phone. Finally he said, 'I can't tell her, Pete. I can't tell her until they know for sure. She's hanging on by a thread, Pete, and I can't lose her as well. Tell me when they know for sure and then I'll tell her.' His voice trailed off, all the anger leaving him exhausted and trembling.

'What about you Doug, how will you cope?'

'Jesus, Pete,' laughed Doug, 'If you think any of us are actually coping you're fucked in the head. Even you and Margie aren't coping. No one copes. We put one foot in front of the other and hope like fuck that we don't hit a wall.'

Any other time Pete would have pulled rank. He would have reminded Doug that he was a police officer and a lot older than Doug. He would have reminded Doug that his father would have taken a belt to him if he had heard him talk to Pete like that. But this was not any other time.

'We're here for you, mate. Whatever you need just let us know.'

'Thanks, Pete, and I'm sorry I . . .'

Pete had heard the tears lock in Doug's throat.

'No worries, mate. You just call if you need us.'

'I will and you'll call when . . .'

'When we know for sure I'll come out. I'll come out and let you know.'

Pete had dropped his phone on the desk. His hand had been shaking and he could feel sweat beading his forehead even in the chilly station.

He was old, he felt so old. What the fuck had happened to the world? How did people like this exist? Who were the kids buried in that yard?

He had known that he wouldn't tell Margie when she came back from doing the shopping. If the news came through . . . if they matched the records . . . Jesus. He would tell Margie then and he would call Doug and they would go out to the farm. He would take Margie with him, and Dr Samuels and the priest. He had felt like a coward for thinking it but he couldn't do it alone. He couldn't tell the boy his son was dead. He couldn't look at his face and not have Margie to hold on to. Dr Samuels would be on hand with injections to numb the pain and those words only he was good at. He usually didn't have much time for Father Richard but he was good when he needed to be. They would all be there and they would tell Doug and Sarah together. They would tell Doug and Sarah that Lockie was dead and buried in someone's yard.

They would tell them and then they would wait until Doug and Sarah were ready, if they ever were ready, and then they would help them pick up the pieces.

That was what mates did. That was what family did. That was what everyone did but it shouldn't have to be done.

It shouldn't have to be done.

Pete focused on the computer again. He tapped at the keys and waited for the time to pass and the call to come.

Tina

The man left the train sometime after Tina nodded off. She felt the train stopping and starting but she couldn't quite wake up to see where they were. She woke with a start and felt her heart race as she looked for Lockie. He hadn't moved. He was curled up on his seat fast asleep. He was covered in the warm sleeping bag and sweating a little in the heated carriage but she supposed that too much heat was better than the opposite.

The man had left his newspaper on his seat. Tina hadn't noticed him reading it. She lifted the paper off the seat and slowly flicked through the pages.

In the middle of the paper was a two-page spread.

House of Horrors!

The house had been photographed from every angle. The back garden had a small digger in the middle of it.

Tina put the paper back down on the seat. She didn't want to know who he had been. She didn't want to read about how much his mother missed him or how good he had been at his job. She didn't want him to be human. He was the uniform— he needed to be just that.

After a few minutes she lost the battle with herself and picked up the paper again.

The uniform's name had been Edwin Bleeker. He had been brought up by his housewife mother and policeman father. His parents had divorced when he was seven years old amid allegations of sexual abuse. The article didn't elaborate on the allegations.

Edwin Bleeker. He sounded like a nerd. He sounded like the guy who ran the computer club and stuttered when he talked. He had been abused by his father and so he made sure the rest of the world suffered as well. Round and round it went.

That's one sure-fire way to break the cycle that all the talking heads are always quoting, thought Tina. Death stopped the cycle right there and then.

Edwin Bleeker had been found after his ageing mother, who was in the early stages of Alzheimer's, contacted the police. She lived alone and her son would visit at exactly five o'clock every evening. When he didn't turn up she called the police. They talked her down. He needed to be missing for twenty-four hours. He was an adult. Maybe he just didn't feel like visiting that day.

But Edwin's mother would not be mollified. She phoned continually until some tired police officer agreed to look into it. One call told him Edwin Bleeker had not turned up to work in two days.

There had been nothing suspicious at the house except for a few newspapers piled up by the door and a window that was slightly ajar. It was freezing and it was raining and the police officer became suspicious. Why leave a window open in such bad weather? Bleeker's car was in the driveway which should have meant he was at home.

The officer called for help. The door was opened and Edwin Bleeker's cold body with its bashed-in head was found. The police called an ambulance and then searched the house for clues. They found a lot more than they were looking for.

The article discussed his collection of child pornography.

'One of the most disturbingly large collections I have ever seen,' Detective Inspector Simms was quoted as saying. 'Some of the images have made even the most hardened of detectives feel sick.'

No one knew who had killed Edwin Bleeker. His neighbours said he kept to himself but that was typical of neighbours. Tina had never heard of a neighbour who said, 'I knew it. I said he was some sort of serial killer but no one believed me.' People only ever had an interest in the world outside their doors when it was on television. In real life everyone kept their heads down and surged forward, buffeted by their own particular winds.

One neighbour—an old man in his eighties—did say that the television had been on all day every day. 'It was a little loud but I didn't like to complain,' he said. On further questioning he admitted that he had sometimes heard shouting and crying but had thought it was the TV. 'And of course I didn't like to complain.'

Keep quiet and keep your head down. That had been Ruby's advice as well. Tina smiled to herself. She hadn't exactly been following anyone's advice lately.

Sometimes trauma brought people out of their houses. They turned off the television and blinked at the misery that had been going on right on their doorsteps while they'd been watching TV detectives catch the killer.

Tina could just imagine the people who lived in the houses on either side of Edwin Bleeker having coffee together and discussing who might have done him in and worrying that the person was on their way back to do everyone else.

In the hospital Tim had been placed in a ward with two beds. The little girl in the bed next to him had the same kind of cancer. The mothers talked in whispers and bonded over their dying children. If you read enough or watched enough television you could almost believe that most kids survived. There was always some brave little soul on the news who had fought the good fight and won. The camera would pan across a smiling family, a little bald child sitting triumphantly among them. Tina hadn't even considered the possibility of any other outcome. When the little girl in the next bed went into remission the staff made her a cake and sent her home. Tina smiled and clapped but really she wanted to spit blood. There was no explanation for why the medicine had worked on one child and not on another. Tina knew that she should be happy for the other family, but she would have sacrificed the girl in an instant for Tim.

People mostly think about themselves. It's about survival.

Tina returned her focus to the paper.

The worst part was yet to come. The sniffer dogs had been brought in to try to find some clues, but they had found the back garden instead. The police had dug with spades and then brought in the digger. Seven little skeletons were found. Seven. Children aged between five and eight. The police were coordinating with the Missing Persons Unit. DNA testing was being done. Dental records were being requested. Parents had been put on standby.

Stand by while we analyse if this little skeleton belonged to your baby. Stand by and hold on tight. It's about to get really rough. Tina imagined all those parents getting a call from the police. How long had they been waiting? Was it better not to know? Was it better to imagine your child somewhere out in the world growing up and living a life you couldn't be part of? Or was it better to know they were no longer hungry or scared?

Tina wondered if her mother thought of her much. Was it every day or only every now and then?

The last thing the paper talked about was the possible connection between Edwin Bleeker and the disappearance of a child named Lachlan Williams from the Easter Show in April. There was evidence of something having been tied under the table in the kitchen. There was speculation about a dog or some other sort of pet.

Tina almost dropped the paper but she pushed her nails through the words instead.

Obviously they were going to mention Lockie. It didn't mean they had connected the dots. They had probably brought out every file for every kid missing over the last few years. Lockie would just be one of the most recent.

The paper said Lachlan's parents had stayed in Sydney for a month in an attempt to locate their missing child but had finally gone back home to their farm in Cootamundra. The paper had contacted the local police but had not been able to speak to the parents. Sergeant Peter Morris—a close friend of the family—was said to be, 'too upset to comment'.

Tina wondered how long it had taken Lockie to give up on his parents. How long had he shouted and screamed and hoped for rescue? Did he stop because of the beatings or did he stop because the uniform told him no one was looking for him?

Bleeker had been interviewed by police when Lachlan disappeared because he was a security guard at the Easter Show. There were a lot of security guards and obviously Bleeker had been very good at covering his tracks.

He must have thought he could get away with anything or he wouldn't have been stupid enough to take Tina to his home. She could not believe he had done that. Maybe he wanted to get caught? Maybe he was tired of hiding the kid? Of hiding who he was? Maybe he thought he was invincible. He had obviously got away with his fucked-up behaviour for a long time. And then there was always the possibility that he wanted something different to add to his collection of skeletons. Mentioning Billy may just have saved her life.

Tina shook her head. Who gave a fuck why he did it?

Maybe the universe had had enough of him. She looked over at Lockie. He was stirring in his sleep. She leaned over and took the sleeping bag away from his skin. She stroked his head and, like the child he was, he settled down.

All those little skeletons in that yard. How come Bleeker was allowed to exist? How long would it have been before Lockie was in the ground as well? What if she hadn't been standing out on the street that night? What if it had been someone who insisted on using the alley or a room nearby? What if. What if.

What if. Her mother used to say, 'If ifs and ands were pots and pans, we'd all of us be tinkers.'

It was a saying from her grandmother and basically it meant that there was no point in going over the ifs and ands. Things just were. Questions got you nowhere.

Tina folded the paper and pushed it under the seat. Then she took it out again and ripped it into squares. She put the whole mess under the seat again.

Edwin Bleeker, the uniform, was dead, and he wouldn't get to hurt another kid. No question about it. Tina would choose dead every time.

———

Lockie woke up and they went to the bathroom. Outside the fields turned yellow.

'What's that in the fields, Lockie?'

He thought for a moment. 'Margarine.'

'Margarine?'

'Yeah, margarine and oil.'

Tina shook her head and then the realisation came to her. 'You mean canola?'

'Yeah, canola.'

Lockie's voice was flat. He should have been jumping around the train with excitement, but she could feel him shutting down. She took out the last sandwich and offered it to him but for the first time since she had met him Lockie wasn't hungry. Something was wrong. She felt a bubble of anxiety rise in her stomach.

'That's Rebecca's farm,' said Lockie, pointing at a field they were passing.

'Is Rebecca a friend of yours?'

'She goes to my school.'

'Oh. It must mean we're really close to your home.'

'Yeah, really close.'

Tina gave up. She was no psychologist. She had no idea what was going through his head and, quite frankly, she was tired of playing mummy. It wasn't exactly the most rewarding job. She wished she had a cigarette and a cup of coffee. She wished she was anywhere but here on this train with this boy.

They stared out at the yellow fields in silence.

Lockie breathed on the window then lifted a finger and wrote something.

Bad boy

Jesus, thought Tina. How was she supposed to deal with this?

Lockie rubbed the words away and wrote them again. Tina racked her brain for something to say. Something that he would want to hear. What did a nine-year-old boy want to hear? She couldn't even decide what she would want to hear if she thought she had been a bad girl. Bad girls survived. Good girls got their hearts broken. That was the absolute truth.

When Tim had been little, about two or three, he had gone through a naughty phase. He wasn't naughty exactly, more like curious. He wanted to understand how things worked. The DVD machine stopped working if you jammed a pen in there. The dog yelped and tried to bite if you pulled his tail. Tina yelled if you tore the pages in her books. Mum got angry if you threw your food on the floor. He just wanted to know where the lines were.

Their mother had never hit him but she had been big on time-out. Some days the poor kid would only be out of his room for about a minute before he had to go back in again. At the end of every day, when Tina was reading him his bedtime story, he would ask her if he was a bad boy.

No, Timmy, not bad. A little bit naughty maybe, but not bad. You could never be bad. You're my little brother and I love you.

Even if I bad?

No matter what you do, Tim, I'll always love you and Mum will always love you and Dad will always love you.

And Buster.

Yeah, Buster will always love you too—but you have to stop pulling his tail, okay?

Okay.

'You know, Lockie,' she said aloud.

'What?'

'The thing about parents is . . . the thing about good parents —and I think your parents are pretty good . . .'

'Yeah, Mum makes cakes, amazing cakes, and Dad takes me fishing even when there's work to do. They're good parents, my mum and dad. But . . . but they didn't find me.'

'I know, Lockie, but I promise they were looking. When we get you home they'll tell you. I promise they were looking.'

'I should have stayed by the stroller. Maybe they're mad and that's why they didn't look. Maybe they know I'm a bad boy.'

'You are not bad, Lockie,' said Tina. She said the words slowly, patiently. 'You are not bad and your parents sound like they're pretty good parents. And you know . . . well, the thing about good parents is that they kind of love you no matter what.'

'No matter what?'

'Yeah, whatever happens, whatever you do, they still love you. Sometimes they shout when you do stuff they don't like but they always love you.'

'What if the stuff you do is really bad?'

'They'll still love you. That's their job.'

'No, I mean what if the stuff you did is really, really bad?'

'It doesn't matter, Lockie. You're just a kid. Nothing you could do could be that bad.'

'You don't know what bad is,' said Lockie, and then he repeated the words to himself. 'You don't know what bad is.'

Tina swore under her breath. He made her so angry. 'Rubbish. Of course I know what bad is.'

'Have you ever been bad?'

'I don't . . . I can't answer that, Lockie.'

'Killing is bad.' The words were almost whispered. Lockie didn't look at her. Tina swallowed. She had almost managed to forget, but that was stupid. What was going to happen when they got to Cootamundra? There was no way she could keep Lockie from telling what she had done. It would come out when they called in the police and the psychologist and the doctor and whoever else was going to be called to get Lockie sorted.

What was done was done. She was taking Lockie home and then she would deal with whatever came after. Maybe they would look kindly on her bringing him home. Maybe she would be out of prison before she turned thirty? Maybe.

'You're right, Lockie; killing is bad. But sometimes . . .'

'Killing a spider is not bad.'

'No, killing a spider is not bad, especially if it tries to bite you.'

'My dad helps Rebecca's dad kill the locusts before they get to the crops. That's not bad.'

'No, that's not bad. I guess they have to protect the crops.'

'Some killing is okay,' he said slowly and Tina could see him thinking through the problem.

'Yeah, some killing is okay.'

'I'll always love you no matter what,' he said fiercely, 'and I won't tell about the killing.'

Tina felt her eyes get hot. Jesus, what had she let herself in for? Her heart turned over and suddenly she felt it grow in her chest.

'I'll always ... I'll always love you too, Lockie, but you don't have to keep any secrets, okay? Tell your mum and dad everything.'

'Not the bad stuff.'

'Yes, Lockie, even the bad stuff. They won't be angry at you. They'll be angry at the uniform.'

'He said they would be mad at me. He said they would hate me.'

Tina saw her hand on the poker again. Some killing was good.

'Lockie, look at me.'

He turned away from the yellow fields and his eyes met hers.

'I've told you before and you have to believe me: everything the uniform said was a lie. Everything. He lied about taking you to your parents and he lied about them not looking for you and he lied about them being angry with you. Whatever he did or you did he made you do it. He made you do it and he was bad and a liar and you are a good kid.'

'He said they wouldn't love me ever again.'

Tina looked out of the window. The thing about being a kid was that you had to hear the good stuff a lot before you believed it. You only had to hear the bad shit once before it began to eat away at you.

She tried again. 'He was lying, Lockie. Everything he said to you was a lie. From the moment you first met him he was lying. Some people are like that. He was a grown-up and he was really, really bad. Do you understand, Lockie? Do you get that it wasn't your fault?'

'It wasn't my fault?'

'That's right, it wasn't your fault. Kids can't control everything. There is nothing you can do about some stuff.'

'It wasn't my fault.'

'Right, it wasn't your fault and your parents will still love you no matter what.'

Lockie turned back to the window. The words had satisfied him for now.

There was nothing more anyone could have done, Christina.

There is nothing kids can do about some stuff, thought Tina. *Even big kids who are really smart. There are some things they can't control.*

It sucked but it was true.

Tina leaned across Lockie and blew on the window. In the mist she had created she wrote: *Lockie is a good boy.*

Lockie laughed, an actual chuckle, and rubbed it out but she did it again. He rubbed it out again and this time he wrote: *Tina is a good girl.*

'That's the truth, Lockie, and don't you forget it.'

'Yeah, that's the truth,' he said.

And then they arrived.

When the train started to slow Tina gathered everything together.

Lockie was quiet but she could see him indentifying landmarks.

It was time for Tina to start thinking again but her brain felt sluggish. She had no plan and no idea what the next few hours would hold for her—or the next few years. She wished there was someone to whom she could just hand everything over. Right at that moment she missed her mother. Not the mother she had been after the divorce but the mother she had been before everything fell apart. That mother had listened to everything Tina had to say. That mother had explained difficult words and played Monopoly. She had read stories and made the best roast chicken. That was the mother Tina missed. That mother would have taken charge and sorted everything out. The mother she had left didn't seem capable of anything anymore, least of all loving her daughter.

Was she any different now? Had she moved on with her life? Had she gone back to being the woman Tim and Tina had known before their father left?

Please, Tina, just give me some time. I know you're taking care of Tim for me and I know you think I've let you down but I've lost the love of my life. I just need some time. But then she found Jack and she only had time for him.

Tina knew now that if she'd been older she might have been able to understand her mother choosing Jack and Jack's way of life over her daughter. If she had just been a couple of years older she could have played along and said her prayers and known that she was close to moving out anyway. She would even have been happy that her mother had someone to take care of her. But she had been too young to tolerate Jack trying to turn her into someone else and too young to watch her mother hand her life over to another man.

If she went back home now it would be impossible to explain who she was to her mother and to Jack. It was hard to explain to herself. But things changed. Tina could feel that the future now held something different from what it had held two days ago. It might hold the terrible spectre of prison but even that wouldn't be forever. It might be possible that there would be a time when she could explain to her mother, when she could try to connect with her again. It could be possible. Anything was possible.

What would her mother say if just she turned up on her doorstep? What would all the people Tina had known say?

'You could be school captain one day if you stay on track,' Mrs Winton had said.

'Please, Tina, don't let go of my hand,' Tim had said.

'I'm the one who's lost a child,' her mother had said.

'Stay away from the drunk ones, they can't get hard and they blame you,' Ruby had said.

'You could take me home,' Lockie had said.

'You won't be back,' Mark had said.

'Go home, Tina,' Arik had said.

What do I say? thought Tina. *What do I say?*

Tina took a deep breath in and let it out slowly, calming her body. Right now she had nothing to say. Right now she was here and she would just have to be here. The sleeping bag was rolled up in her arms and her bag was on her back.

They stood by the doors as the train eased into the station. Lockie held her hand in a tight grip.

'Put up your hood, Lockie, it looks cold outside.' She wanted his face obscured until she knew where they were going and what to do. It wasn't a big town. It wouldn't be long before someone recognised him.

What to do, what to do . . .

The doors opened and they stepped out onto the platform. They were the only people getting off the train. There was someone working in the ticket booth but he was engrossed in his newspaper. They stood in the cold for a minute.

'We're here,' said Lockie.

'Yeah, we're here. Do you live far from the station?'

'Yup.'

'Okay.'

What to do, what to do . . .

'I think . . .' said Lockie.

'Yeah?'

'I think we should go and see Pete.'

'Pete?'

'Yeah.'

'Pete the policeman?'

'He's one of the good guys,' said Lockie. The words were meant for his own ears. 'He's one of the good guys. He has a car. He'll take us home.'

It's not my home, Lockie, Tina wanted to say. She wanted to say it and she didn't want to say it. Somewhere inside her she wished it was her home.

Lockie was in charge. He guided her out of the station.

'How far is the police station?'

'Not far.'

It was lunchtime in Cootamundra. People were on the streets but the wind was there to help as everyone kept their heads down to avoid it.

Lockie didn't hesitate. He knew where he was going.

Tina looked around. Brick-faced buildings that looked like they dated back to a time when there were horses and carts sat quietly beside wide, tree-lined streets. Cars were parked at ninety degree angles and there was still room to spare. There was more air here in the open spaces. The town was busy but it felt like time moved a little slower. The post office with its large tower and embedded clockface was the tallest building Tina could see. She identified wattle trees and was pleased that she had remembered something from her year eight biology lessons.

As they walked, they passed some winter tourists studying maps and taking pictures of the beautiful buildings. Tina wanted to be them. She wanted to have nothing else to think about except where to go for lunch.

Lockie was right. It wasn't far to the police station. At the door they both stood still for a moment. Despite the biting wind Tina almost wished the walk had been longer. She felt like she needed more time. The buzzing in her head was back again. She couldn't get the thoughts to line themselves up. All she could do was follow Lockie.

She knew she should be the one pushing Lockie inside but she could feel his hesitation. She wasn't hesitant. She was terrified. Once the two of them stepped through the door everything would change. She knew that she could just leave him there. She could turn and bolt to the station and get on a train heading anywhere but back to the Cross.

Lockie would go into the station by himself. He trusted Pete. Pete was one of the good guys.

But she had done enough running. She had been running from everything for such a long time she couldn't go one more step. It was time to stop.

'Ready, Lockie?'

'Yeah, ready.'

Tina stepped forward and pushed the door.

'Tina?'

'Yeah?'

'I'll always love you no matter what.'

'I'll always love you too, Lockie.'

She swallowed the lump in her throat and they walked in together.

It wasn't like any kind of police station Tina had ever seen. When she and Mark had been into the one in the Cross to ask for help with Ruby noise had filled the air. They had chosen to go in the early hours of the morning, hoping to find one tired police officer willing to listen, but no one who worked in the Cross had the luxury of being tired.

The station had been filled with people. Drunks sobering up and junkies coming down ranted at men and women with bored expressions on their faces. A man held a rag to his bloody nose and one of the girls Tina knew looked in the other direction. The phones rang and the acrid smell of urine filled the air.

No one had wanted to listen. They kept asking about drugs and who Tina and Mark thought they had killed. Mark had been flying but Tina was just Tina and still they hadn't wanted to listen.

The cop at the front desk had said, 'We've got bigger fish to fry than what you think has happened to your imaginary friend, kids. Off you go. Stop wasting my time.'

And so off they went and Ruby died alone, locked in her flat.

In Cootamundra the station was quiet. Tina looked around but before she could see anyone she saw the poster on the wall. Lockie saw it too. It stopped him mid-stride.

It was surrounded by For Sale notices and babysitting flyers.

Over the months it could have become covered over as hope was lost but it hadn't been. Right in the middle, with some clear space around it, was the colour poster of a blue-eyed boy. His head was covered in golden curls and he had a deep dimple on his right cheek. His face had been enlarged so that every freckle could be counted. He was Lachlan Williams and in this town they were still looking for him.

He looked nothing like the pale, skinny boy Tina was with.

Underneath the picture were the words:

Missing:
Lachlan Williams
Aged 8
Disappeared from the Easter Show April 2010
If you have any information please contact:

There were a whole lot of numbers and a website address.

Lockie stared at the poster for a minute. He pushed his hood back down and ran his hand over his brush-cut blond hair.

'What—' Tina began.

'He shaved it,' said Lockie before she could complete the question. 'Every few weeks, when it got longer, he would shave it again.' His voice was two hundred years old.

Tina saw her hand on the poker and felt a surge of triumph at what she had done. Some people just deserved to die. It wasn't a nice thought but it was true. You couldn't change someone who was fundamentally evil.

Of everything Lockie must have suffered, and Tina could not even wrap her mind around what he must have gone through, the shaving of his head seemed somehow the worst.

The uniform had changed who Lockie was. He was a golden boy with golden curls and the uniform had taken the gold from him. Lockie looked nothing like the poster. His face was all angles and his smile was lost. He hadn't needed to conceal himself beneath a hood. No one would have recognised him anyway.

They walked slowly over to the desk at the front of the police station.

There was a large man standing behind it. His hair was grey and his skin was deeply creased. His beer belly was just beginning to strain the buttons of his shirt. He was tapping on a computer, leaning against the counter. He gave the two of them a cursory glance. He clearly hadn't heard them come in. 'What can I do for you kids?'

Tina could feel her heart racing and she could see Lockie's pulse in his skinny neck.

'Hey, Pete,' he said quietly.

The man looked up again and gave the two of them a closer look. He stared at Lockie for a moment and then his eyes widened. He looked over at the poster on the wall and back at Lockie.

'Jesus Christ, Jesus Christ,' he said, backing away. He rubbed at his eyes. 'Jesus Christ . . . Is it you, Lockie. Is it you?'

Lockie nodded.

'Jesus, Jesus, Lockie, oh god, Lockie . . . Where have you been?'

The policeman came out from behind the desk and grabbed Lockie gently by the shoulders. He studied his face, searching for the boy he knew. He ran his hands over Lockie's hair and felt up and down the boy's skinny arms.

He looked from Tina to Lockie. Tina could see him trying to get his breathing under control. He looked like he was going to have a heart attack. She stood silently next to Lockie. The thing had to play itself out.

'Margie,' shouted Pete. 'Margie, get out here!'

'What now?' came a voice from behind a door at the back of the room.

'Margie, you have to get out here.'

Tina heard a loud frustrated sigh but the door opened and a small woman with hair as grey as Pete's stepped out. She wasn't wearing a uniform and Tina guessed she must be Pete's wife. She peered across the counter and gave Tina and Pete a questioning glance.

Pete pointed wordlessly to Lockie.

The woman looked at him, trying to identify him and then: 'Lockie!' she screamed. 'Oh my god, Lockie.'

Margie reacted the way a woman reacted. She kneeled down and grabbed Lockie in a big bear hug.

Then she leaned back and looked him over.

Lockie stood with his arms by his sides as she ran her hands over his hair and squeezed his arms. Tina could see how uncomfortable Lockie felt at being touched. Margie hugged him again and again. She didn't notice Lockie's face or she would have stopped.

When Margie stood up she was crying.

Pete, meanwhile, was watching Tina.

'Start talking,' he said to her and Tina could see he had already decided who was to blame for Lockie's disappearance.

'Her name's Tina,' said Lockie. 'She saved me. Can you take us home, Pete?'

Pete looked at Lockie. 'You know I will, Lockie, but first —'

'Please, Pete,' said Lockie. 'Can you just take us home?'

'Oh god,' said Margie. 'Doug and Sarah—we have to call them. We have to let them know.' She kept touching Lockie, on his head, on his arms and on his back. Tina could see Lockie wince. People wouldn't know that they needed to be careful when they touched him. Some touches can make you feel sick.

'I think . . .' said Tina.

Pete and Margie turned to her.

'I think Lockie could use something to eat.' Tina didn't know if he was hungry but she wanted to give the woman something to do so the touching would stop.

'Oh god, yes,' said Margie. 'You're so thin, Lockie. Why are you so thin?' She wasn't really expecting an answer, Tina knew. She would know that whatever had happened to Lockie, it wasn't good.

Margie led them into an office and they sat down on a small leather couch. Then she left them alone.

Tina and Lockie sat in silence. Lockie was alert, waiting for what was to come. He rubbed his hands together and stared at the wall.

In the silence Tina thought, *Now*.

This was her chance to leave. She could bolt out of the door and go somewhere, anywhere. She had done what she had promised to do. Her part was over.

She could, but instead she sat and she waited, and then Lockie reached for her hand and it was too late.

A minute later Margie appeared with a jar of biscuits.

'There's not much here but we could send out for something . . . I don't know.'

'I want to go home, Margie,' said Lockie with his flat old man's voice.

Tina saw a spark of fear in Margie's eyes. He must sound so different to the boy they had lost. Tina had only ever known this Lockie but there was obviously another Lockie, another boy who had never even been able to conceive of a man like the uniform. That was the boy these people had known. That was the boy they had missed. This thin, almost wasted child who spoke in short sentences without a smile to accompany his words was not the Lockie they knew.

Margie ran back out to Pete and some furious whispering began.

Lockie took a biscuit and ate it slowly. He looked over at her before he took another one out of the jar.

'You can have as many as you like,' said Tina.

When Lockie hesistated Tina leaned forward and stuck her hand in the jar. She grabbed five biscuits at once and shoved them in Lockie's pocket.

Lockie gave her one of his small smiles.

A few minutes later Pete came into the office.

'The landlines are down and your mum and dad aren't answering their mobiles, Lockie. We'll have to just go out there and surprise them.'

Lockie grabbed Tina's hand.

'I'm sure they'll be excited to see you,' said Tina.

Tina saw Pete glance at Lockie's white-knuckled grip on Tina's hand.

'Yes, oh yes. They'll be really happy, Lockie. They'll be happier than they've ever been in their lives. They've missed you so much. Every day they've missed you and we ... we've missed you, too. Everyone will be so happy, mate. Don't worry, Lockie, everything will be right. So why don't you and I go out to the farm, while Tina stays here and talks to Margie?'

'No,' said Lockie quietly. And then, louder, 'No. Tina saved me, Pete. She saved me from the uniform. She's coming home with me. She saved me and she's coming home with me.' Lockie wasn't asking, he was telling. There would be no discussion.

Tina met Pete's eyes. 'Just let's get him home, okay? I can tell you everything later. Let's just go.'

Pete nodded. Tina knew that inside him his confusion and his joy and his fear of the truth would be colliding.

Pete was not Lockie's father but it was obvious that Lockie belonged to more people than just his parents. Lockie belonged to Pete and Margie as well and Tina had no doubt that he probably belonged to the whole town too.

Out front Margie was dialling the phone, trying again to get hold of Lockie's parents.

'You keep trying, Marge; we'll take a drive out there.'

She nodded, then bent down to give Lockie another hug.

'We've missed you, Lockie. We've all missed you so much. You have no idea . . .' She couldn't finish the sentence. The tears began again. She grabbed a tissue from a box on the counter and went back to dialling the phone.

You have no idea, thought Tina sadly. *No idea at all.*

Out the front of the police station Lockie and Tina got into the back of the police car.

Pete started the car. As they pulled away from the kerb Lockie said, 'They were looking for me.'

'Of course they were,' said Tina. 'I told you: parents love you no matter what.'

'No matter what,' said Lockie, uncertainty in his voice.

'We were all looking for you, Lockie,' said Pete. 'We've been looking for you for four months and we would have looked for you forever.'

'Tina found me,' said Lockie.

'Where did she find you, Lockie?'

'Please Pete,' said Tina. 'I promise I'll give you the full story but he's tired and he needs to go home.'

'Home,' Lockie repeated softly.

'Yeah,' said Tina. 'Home.'

———∞———

The drive to the Williams' farm took forty minutes. Pete was silent the whole way.

Tina could sense him biting back the questions—questions she would have no choice but to answer. But what would be the right answers?

Lockie would lie for her, she knew he would, but she also knew that there were some things too heavy for a kid to carry. Lockie would have enough to deal with without having to live with the lie of the uniform's death.

How many years did you get for manslaughter? Isn't that what they called it when you killed someone but hadn't really planned to kill them? Had she planned to kill him?

She hoped she wouldn't have to answer that question.

Tina had no doubt that Margie would talk herself hoarse on the phone. Soon, everyone in town would know that Lockie was home. The wheels were in motion. The train could not be stopped. Clickety clack, clickety clack.

She looked at Lockie. His body was tense and his eyes darted over the landscape.

She put her hand over his and he grabbed it. She let him hold on and after a few minutes she felt him relax and then she relaxed as well.

His head dropped onto her shoulder and then his eyes closed. After a few minutes Tina felt her own eyelids droop.

She thought about the last car ride she had taken. It had only been a few days ago but it felt like she had journeyed for a lifetime since. The universe worked in strange ways. What if everything that had ever happened to Tina had happened so that one day she could rescue Lockie? It seemed too cruel an idea but you never knew. Or maybe she was just in the right place at the right time. Shit just happened . . .

Tina and Lockie woke up when the car stopped.

Pete got out first and stretched his arms over his head.

Lockie rubbed his eyes and sat in the car looking at his home. Then he opened the car door and got out to stand next to Pete.

Tina scrambled out and stood next to him. She put her arm lightly across his shoulders. He was trembling.

Pete had stopped the car at the bottom of a long brick driveway. Tina saw a large low house that stretched across the open space. It looked like an ordinary suburban house, with white painted cladding. She could see curtains in the windows. All of them were open.

Tina could imagine Lockie's mother walking into his room every morning to open the curtains and then staring at the empty bed where her son should have been.

Her mother had left Tim's curtains closed when she knew that he would never make it back home. There was no need for light in the room anymore and no need for air.

There was a garden in front of the house, filled with the hardy kind of plants that could survive anything, including winter.

She scanned the open spaces surrounding the house. There were cows nearby and sheep in the distance and huge squares of margarine yellow. There were reds and deep greens and a few splashes of orange. There was colour everywhere you looked. Colour and beauty and she understood how desperately Lockie would have missed his home. Under the table in that cold stark kitchen he would have held on to what he had known all his life and it would have helped him hold on to himself. That was what you did when you couldn't see a way out; you held on to the past, hoping it would become the

uture. You grabbed on to the good stuff and tried to believe
hat everything would be okay again. It was stupid but it was
luman nature.

Lockie clasped her hand and just looked, drinking in his
lome and shivering with fear and excitement and joy and
·elief and whatever else he must be feeling. There was a swing
;et in the garden, and on one of the swings sat a little girl with
ong golden curls. She was dragging her feet on the grass to
;top the swing.

It was cold to be outside in the garden but the little girl was
·ugged up with a beanie and a scarf.

The air was filled with a silence broken only by the wind
ind the cows and the metal scraping sound of the swing
>eing halted.

There was a man in the garden with the little girl. He was
.urning over the soil in a garden bed. He had obviously heard
.he car, because he raised his hand in greeting, but then he
lad gone back to his work. He had actually turned his back
>n the car.

Tina thought she knew what that meant. The man had not
wanted to see Pete the policeman. Maybe he thought Pete was
>ringing bad news.

Tina smiled. Here was good news. Finally, here was good
lews for this family.

The man dug the garden fork into the soil with a little bit
>f effort. He was deliberately not looking at Pete.

The little girl walked down the driveway towards them.

Pete said quietly, 'No real way to prepare them. You go
thead, Lockie.'

Lockie squeezed Tina's hand.

'Go on, Lockie, it's your dad. He's been looking for you for a long time. Go on.'

She pulled her hand slowly out of Lockie's grip. She wanted to save him from his fear, but she had saved him once. Lockie would have to do this by himself.

The little girl who was surely Sammy looked back at her father, but he was still concentrating on his work.

She smiled in Pete's direction and then she focused on Lockie.

She stared at him, as if trying to work out exactly who he was.

Lockie pushed his hood back, exposing his short blond hair. He stood, and Tina could sense him holding his breath, waiting for his sister to see him. To really see him.

Sammy stared hard at Lockie now, frowning. And then Tina saw recognition light up her face. She looked at her father who had still not looked up.

She looked back at Lockie.

She started jumping up and down.

'Lockie!' she screamed. 'Lockie, Lockie, Lockie!'

Lockie smiled.

The man jerked upright and dropped the garden fork. 'Stop that, Samantha,' he whispered angrily. 'Jesus, stop that. Be quiet. Stop that.'

'Lockie, Lockie, Lockie!' The little girl flew down the driveway and launched herself at her brother, who went, 'Oof,' but he steadied himself and wrapped his arms around her.

'Lockie, Lockie, Lockie,' she repeated, as if to make the moment real for herself.

The man stood and stared at his children, still without realising that he was indeed looking at both his children. He started walking down the driveway.

He began with an angry quick stride but the closer he got the more unsure his steps became. He was a big man in charge of a big farm but his steps became small and faltering.

Tina could see the disbelief spreading across his face.

Sammy let go of Lockie and took his hand. She started pulling him up the driveway. 'It's Lockie, Dad. Look, it's Lockie, come look, Dad, Lockie's home. He's home, Dad. I knew he would come home. I told you, Dad. Look its Lockie. Lockie, Lockie, Lockie's home. Lockie's home.'

The man stopped a few feet away from Lockie. His mouth was open. He moved it once or twice, but no words came out, and then came a sound that Tina had never heard before. It was a moaning, keening sound, but rough with the depth of his voice. It was four months of agony and the ecstasy of this moment all rolled into one. It was his heart right out there in the open for everyone to see.

He opened his arms and dropped to his knees.

Lockie let go of Sammy's hand and continued alone up the driveway towards his father. He was twisting his hands and pulling at his jumper. He walked into his father's arms and was completely surrounded by the large man.

'I'm sorry, Dad,' he said. 'I'm sorry, Dad, I'm sorry.'

At the bottom of the driveway Tina watched Lockie and his father. Lockie's voice was muffled by his father's arms, but Tina could still hear him repeating, 'I'm sorry.'

Say it, Tina begged the man silently. *Please, please, just say it.*

'Oh, Lockie,' said the man through his tears, his large shoulders heaving. 'It wasn't your fault. It wasn't your fault. I'm sorry, Lockie. I'm sorry. I've been looking for you, Lockie. Where did you go, mate? Where did you go?'

Pete

Doug stood up with Lockie still in his arms. Lockie's legs were wound tightly around his waist and Pete could see the man's hands moving along his son's body, feeling the changes.

They stood like that for a few minutes. Samantha ran up the driveway to join her father and her brother. She wrapped her arms around her father's leg and put her thumb in her mouth.

Tina and Pete stood together.

Pete knew he should be grilling the girl, getting the full story before details were lost, but he was too spellbound by the reunion.

The boy he was watching was so different.

There was no way to avoid the truth. Someone, a very evil someone, had hurt his boy. Pete felt his fists clench. Whoever it was that had turned Lockie into the skinny kid trapped behind his pain, he would pay. If he had to spend his whole life looking for him, Pete would find him and then he would make him pay.

The girl had obviously helped Lockie. He had no idea if she had found him or if she had been with him the whole time, but Lockie kept saying that she had 'saved' him. He was a clever kid and he knew what the word meant.

Pete liked the way she looked at Lockie—like a lioness, like a sister, like a mother.

The skinny girl with short messy black hair could have been anyone. She looked about fifteen but when she spoke she sounded a lot older. She was wearing a big coat but underneath that Pete had caught a glimpse of a short skirt and a tight red top. Not the kind of thing a nice girl would wear. Maybe she wasn't a nice girl but she was smart. That was easy to see. She was watching Lockie with his dad and Pete could see her body sag with relief. She was relieved to get him home. It must have been a promise she had made the boy. Pete had no idea how she'd got him home. She didn't look like she had a cent to her name.

He sighed. So many questions to answer and the worst part was that some of the answers would be things he did not want to hear. Some of the answers would keep him up at night for the rest of his life. He wished he didn't have to know, but he figured that if Lockie had been through it his family should know about it. If Lockie had been one of the small skeletons buried in the yard in Sydney they would have only been able to imagine what he had suffered. Now they would know.

Which way was better?

Pete thought about all the other parents who were waiting for the results of tests from the police. For a moment he let go of what needed to be done and what was to come and he offered up a prayer of thanks. Then he offered up a prayer for strength for all those other parents who would never again get to feel their kid's arms around their neck.

And then he wiped his eyes because he was a grown man and a cop and he really shouldn't be standing in the driveway crying.

Doug

It was getting really cold out in the yard, but no one was going anywhere. Doug could feel his body swaying. Swaying like it had when he held Lockie as a tiny squalling creature who refused to sleep. Swaying to comfort and calm the boy. Swaying to calm himself.

He turned to walk back into the house and felt Sammy curl her arms tighter around his leg. He looked back at Pete and said, 'Keep Sammy for me.'

'No, I want to come,' said Sammy.

'You come stay with me Sammy, we can play in the yard— I'll push you on the swings,' said Pete.

'No,' said Sammy, holding on tight.

'Samantha, please stay with Pete,' said Doug.

'I want to go with you Dad.'

'Come, show Tina your cows,' said Pete. Doug felt Sammy loosen her grip. She loved showing off the cows. For the first time, Doug noticed the girl standing next to Pete.

He had no idea who she was, but that was unimportant right now.

Right now he needed to concentrate on keeping himself under control. Inside, his gut churned. There was a war going on.

The joy of holding his son again clashed with the waves of anger that rose higher and higher with each passing moment. He thought he had known why Pete had arrived at the farm. He had pushed the fork into the soil and watched the earth turn over sure that the truth of their tragedy was about to be laid before them. He had watched the dry earth give up the rich brown soil and wanted to stay there forever in the cold garden just watching his fork move the earth. He had not wanted to hear what Pete had to say.

And now this . . . this . . . What did you call this? A miracle? What else could it be?

But this miracle was tainted.

He was not holding the same boy he had taken to the Easter Show. This thin child with shaved hair was not the Lockie he knew. Someone had taken that child.

They had taken his child and he could feel by the weight of him they had starved him.

Before the Show he had started to envisage a time when the wrestling game they played would involve real strength. Lockie was getting stronger every day and he remembered feeling proud that his son would probably grow up to be a bigger man than he was.

The boy he was holding now was lighter than Sammy.

Someone had done this to him. They had done this and god knew what else.

Doug walked slowly into the house, trying to find the right way to break the news to Sarah.

She was lying down in the bedroom again. These days she spent more time there than anywhere else.

As he walked Lockie dropped his head and closed his eyes.

Doug took a deep breath. Lockie would have to wake up. He would have to wake up and say hello to his mother.

Doug walked slowly through the house to the main bedroom at the back. It was the only room in the house whose curtains were permanently closed.

How damaged was his child? Would he ever be the same boy they had taken up to the Show? What had been done to him? Dear God, what had been done to him?

His ribs stuck out even under the jumper he was wearing. It was not his jumper. He had been dressed in shorts and a T-shirt, perfect for the warm day. He had a cap with a Bulldogs logo. What could have happened to his clothes? How long had he had the jumper?

Doug bit his lip. First things first.

He opened the bedroom door cautiously and looked into the gloom. Sarah was on her back. Her mouth was slightly open. She was fast asleep. The room smelled musty with the heater on. Sarah slept tightly wrapped in her covers.

Doug swallowed. He wanted to run into the room whooping and shouting that Lockie was home but Sarah was so fragile he had no idea how she would react. He walked over to the window and opened the curtains. Outside it was getting dark already but enough light entered the room to wake Sarah up.

She moaned and opened her eyes.

'Oh god, Doug, please just close them. I'm so tired.'

Doug sat down on the bed and Sarah turned her back to him. She had not looked at him.

Lockie opened his eyes and looked around the room.

'Ready to say hello to Mum, mate?' Doug asked.

'Hi, Mum,' said Lockie to his mother's back. His voice had changed. It was deeper and had an edge to it. He sounded older. He sounded like someone who had seen too much. But Sarah would know it was her boy.

Doug saw Sarah's whole body tense at the sound of Lockie's voice and then she reached her arm behind her and twisted the skin on her back with such force Doug knew she would have left a mark.

'It's not a dream, Sarah,' he said quietly. 'He's home.'

Sarah sat up, her eyes wide.

'Hi, Mum,' said Lockie again.

'Hello, my boy,' said Sarah softly.

Softly, as though he hadn't been missing for four months.

Softly, as though he had just been away for a day.

Softly, as though she hadn't been trying to die slowly.

Softly she said, 'Hello, my boy.'

Doug could see her chest heaving.

'We've been looking for you,' she said, and then she held out her arms.

Lockie climbed off Doug's lap and onto his mother's legs. She wrapped her arms around him and pushed her nose into his neck, finding his scent and identifying her child.

Lockie buried his head against her breasts and then he began to cry. Just soft little sobs that were soon matched by his mother's tears.

Doug wanted them to stop but tears were good. He would have to get used to tears.

They sat like that for a while until Sarah pulled away a little and got a tissue. She wiped her nose and face and then put the tissue to Lockie's nose.

'Blow,' she said, and Lockie did as he was told. He was too old to be treated in such a way but Doug could see that he would have to go back a little before he could move forward again.

When the call had come from Pete about the security guard, Doug had known that he was the one who had taken Lockie. The certainty was a stone in his throat.

It was too coincidental. The police had interviewed every security guard at the Show and Doug had even watched a few of the interviews but he couldn't have picked Edwin Bleeker out of a line-up. That was the man's name. Edwin Bleeker. He was a small, scrawny person who looked like he would have trouble growing a proper moustache.

Doug had read about him online in the early hours of the morning after Pete had called. He knew the newspapers would have the story. They always did. He didn't want to know but he had to know.

The rage had burned. Rage at the police for missing the man and rage at himself once again for having left his children alone. Lockie would have trusted a security guard. He had grown up knowing that the police were there to help. He would not have been dragged away kicking and screaming. He would have gone willingly.

Maybe he had stepped away from the stroller and found himself lost and even turned to the security guard for help.

What kind of a world was this?

Doug had known that he was the man who had taken Lockie and he knew that it was only a matter of time before the call came to confirm that one of the little skeletons found buried in the man's garden belonged to Lockie.

He had not been able to tell Sarah. He had not been able to tell her and he had done his best to put it out of his mind until the end. He was glad the man was dead. A man like that needed to be killed. He needed to have his life ended in the worst possible way.

Doug had moved soil and milked the cows and he had carried his phone everywhere. He knew that he needed to be the one to take the call. He needed to be the one to tell Sarah.

Today he had woken up sure that it would be the day for the call. The landlines were down and he had let his mobile run flat.

He hadn't really meant to do it.

He had meant to do it.

A few more days of hope for Sarah. It was the only gift he could give her.

And now his son was home. He had not been buried in the yard with the other kids. Doug did not have to be one of those fathers who had to choose a small coffin for his child.

He was home and he was safe and Doug could not believe his luck.

The man had surely been the one to take Lockie and yet here he was and the man was dead.

Doug couldn't get his head around it.

He stroked Lockie's head. He was lying on the bed next to his mother and she was singing softly—a song about a train full of sleeping children. Lockie's eyes were closed again.

The boy was obviously exhausted.

He would leave them alone for a while. They would need the time.

Sarah began to talk quietly, keeping her voice low so that Lockie would keep sleeping. She whispered words that told him how things would have to work. Doug could hear the old Sarah knocking. The clever, educated Sarah trying to get through. He nodded. They would do things her way. He was fine with that. Right now he was fine with anything.

He had left Pete and Sammy out in the garden with the girl Pete had brought with him. She was obviously connected in some way to this whole thing, but how?

He stood up to go and find out.

Tina

Sammy was chattering away. She had dragged Tina to the side of the garden and clicked her tongue to summon her cows.

Tina didn't want to touch them but to please Sammy she ran her hand over a brown and white body, her mind on what was happening in the house.

Pete wandered over to the fence and stood next to her. 'I reckon we'll give them some time in there. I hope she'll be okay—his mother, I mean.'

'I think she'll be more than okay.'

'There are a lot of questions. We've been looking for this boy for four months. We had a call from the city about that house with all the dead kids ... I didn't think Doug would survive it. I don't think he said anything to Sarah.'

'I read about it,' said Tina, giving nothing away.

'I thought it would finally kill her if Lockie turned out to be one of them. She couldn't have taken it.'

Tina thought about the idea of how much a person could take. People only survived because they turned the real into the surreal. If it was outside your comprehension you didn't have to deal with it, to feel it.

If you woke up each morning and thought that it had all been a bad dream, then you fell into the darkness of the truth. But if you simply pretended it hadn't happened you didn't need to deal with it at all.

She had tried that for a while after Tim. She would walk into a room, knowing that he wasn't in there, and she would say to herself, 'I wonder where Tim has got to. I'll look for him in a little while.' And then she would eat dinner or watch television or do some homework and she would not think about it and she would get through that hour, that day, that night.

But shit came back to get you in your dreams. She would wake up shaking and sweating and even without being able to remember the dreams she would know what they were about.

Once she made it to the Cross, sleeping during the day had helped. For some reason the nightmares could not find her during the day. Complete exhaustion helped as well.

In the garden with her hand on a cow, Tina felt like she could sleep on her feet, despite the cold. If she did manage to find a bed then she would be safe from the dreams. Her brain would just switch off.

Pete was looking at her, waiting for something, anything.

Tina met his stare. He deserved an answer. They all did.

'I haven't had him for four months. I've only had him for a few days. He asked me to take him home and I have.'

'Simple as that?'

'No. No, so much more complicated—but I'm so tired,

Pete. I'm not going anywhere. If I could just stay somewhere in town or something for a few days I'll tell you the details, but I'm so . . . so . . .'

To her surprise Tina was crying. She wasn't just choked up she was actually crying. The tears came while she talked. They ran down her face as if she were overflowing. Inside her a hole had opened up. She had held herself together for so long but here was this hole and the longing for Tim and her family leaked out into her soul and her body spilled it onto the cold soil in the garden.

The tears kept coming and eventually Tina had to cover her face. She was ashamed to cry in front of this man and this child.

'All right, all right,' said Pete, giving her an awkward pat on the back. 'Don't upset yourself, luv. Lockie obviously likes you so you must have done something right. We'll talk in a few days.'

'You can stay in my room,' said Sammy, seeing adventure in everything. 'I've got a pink bunk bed and you can sleep on the bottom. I can move my toys.'

'Thanks, Sammy. My name's Tina, by the way.'

'My name's Samantha.'

Tina smiled and sniffed. 'Yeah, I know. Lockie told me.'

'Lockie got lost.'

'Yeah, he did.'

'But you found him.'

'I think we kind of found each other.'

The air turned up the chill and darkness crept into the garden.

'I'm cold,' said Sammy.

'Do you think we can go inside?' asked Tina.

'I reckon we don't have a choice. I don't know how they're going to feel about you ... you know, staying, but you can come home with me. We've got plenty of space.'

'Thanks, Pete.'

They moved towards the house as a little group. Doug came outside and stood on the porch. He nodded at Pete. 'Beer, mate?'

'Christ, yes.'

'And you—what about you ... Sorry, I don't know your name.'

'It's Tina.'

'Can I get you something to drink, Tina?'

'Um, yeah ... Could I have a Coke or coffee or something?'

'We don't have Coke but I can do a coffee.'

'That'd be great, thanks.'

'Milk and sugar?'

'Yeah, thanks.'

The living room held two worn leather couches. A gas fire burned brightly, filling the space with warmth and mellow light. Tina sighed gratefully and felt her body begin to thaw. She didn't want to take off her coat. In this house, with these people, she was ashamed of what she looked like.

Pete watched her for a while and then Tina heard him whispering to Doug in the kitchen where coffee was being made.

A minute later Doug came in to the room holding a jumper.

'Ah, Pete said, well he ... ah, this is mine and it'll be a bit big, but ...'

'Yeah,' said Tina, smiling and taking the jumper. 'Thanks.'

In the bathroom she pulled the jumper over her head. It

hung below her knees. She didn't look in the mirror. She knew she looked like shit but she would worry about that tomorrow.

Doug came into the lounge room with the coffee and Sammy trailed behind him holding two beers.

After she had handed Pete and her father a beer each she ran back to the kitchen and came out with a juice bottle with characters from *The Little Mermaid* painted on the side.

Only the sound of liquid being swallowed filled the room.

'So,' said Doug, clearing his throat. 'I . . . I don't really know who you are . . .' He wasn't looking at Tina; he was looking past her.

'Tina found Lockie,' said Sammy. 'And then she bringed him home.'

Doug took another swallow of beer and looked at Tina.

Tina nodded.

'I'm sure Tina can fill us in later, Doug. Maybe even tomorrow. I could take her home with me and we could come back tomorrow.'

'You found my boy?' said Doug.

Tina nodded.

'Was he in that man's house?'

Tina nodded again.

'And you brought him home.'

Tina just stared at Doug now. She really wanted it to end there. She wasn't going to keep any secrets but she didn't really feel capable of words.

Fortunately, Doug accepted the silence.

'You'll stay here with us for a few days. You look tired. You'll stay here.'

'Thanks.'

'We can make burgers for dinner,' said Sammy. 'They're Lockie's favourite.'

'Right you are, little girl,' said Doug.

'It's good that he's home now,' said Sammy.

'It is,' said Doug slowly. 'And I think . . . I think that we are going to have to talk about a lot of stuff with you and Lockie. You know, about how we're feeling. But we'll get a good night's sleep first. You can ask me anything you like Sam, about Lockie . . . you know.'

Doug sounded uncomfortable, as though the words didn't quite fit in his mouth. Tina thought they would have come from his wife.

Tina wanted to meet her. And she wanted to see Lockie now that he was here where he belonged. Now that he was home.

Sarah

In the bedroom Sarah lay next to her son. She could hear movement in the kitchen and wondered if Doug had started preparing dinner.

She longed for something sweet to eat. She had not been hungry for days, for weeks, for months, but now, with her son lying near her, she wanted the taste of sugar on her tongue.

She would not move though. She didn't know if she would ever be able to leave his side again.

Lockie's breathing was deep and even. He was so tired but she would wake him soon. He needed to eat. He needed to eat and eat and eat.

Her hand was on his waist and she could feel his hipbones jutting through the washed-out pair of pants he was wearing.

The last four months tumbled through her mind. Images of herself and her family made her shiver. She saw Doug's face and Sammy's face and she saw her own terrible haunted face in the mirror. A small part of her had believed that the torment would never end, that they would be trapped in the grey area of not-knowing forever.

And now here he was.

He didn't look like the Lockie she had taken to the Show. He was so skinny and his hair—what could have happened to his hair?

This was not the Lockie she knew but it was Lockie and he was here.

She wanted to start feeding him right now. Her instinct was to rush to the kitchen and gather everything she could and just sit and watch him eat, but she would wait. She had spent so much time trying to feed her children. Making sure they had the right amount of fruit and vegetables, weighing them when they were babies, measuring every change.

Lockie had been such a long skinny baby that every kilo he had managed to put on had felt like a triumph.

He had not said anything to her since arriving home except 'Hi, Mum' and 'I got lost.'

Lockie had never been one for sharing his distress. Sarah remembered him at five after he had broken his wrist. He had only mentioned that it felt a little sore and she had watched him holding it gently, keeping it from harm, and she had known that it was broken.

Something inside Lockie was broken and she could see it in his eyes. She could feel it. She just knew that the story behind where he had been would be a terrible one.

The miracle of his return was the beginning of a long journey that her family would have to make together.

'Something terrible has happened to him, Doug,' she'd said when he stood to leave the room, after handing Lockie to her.

'Sarah, you don't . . .' He stopped.

'What?'

'Pete called me about someone, some man. They found some kids buried in his backyard . . . I think he might have had Lockie.'

'*What?*'

'It's . . . God, I can't really explain it. I was going to tell you later.'

'When?'

'When we knew if Lockie was one of the dead ones or not.'

'Jesus, Doug.'

'Look, we'll get there. Rest now. Be with him. I'll take care of things.'

Sarah put the man and the other dead children out of her head. Later, perhaps, she would watch Lockie out in the garden and cry for all the mothers who would not see their children again. Later she would weep for the sadness of their loss and the joy of her own luck, but now she only had eyes for her boy, her little man, her Lockie.

She ran her hands over his body, lifted his shirt a little and caught sight of a yellowing bruise.

The air caught in her throat.

'Oh Jesus, Jesus, Jesus,' she whispered.

Someone had hit him. She wanted to undress him right then to see the damage but Lockie was so fast asleep. She knew he wasn't just sleeping because he was tired. He had gone to the same place she had been in for months.

She and Lockie looked alike now. The angles on his face matched hers and in a way she was glad.

She had suffered along with him.

And now here he was.

Sarah pulled him closer to her and breathed in and out with her son, her boy, her Lockie. She sniffed at his hair which smelt faintly of cheap shampoo.

She would bathe him before he ate. She needed to see his body. She needed to touch his skin.

She didn't know if she would ever be able to let go.

Tina

When Sarah and Lockie finally emerged from the bedroom Lockie was wearing pyjamas, a dressing gown and slippers. The pyjamas had creases in the legs, as if they were still new. His mother had bought him winter pyjamas even though she had lost him when the sun was still burning its way through an Australian autumn.

'We're making burgers, Lockie,' said Doug as soon as he saw him. 'Your favourite.'

Tina studied Sarah. She was almost as thin as her son.

There was a picture on the fridge of the family on a beach, probably on holiday. In the picture Sarah was wearing a long T-shirt. The kind that covers up any flaws women might feel they have. Her face was rounded and she had her son's deep dimple.

Sarah sat Lockie down at the table and helped Doug hand out plates of homemade burgers with salad on the side.

Lockie looked at Tina and smiled his small smile and then he ate while the adults talked of the weather and the government as though they were at a dinner party.

Doug and Pete drank beer and Sarah had wine, but Tina was given juice like the children. She wanted to laugh. If they could have seen the things she was offered on a daily basis! But they hadn't seen and they didn't know. Tina was happy to keep it that way.

Lockie was not asked any questions. His mother ate, taking bites of food only when Lockie did. She did not take her eyes off her son. The whole table was focused on Lockie.

When he began cramming in the bites of burger Tina and Sarah both said, almost at the same time, 'Slowly, Lockie.'

Lockie slowed down and Sarah looked at Tina and seemed to see her for the first time. They locked eyes and Sarah nodded slowly as if acknowledging Tina, acknowledging who she was to Lockie. Acknowledging what she had done. Lockie must have told her just as he had told Pete and his father.

Tina allowed herself the luxury of a smile and then she dropped her head and concentrated on the salad, savouring the fresh vegetables and the tang of the dressing, but mostly savouring the feeling of being with a family around a table.

Sammy kept up a conversation by herself. Anyone could join in or not, she didn't seem to care. She told Lockie all about what had happened at school before the holidays and how good she was getting at riding Fairy Queen, her pony. Then she told him about a fight she'd had with her friend Jennifer.

'She said you were never coming back and I said yes you were and then she said that her mum said you were probably deaded and then I cried but I also hit her and Mrs Watson came outside and gave us both time out on the reflection couch.'

Tina could see Doug and Sarah holding their breaths at this speech. How would Lockie react? There would be many moments like these for many months to come. Moments when Lockie's four torturous months would be thrust into the light by a careless comment or question. Moments when they could lose Lockie forever if he chose to close the door and act like it hadn't happened.

Tina could see it would all begin with this one little remark by his sister. How would Lockie react? The whole table waited.

Lockie swallowed his mouthful of burger and said, 'Jennifer's stupid.'

'That's what I think,' said Sammy. 'She's going to be really mad when you come back to school next week after the holidays.'

'Maybe not next week,' said Sarah softly. 'We'll give Lockie a little bit of time, won't we, Lockie?'

'Yeah,' said Lockie. 'But then I'll be back and I'll show stupid Jennifer.'

'Yeah, stupid Jennifer,' said Sammy and she giggled.

Later, when she went to use the bathroom, Tina passed Lockie's room. Racing cars zoomed across the walls and his bed. He was asleep next to his mother. He was curled in the foetal position with his legs jammed into his mother's stomach. If you had thrown a blanket over the two of them Sarah would have looked like a woman in the last stages of pregnancy. Lockie was back where he belonged.

———

Doug and Tina sat in the lounge room of the silent house. Pete had gone home. They were both drinking coffee. Doug had added a drop of whisky to his and when Tina held out her cup he had only raised his eyebrows a little before adding some to hers as well.

'I hope you'll be okay bunking with Sammy for a couple of nights. I need to get the guest room cleared out. No one's ever really used it,' said Doug.

'Don't you have family come and visit and stuff?' said Tina.

'Nah,' sighed Doug. 'Not really.'

Tina could hear a whole story behind the words but she was aware that she was the one who had to do the talking now. She had told Pete to give her one more day to rest but even though it was late she felt re-energised. Her heart was a fast drum solo in her chest while she worked out what to say to Doug.

Doug would not wait one more day. Doug needed to know now so that he could tell Sarah and when Lockie woke up tomorrow his parents would know how much there was to be done. They would know where their boy had come from and they would be able to help him move on to another place. A different place. A place where he could be a nine-year-old boy again.

'I know that you may not want to talk about . . . you know . . . what happened,' said Doug.

'I do want to talk, Doug . . . I do. It's just that I'm not exactly who you think I am. I'm not just a nice girl who rescued Lockie.'

Doug gave a small sharp laugh. 'I know that, Tina. I can see that. I'm just a farmer but some things are obvious. I want to make it clear before you say anything that I believe you saved Lockie. He kept telling me that again and again and I know it's true. Whatever else you may have done, whoever you may be, the most important thing right now is that you saved Lockie. Okay?'

'Okay.'

Tina closed her eyes and let the warmth of the whisky make its way through her veins. Soon it would be time for a shower—a real shower and bed. Sarah had given her some clothes and pyjamas before she put Lockie to bed and she had only asked two questions.

'Doug thinks Lockie was with the man who killed some other kids, the one Pete told him about. Was he?'

Tina nodded.

'What happened to that man?'

'He's dead,' said Tina.

Sarah's face was stony. She gave a curt nod of her head. 'Good,' she said, and that was the end of the conversation.

'How old are you?' asked Doug into the silence of the room.

'Seventeen,' said Tina.

'And how old were you when you ran away from home?'

Tina's eyes flew open and she found herself staring into Doug's blue eyes. The knowledge of the world was on his face. For a moment she felt trapped by what he had figured out. Trapped and hunted. Doug would get the truth no matter what. But then she felt something else flood her body. It was the relief she had felt on the train. She didn't have to run and she didn't have to hide. It would be okay to tell Doug the truth.

And if it wasn't okay? Well then, she would just deal.

She began at the beginning. She needed to talk about who she had been before she got to who she was.

She talked about her father and she talked about Tim. She talked about Tim for a long time and all Doug did was listen. She talked about the divorce and her mother and she talked about Tim. In the lounge room lit mostly by the light from the gas fire she talked about Tim the way she had never imagined she would talk about Tim. She told Doug, a stranger, everything she had seen and everything she had felt because she knew that he had lost a son as well. He had lost a little boy too and even though he was back he would never really be back. Tina talked to Doug because she could see that he knew what it felt like. And she talked to Doug because after her years of silence she needed to talk or she would burst.

Finally, she needed to talk.

At some point Doug got up to get her some tissues so that she could stem the flow of tears and blow her nose but otherwise he only listened.

When she was silent for a while he made some more coffee and added more whisky.

Outside the night worked its way towards dawn and inside Tina talked. When she got to the part about seeing Lockie in the uniform's house she watched Doug's face. She didn't spare him anything because Lockie hadn't been spared. She talked about the rope and the cold and the way Lockie froze when the man touched him.

Doug's skin became the colour of chalk and his fists clenched.

She wanted to spare him the details but he needed to know.

When she told him about letting Lockie hit the uniform with the poker a grim smile crossed his face. Tina understood the smile. People never really got beyond the concept of an eye for an eye. Especially when someone took your child.

She talked about feeding Lockie and showering him and bringing him home. And when she was done she was proud of herself for not leaving anything out. Not the nights on the street or her friendship with Mark and Ruby or what she had done to survive.

Finally she was silent and she waited to see what Doug would say. Mentally she located her backpack and tried to work out how to get to town. She was completely sure of his condemnation.

It didn't matter what he thought. She would survive no matter what happened now, and if she had to go to jail or whatever she would survive that as well.

Doug looked at her for a long time. She felt him judging her, studying her, observing her, but she didn't know if he was trying to understand her or if he was just getting ready to dismiss her.

'Well, I reckon you must be ready for some sleep,' he said.

'I . . . yeah, I guess I am,' she said. The words were an anti-climax. After everything she had said, this was not the reaction she had expected. It was like he hadn't even heard her.

'You've got everything you need for a shower and stuff?'

'Um . . . yeah, I think I'm good.'

'Well, I'll say goodnight then. I might just clean up a little and get things ready for the morning.'

'I could . . . I could help.'

'Not tonight, Tina.'

'Okay.' Tina's heart was a stone. She knew what he was trying to say.

'But from tomorrow, when you've had a bit more rest . . . we'll get you sorted out. There'll be lots to do come spring.'

Tina listened to the words in her head again. 'There'll be lots to do come spring.' Spring was a month away.

She felt a red glow heat up her face. She wanted to hug him but she clasped her hands together instead. Doug obviously wasn't one for effusive words. He said what had to be said. Tina understood his message.

'Yeah, okay . . . Goodnight.'

She picked up the things Sarah had given her and left the room. When she got to the door Doug cleared his throat and she turned around.

'Thank you,' he said. 'We'll say it again and again and I'm sure you'll get sick of hearing it, but thank you. Thank you for saving my boy.'

Tina felt the tears begin anew. She nodded, then she went to have her shower and sleep in the pink princess bunk bed and she left everything in the hands of the universe because it didn't seem to be doing too bad a job.

Doug

Doug watched the fire and heard his words again. 'There'll be lots to do come spring.'

He knew what he was doing. Questions would be asked. The girl had come from nowhere and she could be anyone. She had saved Lockie but she had lived on the streets and done god knows what and questions would be asked. There would be whispers and difficulties but Doug had made his decision. He would tell Sarah and she would agree. They had both watched Lockie at dinner while Lockie watched Tina. Occasionally the boy would take her hand and Tina held on tight.

What kind of family took in some stray girl who had done things they only ever read about? They weren't any kind of family anymore. They were so broken. They were all so broken, and who knew if this broken girl and his broken family could create some sort of jagged whole? There was no clear way forward for any of them but Doug felt a small seed of certainty that the girl needed to be with them, with Lockie.

Questions would be asked but for the first time in four months Doug would not be short of answers.

Lockie

It was almost too warm in his bed but Lockie didn't want to move enough to throw off one of the blankets. His mum had given him two extra blankets even though there was a heater in his room as well. She kept asking him if he was warm enough. He liked to be warm now. He wanted to be warm forever. His mum had asked if he wanted her to sleep with him again but he didn't, not really. He had to sleep on his own like he had before. If you were nine you didn't sleep with your mum and he was nine now.

Soon he would be going back to school and there was no way he wanted Tyler and Matt to find out he still slept with his mum.

His mum had made a cake for his birthday and she had kept it in the fridge out back. It was a Ben 10 cake and it was chocolate on the inside and he and Sammy got to have cake every day now. Mum said he could have a party when he was ready. A party would be the best. She would make another cake.

He had so much stuff for his birthday but the greatest thing ever was the Xbox. It had cool games and only he and Dad could play 'cos Sammy was too little—but Tina could play too and she was really good at racing.

There was lots of stuff from everyone else as well and when people came to visit they brought more presents. Mum got cross when too many people came but Lockie could see her trying to smile for everyone. He tried to smile too but sometimes he had to go to his room and be quiet for a while and then Sammy and Tina wouldn't let anyone in.

There was a special night-light plugged into the wall so he could see everything in his room and under the covers he was holding onto his soft Bob. He didn't want Tyler and Matt to know about soft Bob either but they had seen him sitting on Lockie's bed since they first started coming to play when everyone was only four. Tyler had an ugly teddy bear on his bed and Matt had a dog. When they played together the dog and the bear and Bob all got chucked under the bed.

He was too big for night-lights and soft toys but his mum said that no one had to know and that it was okay for him to hold on to Bob for as long as he needed him.

She also told him that the things that had happened weren't his fault.

His dad said the same thing and so did Tina. Pete and Margie, too.

Lockie was getting tired of people telling him that it wasn't his fault but maybe they kept saying it so much because it was true. If his mum said something over and over again t was usually because it was important and true. She said things like, 'Brush your teeth and vegetables are important for healthy bodies and people like it when you say *please* and *thank you* and you can do anything you want with your life when you grow up.' She said those things over and over because she really meant them so maybe she was telling him it wasn't his fault all the time because she really meant it.

He squeezed Bob and poked one foot out of the blankets.

There was a lady coming tomorrow. His mum had told him about her after dinner and two bowls of ice cream and cake.

The lady's name was Amber.

Lockie liked the word Amber. It was a name but it was also a colour. Amber was a kind of golden honey colour. He liked honey on his oats and honey on his toast. He would ask Mum to give him some honey tomorrow at breakfast.

Amber was coming to talk to him about what had happened and she would come and talk to him every week until he didn't feel like talking anymore. 'You can tell Amber anything you want,' his mum had said.

Lockie hadn't been sure about that but then Tina said, 'You tell her everything, Lockie. You can tell the good stuff and the bad stuff. Amber is only going to listen to you. That's her job.'

His mother had nodded, agreeing with Tina. He liked that Mum and Tina made dinner together. Tina was going to stay with them and he liked that too. She was going to go to school with him and Sammy. Well not exactly with him and Sammy. She was going to be at the TAFE but Mum would drop them all off in the morning and pick them up in the afternoon.

He was a bit scared about going back to school. Maybe he could tell Amber about that?

His dad said he could talk to Amber if he wanted to but he didn't have to talk if he didn't want to.

His dad had come to lie next to him before lights-out time. He was so big his feet hung off the edge of the car bed. He was bigger than the uniform. A lot bigger.

If his dad had known about the uniform he would have found him. He looked and looked but no one could find him 'cos the uniform had hidden him away. If his dad had known he would have found him but Tina found him and that was okay.

Lockie's eyes began to close. Sometimes in the night he had to open them in the middle of a dream to make sure he was home.

The uniform was in some of the dreams so he had to open his eyes quickly and see the racing cars on his wall and then he knew he was safe.

Tina had saved him and she had killed the uniform.

He had killed the uniform as well but only a little bit and even his dad said that some killing was okay.

Pete came to talk to Tina a lot and then a lady who was a lawyer came. Lockie didn't know what a lawyer was but Tina liked her. He wasn't allowed to listen to Tina and the lawyer talk but he had walked past the lounge room and the door had been open and he heard the lawyer say, 'Self-defence—no question.'

He didn't know what that meant but Tina smiled more now.

Tina smiled and Mum smiled but sometimes she cried as well and it was okay to cry. It didn't mean you weren't brave, it just meant that you were feeling a bit sad that day.

He felt his eyes close again and he squeezed Bob under the covers.

In the morning he would ask for honey on his toast.

He would have honey on his toast and play on the Xbox after he did some homework Mrs Watson had sent home from school and then he would eat morning tea and then there would be lunch.

There was lots of food in the house and his mum let him keep some muesli bars under his bed just in case he got hungry in the night.

In the morning he would talk to the lady but only if he wanted to. He would tell her about how Tina saved him and maybe he would tell about the uniform but maybe not.

And he would play with Sammy and read with Tina and have a really big breakfast.

In the morning he would . . .

Acknowledgements

Once a novel has been written it needs a team of people to get it published.

To that end I would like to thank my agent Gaby Naher for her tremendous support and guidance through this process.

I would also like to acknowledge the wonderful team at Allen & Unwin: Jane Palfreyman for understanding the work from the first page, Ali Lavau for her insightful structural edit and Vanessa Pellatt for her suggestions, for patiently answering all my questions and for her incredible attention to detail.

I want to thank my mother Hilary who asked when she could have the rest of the novel, corrected typos, gave constructive criticism and has been the head cheerleader on this journey.

My father Hylton who read a hundred pages in one night and talks me through the difficult days.

And, of course, David who has printed thousands of pages and who always believed this day would come.

And finally my three children—thanks for giving me time to work and making me laugh when I needed it.

If you found *The Boy Under the Table* compelling, you'll be gripped by Nicole Trope's new novel, *Three Hours Late*.

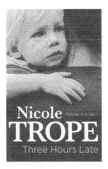

Once, so very long ago, she had watched him like this when he came to pick her up for a date…Her stomach fluttered and burned with infatuation and desire. She would watch him walk up the path and think, 'This must be love.'

But that was so very long ago. Now Liz is wary and afraid. She has made a terrible mistake and it cannot be undone. Alex believes that today will be the day she comes back to him. Today will be the day his wife and young son finally come home. Today they will be a family again.

But Liz knows that some things can never be mended. Some marriages are too broken. Some people are too damaged.

Now the most important thing in her life is her son, Luke, and she will do anything in her power to protect him.

So when Alex is a few minutes late bringing Luke back Liz begins to worry and when he is an hour late her concern grows and when he is later still she can feel her whole life changing because: what if Alex is not just late?

The terrible secrets of a marriage, the love that can turn to desperation, the refuge and heartbreak of being a parent, the fragile threads that cradle a family…*Three Hours Late* is a gripping and deeply emotional novel of almost unbearable suspense from a writer of great insight and empathy.

ISBN 978 1 74331 315 2

Read on for a taste of the tension…

Three hours late

'Aiden, we've been around this block twice already. Don't you think that if the guy was here we would've found him?' asked Julie.

'I know, I know,' said Aiden. 'But it just feels . . . I can't explain it, Jules. Maybe it's a little of that police instinct we're all supposed to have. Besides, the last call he made came from this tower.'

'Yeah, but that was an hour ago. The choppers have been over this park at least twice. They would've seen the car if he was here. Let's go check out some of the shopping centres. He told his wife he'd taken the kid to an arcade earlier today. Maybe he went back there. Shopping centres are a great place to hide. Let's start at the first one we come to and go from there. We're wasting time here.'

'I don't know, Jules. I think this guy will be closer to home.'

Julie pushed some blonde curls back behind her ear. 'I think he's hidden away in the dark somewhere far from prying eyes, just like the rat he is.'

'Don't make me pull rank, Jules,' said Aiden.

Julie and Aiden hadn't been partners long but they had clicked from the beginning. Julie never needed to be told who was in charge.

Now she looked at Aiden, hurt by the rebuke, but relaxed when she saw he was smiling.

'Fine, but this is the last time, okay? Go around once more and then we'll start on the shopping centres.'

The police cruiser crawled past the park again.

'I know it looks deserted but I just want to check out the bush at the back,' said Aiden. He pulled off the road into the dust and stone area that served as a car park and the two police officers climbed out of the car. In the dying light of the afternoon the empty swing moved back and forth as if waiting for a small body and pumping legs. The slight creak of the metal chains sent a shiver down Julie's spine. Even as a kid she'd never been a fan of the park. There were too many big kids, too many unknowns.

'There's nothing here,' said Julie, wrapping her arms around herself.

'Looks that way,' said Aiden. The bushland surrounding the park looked undisturbed.

•

White lines chased each other around the freshly marked oval. There were three schools close by that were probably getting ready for their sports carnivals. Aiden glanced across the empty stone steps that served as stands for watching parents. He didn't understand his certainty that the guy was here. It would be a stupid place to hide. It was too close to the house where the kid lived. The guy was probably hiding out in a giant car park where he would be almost impossible to find. Or maybe just maybe he was long gone by now. He could be on the highway heading out of Sydney on the way to Queensland. Or he could be hiding out in some small country town already. He could be anywhere.

'So why do I think he's here?' muttered Aiden.

He closed his eyes and tried to work out what was bothering him. He felt like there was something he was missing. But whatever it was it remained out of reach. He opened his eyes with a sigh.

The park had a small play area off to the side but was dominated by the oval in the middle. All around houses stood on sentry duty in the quiet Saturday afternoon. It was a little cold now for kids to be out but even so the park was eerily empty.

He turned to walk back to the car as the sun dipped a little lower on the horizon and then he caught something in his peripheral vision. He turned around and waited for it again.

And there it was: a flash as the last rays of the sun hit something metal. There *was* something in the bush.

Aiden started walking towards the place where he'd seen the flash. Crossing the oval, he noticed tyre tracks. He broke into a run.

He knew what he would find when he got to the cluster of gum trees, banksias and tangled undergrowth. He knew they would be there.

As he drew closer he saw the outline of the car, a blue Toyota sedan. He knew that when he checked the licence plate it would be WVX 217.

His heart was pumping now and despite the cold he was beginning to sweat. He slowed down and made himself a cat. If they were still in the car he didn't want to startle the man into doing anything stupid, and if they were outside the car he didn't want to alert the guy to his presence.

He crept forward, trying to avoid hidden twigs; cursing the gold-red fall of leaves that carpeted the ground.

The car's engine was running, just purring gently. Aiden wondered how long it had been running for. How long could a tank of petrol last if the car was parked?

He grabbed his taser from its holder. A gun would freak the kid out but he wouldn't know what a taser was.

He stepped forward and peered through the rear window.

When he couldn't see anything he moved around to one of the back passenger windows.

If the kid was in the back seat Aiden would have to signal to him to keep quiet. He already had his finger against his lips. Hopefully the kid would be more curious than terrified by the sight of a police officer looking through his window.

The man would probably be in the front seat and wouldn't see him. Unless of course they were both in the front seat and neither was in a position to see him. Unless neither of them was in a position to see anything.

Aiden looked back at the oval and saw Julie jogging across to meet him. He put his hand up, indicating that she should stop; the last thing he needed was more noise. Julie obliged and became a statue. She wouldn't move again until he told her to.

He refocused on the window. He saw a booster seat covered in pictures of Winnie-the-Pooh and his friends. Eeyore stared out the window at Aiden, his tail drooping and face resigned. There was no sign of the boy.

The park and the car sat together in the silence of the day. Aiden stepped forward again, straining his muscles to keep his body light on the ground. Holding his breath, he looked into the front seat.

He put his taser back into its holder.

He stood up straight and waved at Julie.

She resumed her run across the oval.